I0536012

SIDEARMS & SILK

A NASH MYSTERY
BOOK 1

VELLA DAY

Erotic Reads Publishing

Sidearms and Silk

Nash Mystery Series
Book 1

Copyright © 2017 Vella Day

www.velladay.com

velladayauthor@gmail.com

Edited by Rebecca Cartee and Carol Adcock-Bezzo

E-book ISBN: 978-1-941835-42-5

Print book ISBN: 978-1-941835-43-2

ALL RIGHTS RESERVED. No part of this book may be used or reproduced in any manner whatsoever without written permission of the author except in the case of brief questions embodied in critical articles or reviews.

This is a work of fiction. Names, characters, places, and incidents either are the product of the author's imagination or are used fictitiously, and any resemblance to actual persons living or dead, business establishments, events or locales, is entirely coincidental.

ABOUT THE BOOK

One missing person, one private investigator, and one deputy. Their passion for the truth and each other ignites in the small town of Kerry, West Virginia.

Private investigator Dax Mitchell had more pressing things to do than solve some mystery in small-town Kerry, West Virginia—that is until some sweet old lady begs him to locate her missing friend. Not even a former homicide detective could turn her down.

Deputy Jessie Nash has enough on her hands, and the last thing she needs is an irresistible investigator interfering with her job. After her boss goes missing, Jessie reluctantly turns to Dax for help. Now, they must work together to solve the case.

The problem? The closer they work, the more intense their desire for one another becomes. As they uncover truths neither wants to face, will it extinguish the passion that burns so deeply between them or make it brighter?

CHAPTER ONE

"The irrationality of a thing is not an argument against its
existence, rather, a condition of it."
Friedrich Nietzsche

Kerry, West Virginia

Nightly rounds sucked.

Seven days a week, Deputy Jessie Nash drove to the edge of
town to check out some half-built cement plant in Kerry, West
Virginia. The good old mayor promised the company that the
sheriff's department—read her—would do everything to ensure
that nothing happened to their precious building. Short of
blowing up the place, there wasn't much anyone could do to
cement. If the town hadn't been so desperate for the employment opportunity, she might have balked at the assignment.

As Jessie drove in to make sure no vagrants were squatting
there, the cruiser's headlights shone on the front of the building.
The top half was encased in a white fog, and the bottom half
looked like a skull with black, looming eyes where the doorways
would eventually go.

Needing to get this chore finished as quickly as possible, Jessie stepped out of her cruiser and stood in the headlight's path to study her surroundings, cold dampness settling in her nose and throat. As she looked for something amiss, tendrils of fog wrapped around her legs. The sight was unsettling and fascinating at the same time.

She glanced toward the full moon glowing through the fog-laden sky. Even she had to admit, the silent orb looked a bit menacing. Maybe Nana was right—the moon might be the cause of all the town's recent problems. Jesse huffed out a laugh. Right, and the mines would reopen tomorrow and give Kerry back its life.

To be fair, three strange events had happened in the last few days to make even her suspect some presence was hovering over the town. The most disturbing of which was the disappearance of Sadie Palmer, Jessie's grandmother's best friend. While Nana was convinced there had been foul play, Jessie believed Sadie was on a trip and had merely forgotten to tell someone. It wasn't as if that hadn't happened a few times before.

Nonetheless, her grandmother was upset, which was why Jessie had begged her boss, Sheriff Clinton DuPree, to cough up some funds to hire additional help to find the woman. Unfortunately, he said there was no money to look for *Flaky Sadie*, as he called her. That meant tomorrow, come hell or high water, along with all her other chores, Jessie was going to talk to the neighbors to see if they had any idea where her grandmother's friend might have gone.

A little voice in her head told her to stop playing around and get on with the inspection or she'd never make it home. With her flashlight in hand, she worked her way around the construction tape and headed toward the building where two large cranes peeked their gangly heads through the mist like giant dinosaurs.

The smell of cement dust was heavy in the air, and as she coughed to clear her throat, a cold breeze trickled under her shirt and made her shiver. She should have worn her Pea coat tonight, but she hadn't wanted to believe winter might be upon them.

Jessie blew out a breath to test for frost but nothing crystalized, implying she had time before the snow arrived.

A night owl hooted in the distance a second before the fog brightened in front of her. She stilled, her pulse racing. Someone else was there, and she doused her light.

Deep inside the blackness, more flashes flickered, and then beams of light swung around in random patterns like some mystical ritual. What the hell? She didn't believe in ghosts or aliens, but just maybe...

Shuffling her feet along the ground to avoid running into anything, she moved closer to the building.

Ouch! Shit!

Despite her caution, she banged her knee into something hard. Feeling around with her hand, she found she'd run into stacks of cement blocks. Luck just wasn't with her tonight. Her leg throbbed, but Jessie wouldn't let some namby-pamby injury stop her from doing her job.

Laughter burst from inside the plant and her shoulders relaxed. From the high, thin tone, it was kids—kids who shouldn't be out here on a school night. Cripes, they shouldn't be here on any night.

Turning on her light, she rubbed her knee and limped forward, careful to avoid the construction equipment this time. It didn't take long to find the trespassers. Fourteen-year-olds Billy Jenkins, Phil Hartner, and Chuck Federer were spraying graffiti on the newly erected walls.

"Hey, you guys. What the heck are you doing here?"

The cans of spray paint turned silent and their lights stopped thrashing about.

"Ah... ah... we were just having some fun," Chuck said, a smile wavering on his lips.

"Well, have some fun someplace else. This is private property." She swept her light around the enclosure looking for signs of alcohol or drugs but found nothing illegal.

"You gonna tell our folks?" Good, Phil sounded scared, as well he should.

"Someone's gotta pay for this mess," she said in her I'm-the-deputy-and-you're-just-a-kid tone. As soon as Jessie flashed her light on their faces, they held up their hands and squinted. "Bunch of juveniles. Go home before I drag you off to jail."

She held in a laugh as they raced out of the plant, looking like they'd been caught naked by their moms.

"Fuck." That would be Phil. Guess he must have tripped over the cement blocks. Served him right coming out here.

***

Dax Mitchell rolled down his truck window and sucked in the crisp, clean air. He swore he'd never step foot in West Virginia again, but here he was. Despite the sun shafting through the turning leaves, it didn't make the state any more inviting.

He searched for signs of the town, but when he found none, he glanced down at the map, figuring he had to be close. Margaret Nash mentioned Kerry was small and isolated, but she'd also said he couldn't miss the place.

Convinced he'd find it if he went a bit farther, he continued along the narrow road. When he crested the ridge, he spotted the village nestled in the valley below. He didn't like how the town sat between the rolling hills. One road in meant only one road out—confining, constricting, claustrophobic.

His gut churned, and Dax pulled off the road to get his bearings, gravel crunching under his tires as he came to a stop. Bearings, hell, he needed to get a grip. He never should have agreed to take a job located in a small mining town—one just like where he'd grown up. It didn't matter the Kerry mine had been closed for almost a year. He'd bet ten bucks there weren't streetlights bordering every road like there were in Baltimore.

It had been dumb to come here, but Margaret Nash had sounded so much like his grandmother, he'd agreed to help. Besides, it couldn't be too hard to find a seventy-eight- year-old woman in a town with a population of six hundred. He'd earn his money and leave—maybe even before dark.

Getting himself under control, Dax slipped back onto the deserted two-lane road. A mile later, he spotted a sign boasting that the town of Kerry was the home of the hedgehog. Christ, if that was the best the town had to offer, maybe he should turn around right now. If only he hadn't promised Mrs. Nash he'd find her friend, he just might have.

He crossed a bridge that spanned a deep gorge with the river sparkling below and was struck once more by the view. It might be pretty, but looks could be deceiving.

As he approached the town, his heart sank. The main drag had about half its storefronts boarded up. The good news was that there were a few signs announcing the arrival of some stores, implying the town might survive. He'd spotted a construction sign a ways back indicating a new cement plant. Perhaps this was fueling the growth. His hometown hadn't had a savior like the new plant. If it had, his mom wouldn't have had to work two jobs to support him and his brother.

Stop remembering. Think of something good.

Kerry did have its advantages. According to Margaret Nash, everyone was aware that Sadie Palmer, the town seamstress, had disappeared three days ago, which might make it easier to question people. Of course, getting them to answer those questions to a stranger was another matter.

Quite a few trucks, most looking like construction vehicles, huddled in front of The Sugar Shack, a building squished between the bank and a used bookstore. Given the pink neon cup that was blinking erratically above the door, he guessed it was the town's diner.

His stomach could use some grub, but he'd have to wait before satisfying his hunger. He first needed to find the location of his new employer. The address Margaret Nash had given him was Nash Road, Kerry, WV. No street number, no directions, no landmarks. Then again, if you had a street named after you, the spread must be impressive.

Unfortunately, his cell's GPS wasn't helping, as he hadn't been able to get cell service out here. He doubted this town had printed maps, and there certainly wouldn't be an information center either. His best bet would be to ask at the sheriff's office.

Dax spotted a separate building at the end of the street and the large, swinging sign on the front porch indicated it was where he needed to go. The all-brick building was about thirty feet wide by fifty feet long, and except for the worn wooden decking leading up to the entrance, it was in moderately good repair. A hitching post, that looked as old as a John Wayne movie, sat off to the side.

He almost laughed. All the place needed was a watering trough, and he could have believed he'd entered some kind of time warp. Dax parked in front, and as he stepped out of his truck, a spasm shot up his left leg. He winced, proving he should have taken the time to stretch on the way down. He rubbed his thigh, but it didn't do any good. Damn injury from the exploding land mine would never heal. Even taking the three wooden steps one at a time didn't prevent the ache from racing straight to his hip.

The large, black door handle and brass sign showed the place had been a prize many years ago, and he bet with a little polish, the building could be a city treasure again. Pots of sweet smelling wild flowers bordered the door, and while it reminded him of his grandmother's house, he didn't need to be spending time admiring what he'd soon never lay eyes on again.

He stepped inside to voices raised in a heated discussion. Dax debated waiting outside, but a man who looked to be in his mid-fifties motioned him in. A white-haired lady stood with her back to Dax, her hands on her wide hips, seemingly oblivious he was even there.

The inside was a little stuffy and a bit dark, but otherwise, it was a nice sized office with two desks and a row of armed, wooden chairs near the entrance. At the end of the chairs were three five-drawer file cabinets, and off to the right sat two empty holding cells.

Dax shifted to the side to peer around the elderly woman and spotted a metal plate on the man's desk that read, Sheriff DuPree. The man leaned back in his chair and kept his gaze on the older woman while Dax stayed put, waiting patiently for his turn to speak with the busy man.

"How many times do I have to tell you, there ain't no such thing as aliens," DuPree said in a patronizing tone to the woman.

"Well, I seen the lights with my own eyes, Clinton. Me, Mary Alice, and Eleanor will tell you the lights came out of nowhere, then disappeared, just like that." She snapped her fingers.

"You saw them next to the mine, right?"

"Yes."

He scribbled something on his note pad. "And Sadie was with you?"

"Yes."

Sadie, the seamstress? Dax straightened.

The sheriff scrubbed a hand over his chin. "So how did she disappear? You see the aliens take her, Margaret?"

Aliens? He hoped this wasn't Margaret Nash, but odds were she was.

"No. She didn't disappear that night, but since she was real curious about why they landed in Kerry, she wanted to look for some evidence they might have left behind."

"Did she find any?"

"Yes. I'm guessing that's why she went back the next night to check them out. It's when they must have taken her."

For a split second, Dax hoped there really were aliens; it would make his short stay more interesting.

The sheriff sat up, leaned forward on his elbows, and

expelled a deep breath. "Okay. Lemme see this *evidence*." He wiggled his fingers, motioning for the found prize.

Margaret opened a large, black cloth bag and pulled out a pair of NVG's, night vision goggles.

The sheriff's expectant face fell, and Dax thought he caught a flash of worry, but it disappeared too quickly for him to be sure.

"And how is this proof of aliens?" the sheriff asked.

"For Pete's sake, Clinton, they're glasses. The aliens wear them to see in the dark," she said with such authority Dax almost believed her. "You need to get out more."

Dax forced his lips not to turn up.

"Oh, okay, Margaret," the sheriff said, taking the goggles from her. "I'm beginning to worry about you. Your memory's not what it used to be."

"I'm as sharp as I've ever been."

"A few fries short of a happy meal," the sheriff mumbled under his breath.

"What was that?" she asked, leaning closer.

Boy, did she ever remind him of his high school algebra teacher—strict and always pissed off.

"Nothing." The sheriff ran a hand over his mouth again, looking as if he needed to compose himself. "Sharp, you say? Don't you remember how you had the town in a tizzy over the crop circles? You just knew aliens had made them. It turned out, the Parker boys had stolen old man Haslett's tractor in the middle of the night and cut down his field."

She flapped her arms, as if she was trying to come up with a good excuse, but DuPree held up a hand. "And how about the ghosts you claimed were in your house? You had me stand watch for three nights waitin' for them to show up, and what were they? Rats. That's right, rats in your attic making scratchin' noises."

"I know. That was a mistake, but this time I'm telling you we saw... alien lights." Her voice trailed off. No doubt even she was beginning to disbelieve her own story.

"And the vampires?" The sheriff tapped a pen on his large wooden desk.

Margaret clicked close her purse and tilted her head high. "Fine. I knew you wouldn't believe me, so that's why I've hired a private investigator."

DuPree's brows pinched together.

That was Dax's cue, so he stepped forward and held out his hand to the officer. "That would be me, Dax Mitchell."

Margaret turned around, slapped a hand over her chest, and took a step backward, her eyes wide. "Oh my, you're the private investigator?"

Sure he had a bum leg, but from his stance, she couldn't tell. He was only thirty-four, a good age to do detective work. "Yes, ma'am."

The sheriff cleared his throat. "Clinton DuPree."

"Sheriff."

"I don't suppose Margaret here told you her granddaughter is my deputy?"

Dax stole a glance at his potential employer. She smiled, looking innocent, and he tamped down his frustration. "No, she didn't." Talk about a wild goose chase. "So why *did* you hire me?" He tried not to show how pissed he was, but he failed.

"Because Sadie disappeared," she stated.

"I mean, why me? Why not ask your granddaughter to look for her?"

Clinton DuPree leaned back in his chair with a smug look on his face and crossed his arms over his barrel chest.

"I... I didn't want to worry Jessie. She has enough to do without searching every house for my friend. I figured you could do it faster, being a big city boy and all. Besides, you found that girl who'd been lost for weeks."

The notoriety of that case had kept him busy for months. Dax turned back to the sheriff. "Any clues?"

The man took a sip of coffee, and the rich aroma nearly killed him. What he wouldn't give for a cup now.

"Nope. Sadie's not at home, I can tell you that. I called her sister in Wheeling, but she hasn't heard from her either, and I asked around a bit here but got nowhere." He looked back at Margaret. "It's not like Sadie hasn't gone off before, you know. Right Margaret?"

Margaret Nash huffed. "That may be true, Clinton, but she always tells me if she plans on going somewhere. No, this time something bad has happened."

Dax wanted to say that if the aliens had taken her friend, his employer surely couldn't expect him to get her back, but he kept quiet.

Margaret grabbed his arm. "Let's get out of here. We need to discuss this in private." She snapped a look back at DuPree.

Dax shrugged then let her lead him into the bright sunshine. Holding on to the rail, she made her way down the three steps, hobbling as bad as he did. She said nothing until she got to the bottom then shielded her eyes. "You eaten?"

He couldn't help but like her feisty attitude. "Nope."

"Well, what are you waiting for? Good food is down a block or two at The Sugar Shack."

"Lead the way."

***

Jessie Nash rubbed her aching back. She hadn't planned on moving a gazillion boxes, a queen-sized bed, and a chest of drawers today, but since Lena Randall's husband had run out on her and left her with nothing more than her income at the diner, someone had to help the poor girl move into a cheaper place.

Lena swiped the sweat from her brow. "Can't thank you enough, Jess, for helping."

"Just doing my job." Jessie was too embarrassed to say, *What are friends for?* She didn't do well with mush and sloppy sentiment. Give her cold, hard facts anytime and she'd be happy.

"Well, I don't see Sheriff DuPree helping."

Jess laughed. "Right. Coal will spontaneously turn into diamonds before that day comes." That got a laugh out of Lena.

A law enforcer's job was to keep the peace, sure, but Jessie wanted to help the community more than that, though she didn't remember any stories where her father or grandfather ever did moving duty when they were the town's sheriff.

"I really have to go, Lena. Call me if you need anything else."

"Sure." Lena's smile came out weak.

As Jess hopped in her cruiser, all she could think about was taking a long, hot shower. Her shirt clung to her chest, despite the temperature being in the fifties.

Fifteen minutes later, she pulled down her dirt drive. Nana's Cadillac sat in its usual spot, but next to it was a beat-to-shit truck with Maryland plates. Sure the state abutted West Virginia, but Kerry didn't get many visitors, and her grandmother received even less. Jessie wouldn't find out the identity of the visitor by sitting there, so she jumped out of the cruiser and raced up the steps, the front porch squeaking as she trod across the old boards.

Gotta get those fixed. Right. As soon as the tooth fairy left her some money.

Jessie pushed open the front door. "Nana?"

The door to the kitchen swung open, and the smell of fresh cinnamon buns sent her stomach grumbling.

"'Bout time you got home," Nana said, the door closing right behind her. She glanced up and stilled. "Oh, my, you look a mess."

"Thanks, Nana." If she wasn't getting some cat down from a tree, she was breaking up a drunken brawl on Saturday night. "What else is new? I usually come home grungy."

"We have company, and I don't want him see you looking like you got in a fight and lost."

"You're exaggerating, Nana." Jessie couldn't help but laugh at the look of horror on her face. "So who's here?"

"Go shower and put on a pretty dress." Nana made a shooing motion.

A dress? Her grandmother had lost her mind. The last time she'd dressed up was when she'd buried her father.

The kitchen door popped open, and an amazing looking man stepped out with a cinnamon roll in his mouth. She wasn't sure which made her mouth water more—him or the scent of the sweet roll.

He finished his bite. "Oh, hello." His dark eyes twinkled— make that incredibly deep, brown eyes as rich as leather.

She tried to form a few words, but her whole body turned to cement, and her usually chatty mouth wouldn't work. "Hel-hello." Shit. She hated it when she stuttered. "Who are y-you?"

Nana swatted at her. "Don't be rude, Jess. He's my guest."

The unnamed man smiled, looking kind, gentle, and surprisingly trustworthy. "Mrs. Nash hired me to find her friend, Sadie Palmer." His voice sounded educated with a slight Southern twang.

He licked his forefinger and stuffed his hands in his worn jeans pocket. The denim hugged his lean hips like a strawberry dipped in chocolate. She hadn't seen a man this good looking in a long time—if ever.

His comment sunk in and anger rushed up her belly. She twirled toward her grandmother. "You hired someone to find Sadie? You know the sheriff is looking into her *disappearance*, and I'm helping."

"That old fart couldn't find his ass in the dark."

Jess's face heated up. "Nana, watch your mouth."

Her grandmother shook her head. "It's true and you know it. Besides, I didn't want to bother you. You don't have the time."

Of late, she had been swamped with work. "I'm planning to look tomorrow. Even you have to admit Sadie's probably off on one of her quests. Don't you remember the last time she left?"

Jessie didn't wait for a response. "She flew to Las Vegas on a gambling junket and told *no one*—not even her *bestest friend.*"

Nana glared at her. "This is different."

"Is not." Jessie didn't want to admit something bad could have happened to Sadie. She cared a lot for the old lady, but the facts were adding up to indicate something had.

Jess turned back and studied the tall stranger. What was Nana thinking hiring him? She bet he cost a fortune, and if they didn't have enough money to fix up the house, they didn't have any to spare on a private investigator. Though from the way he was dressed, and the condition of his truck, it didn't look like he held many jobs. She could only hope he came cheap, or was maybe even free.

"I'm afraid there's been a mistake," she said with as much sympathy as possible.

The man had the audacity to smile, and crinkles formed around his sexy eyes. On him, wrinkles looked good. On her, all of her lines made her look old—or as old as a twenty-nine-year old could look.

He stepped forward. "Dax Mitchell."

He held out a hand, and she took it. "Jessie Nash."

His clasp was solid, assured, and nice. As he pulled his hand away, she noticed his nails were clean and trimmed. While his jeans were tattered, his loose fitting sweater was nice. Too bad they probably covered a few bulging muscles, preventing her from seeing all of his shape. He smelled nice too, like fresh springtime with a hint of spice.

Stop it, Jessie.

He cleared his throat. "It's getting dark. I'll start looking around first thing tomorrow morning for your friend, Mrs. Nash. I'll need a room for the night, so if you could recommend a hotel in town, I'd appreciate it." He glanced from Nana to Jessie.

Nana stepped forward and grabbed his arm. "You'll do no such thing, young man. You'll stay right here." She wagged a finger at him. "And no arguments." She turned to Jess. "Fix up the room next to yours, okay, dear?" she said, just as sweet as could be.

Before Jess could protest, a misfiring engine raced up the drive, the brakes squeaking as the car came to a halt.

Feet pounded on the porch, followed by loud knocking. "Deputy Nash," he yelled through the front door.

Jessie would deal with the new houseguest in a moment. She raced to the door and pulled it open. Bradley Williams, a man who worked at the Coal Mine Bar, stood rigid, his eyes darting right and left.

"What happened?" Her blood pressure soared.

"Someone killed the sheriff."

CHAPTER TWO

When Jessie's knees buckled, Dax reached out to keep her from falling, but she managed to steady herself on the doorjamb before he could lend a hand.

"Ohmigod. C-Clinton's d-dead? When, how, where?" Jessie's body stiffened.

Brad wrung his hands and glanced to the ground. "I'm not sure. I just got to the bar and was taking the garbage out back when I saw him lying there." His face contorted. "He... he had lots of blood on his forehead and everywhere."

The man's face paled, and Dax's homicide detective instincts kicked in. "Are you sure he was dead?"

Jessie looked up at Dax, acting a little startled, as though she'd forgotten he was standing next to her.

Brad ran his gaze from the top of Dax's head down to his scuffed up boots and back again. "Sure, I'm sure. His eyes were open." He puffed out his chest.

The man was defensive but confident. That was a good sign.

"Did you touch the body or move him?" Jessie asked.

Brad straightened. "I shook him to see if he was drunk or something. That's all."

"Then you came right here?"

"No. I ran inside, got a tarp, and tossed it over him so no animals would mess with him." He glanced down. "The sheriff doesn't deserve to have anyone see him like that. It ain't respectful."

"Thank you, Brad," Jessie said. "I appreciate you coming all this way to t-tell me."

"Thought you should hear it in person." The anxious man looked relieved his ordeal might be over. "Can I go now?" he asked.

"Sure. I'll stop by later and take your official statement once I check out the scene."

Poor Jessie. Her pretty face had paled and from the way she was rubbing her hands up and down her legs, this news had understandably devastated her. The informant spun around and sprinted back to his car. Dax found it odd that the man would run, but if he'd had anything to do with the sheriff's death, he wouldn't have told DuPree's deputy about the murder in the first place.

Jessie looked up at Dax again, her green eyes shining and her face tight. She appeared to be using all her inner strength to hold in her grief.

Brad's tires spun down the dirt drive, and his engine misfired once more.

Jessie visibly shook. "Nana, can you call Doc and tell him to meet me behind the bar?"

Dax removed his cell from his pocket and held it out. "You want to use my phone?" Jessie might be able to explain the situation better than her grandmother.

She waved a hand. "They don't work here since we don't have any cell towers nearby—at least not yet."

No reception? He wasn't used to being in an area without service and not having it might hinder his investigation.

"I can't believe it," Margaret said rising slowly from the sofa, her face slack. "We were just talking to him." She lifted her head to meet his gaze. "Who would do this to Clinton? Everyone loved him."

Apparently not everyone.

"Nana, I have to check on Clinton." She rushed to the closet, slipped on a jacket, and as she reached for her service weapon on the side table, knocked it off. When it bounced on the floor, Jessie sucked in a breath, scurried to it, and snatched it up. Her pretty face reddened.

Turning her back to both of them, she slid her piece in the empty holster, and then faced Dax. "Good luck finding Sadie."

He couldn't tell if she was still pissed that her grandmother had asked for his help, or if she was relieved she didn't have to deal with a missing person when she had a murder on her hands.

"I can help investigate the murder if you'd like."

Oh, Christ. His inner censor must have thought he'd issued a cease-and-desist order on thinking. He'd planned to stay only long enough to find the missing woman, but something about Jessie had drawn him in. She seemed focused and caring, two traits he admired.

Be honest, Mitchell. She's hot.

She waved him off. "That's all right. We can handle it."

He shoved down his relief until her words registered. "We? Is there another deputy on the force?" There had been only two desks in the sheriff's office.

Her jaw clenched. "No, I guess I forgot it's just me now." She pulled open the door and a blast of cold air rushed in.

"Have you ever handled a homicide before?" Dax asked.

Her shoulders stiffened. *Way to go, Mitchell.* The chances of many homicides in this small town were slim, so it was wrong to rub her inexperience in her face.

"No."

He admired her honesty, and a bit of guilt mixed with his need to help. "Then I'm coming with you."

He figured he'd get nowhere locating Sadie until this case was solved because folks from small towns tended to focus on one major event at a time. They wouldn't be forthcoming with information until their sheriff's murderer was caught and brought to justice.

Her shoulders sagged, looking as if she carried the weight of the world. She spun around to face him. "Suit yourself, but we take separate cars."

She seemed too upset to drive. "Why?"

She blew out a breath. "I might have to stay all night, and I don't want you to have to hang around. I know you need to find Sadie." She shot a sympathetic glance back at her grandmother.

He liked that she was thinking again. "That works."

Jessie looked over at her grandmother. "Stay by the phone, Nana. Okay? I might need you. And don't forget to call Doc."

Margaret's face lit up. "Sure, honey, just be careful. You want to take some rolls with you?"

"I'm not hungry any more, but thanks."

Jessie raced to her cruiser before he made it to his truck. She slipped in and then glanced over her shoulder. While she couldn't help notice his limp, she showed no signs of disgust at his condition. Perhaps the town folk often came back injured from the war, but he bet not many had been as close as he'd been to a landmine.

During the four-mile drive to town, Dax was barely able to keep up with her. Lights flashing, she whipped around corners faster than a racecar driver, and what was left of his shock absorbers took a beating.

Once they reached the main drag, he checked the streets, looking for something suspicious. The Sugar Shack sign still flickered, and despite sampling the batch of cinnamon rolls, his stomach needed filling. He'd have to stop and buy something to eat before he headed back to Mrs. Nash's.

He must not have been paying close enough attention because one minute Jessie was right in front of him and the next she'd disappeared. He made a quick right turn down a dark alley and nearly clipped his front bumper on a boarded up building in the process. Shit. The narrow rutted road bounced him around as he ate her dust, and he wondered what the hell he'd gotten himself into. The two-story buildings on his right and left closed in on him, and his heart raced. He pressed his foot to the pedal, needing to get out of the confining space before the panic consumed him.

Jessie made it through the gauntlet in one piece, whipped around the end of the building, and once more disappeared from sight. Dax shot through the darkness to the same back alley where a few lights above some doors sporadically lit the roadway. The moment he turned the corner, he let out a long held breath.

As he pulled to a stop behind Jessie, she stepped out of her cruiser. The top of her head might only come to his shoulder but without a doubt, the woman had the longest legs he'd ever seen.

In need of fresh air and a clearer head, Dax swung out of his truck and scoped out the alley and the surrounding buildings. A sign on a door next to where Jessie had parked read, "Coal Mine Bar entrance. No parking."

In order to effectively analyze the scene, he couldn't have his leg pain distract him, so Dax stretched his thigh before making any sudden moves. As he headed toward Jessie, a whiff of rancid garbage made his nose wrinkle.

She must have smelled it too, because she rushed over to the dumpster and peered around it. She bent over and moved something. She then stalked off to the far end of the building before striding back.

With her hands planted on her hips and her feet wide, her gaze continued to sweep the area. "What the hell?" she said to no one in particular, looking like a spitfire ready to explode.

Dax reached the dumpster a second later. "What's wrong?"

"What's wrong? I'll tell you what's wrong. The body's not here." The expression on her face said, *Don't mess with this woman*.

The wind picked up and some of her pretty brown curls escaped her ponytail and framed her face. Her comment finally sunk in. "Missing? Are you sure?" Dax waved a hand. "Maybe the sheriff was merely unconscious when Brad found him and your boss woke up and walked away."

A hint of hope flashed across her face. "Do you think that's what happened?"

"It's possible."

She looked down the alley, her breathing heavy.

He tried another option. "Could this have been some kind of hoax to lure you out here?"

A cool breeze shot around the corner, and Jessie pulled her jacket tighter before crossing her arms. "No. Brad would never be part of something so cruel."

"Would anyone want to keep you away from your house to get to your grandmother?" He was grasping at straws, but occasionally he hit upon the truth.

She looked at him as if he had two heads. "No one would want to harm the sweetest eighty-year old in town. Besides, everyone knows she can handle a shotgun better than any man I know."

Dax didn't picture Margaret being a modern day Annie Oakley, but he'd been wrong before about people, and arguing with Jessie didn't seem like it would do any good, anyway.

A second later she stomped past him and ripped open the back door to the bar. Fearing she'd get into trouble, he followed her. The bar smelled musty and damp, like the place had been closed for months, but Brad was there, carrying a case of beer to the bar.

"Where's Clinton?" she demanded. Given the man was less than ten feet away, she shouted louder than necessary. No hello or how are you handling finding a dead man?

Brad slammed the case on the counter and faced her. "That's what I'd like to know. I went to your place as soon as I saw the sheriff. When I returned, he was gone. I called your house, but your grandmother told me you were headed over here."

Keeping his gaze on Brad, Dax stepped up next to Jessie.

"Can you show us where you found the body? There might be some evidence we can process." He kept his voice low and calm, hoping to diffuse the tense situation.

Brad wiped his hands on his dirty apron and headed out, flicking on the light that shone above the back door. He led them to the dumpster and pointed to the tarp. "He was right here, so help me God." He held up a palm.

Using his foot, Dax slid the canvas cover to the side then crouched down to examine the crime scene. Damn, he needed his flashlight. "Hold on a sec."

He rushed to his vehicle, and a moment later returned with a light in hand. Square foot by square foot, he searched for evidence.

"You see anything?" Jessie asked, her voice shaky.

Was she anxious about him doing the CSU work or just hopeful they'd find a clue to DuPree's disappearance? "Excluding the empty beer cans and leftover food, all I see is what looks like blood on the back wall. If it is, I'm betting it belongs to the sheriff and not the killer." He looked back over his shoulder. "You have any kind of crime scene kit around?"

"What do you need?"

He appreciated that she was willing to cooperate. "A high resolution camera for starters, and some swabs to take a blood sample."

Her back straightened. "The department has a digital camera, but I can't say it's real high resolution. We're a small town, Mr. Mitchell. We haven't had a major investigation in a long time." Her voice rose with each word.

"Hey, I was just asking." He shot her a brief smile, but it wasn't returned.

"Sorry. I didn't mean to yell. I'm upset, that's all. I'll gather what we have."

Dax nodded, appreciating how much it must have taken on her part to cooperate.

Drag marks indicated the sheriff might have been moved, convincing him the victim hadn't walked away.

In no time, Jessie returned. "This is all we have." She sounded more apologetic than mad as she waved the small digital camera. "And here are the swabs and vials."

"Excellent."

She cleared her throat. "How about I take the photos while you gather the evidence?" She finally gave him a half smile, and the change in his pulse rate had to be the excitement of the hunt and not due to his stupid libido. Jesse was cute, but hardly the type to want someone like him.

"Perfect."

She snapped away. "I didn't think private investigators did criminal work. How do you know about this stuff?"

"It's a long story."

The crunch of gravel caught their attention, and Jessie whipped around. A station wagon, age indeterminate, rolled to a stop. Given gawkers would only contaminate the scene, he needed her to shoe them away. "Can you tell them this is a crime scene?"

"It's the Medical Examiner, but I'll tell him there's nothing to examine."

CHAPTER THREE

Dax sat in a back booth of The Sugar Shack and warmed his hands on a cup of hot mocha deluxe coffee. He inhaled the pungent smell and waited for that relaxing coffee-calm, but it never came. He hoped like hell he'd get lucky today and learn what had happened to Sadie Palmer. He had wanted to be back in Baltimore, but now that the cop in him had become involved in the sheriff's case, he'd be sticking around. Having Jessie Nash to look at was an added bonus. Too bad, the sexy deputy hadn't shown any interest in him, which meant he probably should look the other way.

Why she of all people had piqued his interest he didn't know. In the past, he never went for the hard-to-get type—and she was as hard to get as Maryland crab cakes in the dead of winter.

It was only a matter of time before she pointed a finger at him. Her beloved sheriff was reported dead a few hours after he'd arrived in a town that hadn't seen a homicide in forever. Though with all the new construction nearby, there were tons of new people about, and any one of them could have had a run in with the sheriff and gone too far.

If by some chance Jessie did ask for his continued help, he couldn't turn her down since he had offered. He should get out of Kerry as soon as possible, but it wasn't like he had anything else lined up back at home.

A soft wind chime sounded above The Sugar Shack's door. He looked up, thankful for the distraction. From his vantage point in the back, he could keep watch over who came and went. Two construction workers barreled in, one dressed in a flannel shirt and jeans, sporting a big gut and a bigger laugh, while the second man, who was in his mid-twenties, looked fit. He must have told a whopper of a joke, one that Dax wished he'd have heard, as he sure could use a good laugh right about now.

He leaned back against the padded cushion, and as he waited impatiently for Margaret and her two lady friends to arrive, he tapped the spoon on the edge of his cup until the guy in the next booth shushed him. Dax checked his watch, wondering once more what was taking them so long.

Because Margaret and her friends were the last to see Sadie alive, he wanted to ask them a few questions before their memories rooted in and took a turn straight toward some alien spaceship.

Jeez, what kind of case had he taken on?

The bell above the door chimed again, and his gaze shot toward the entrance to find Ms. Jessie herself striding in. Even though she was still dressed in those drab pants and that bulky shirt, she looked good.

He tossed the spoon down in disgust, needing to get a grip. He was here to do a job and nothing more.

With a hand on her hip, she scanned the restaurant. Dax was about to raise his hand to get her attention when she spotted him, nodded without smiling, and headed straight for the opposite side of the restaurant.

Given they were unofficially working together, he'd expected at least a wave. Then again, this was business. Maybe she was meeting someone to get more information about Clinton DuPree's death and didn't need him butting in. He *had* come on a little strong in the alley behind the bar, but that was because he was best suited to process the crime scene.

A waitress walked by his table carrying a tray full of wonderful smelling French Fries and a juicy hamburger, making his stomach grumble, but he decided to eat after he spoke with the ladies.

The door opened again, and this time Margaret and her two friends strolled in. She spotted Dax immediately, waved, and headed toward his booth. Shoulders back, Margaret seemed to concentrate on making sure she didn't lose her balance as she wove around the tables. Bless her soul, Jessie's grandmother looked so much like his Granny it wasn't funny.

The short woman next to her was as frail as a winter snowflake, and the third woman was six feet if she was an inch and looked like she'd spent her life enjoying her own home cooked meals—a real Julia Childs look-a-alike.

"Howdy, Dax." Margaret sat next to him and patted his hand like a child, while her two friends slipped in across from him.

It was nice to see a friendly face for a change, but holy shit, one of the three old-timers must have lost her alien-loving sense of smell. His eyes watered from the overwhelming scent of perfume, but a quick sip of coffee saved him from coughing.

Margaret introduced her friends. Both women seemed fully functioning in the brain department, which was a good start, but he wondered if they shared Margaret's enthusiasm for aliens.

His waitress, Lena, came over, pen and pad in hand, looking frazzled. "Hi, Margaret, Eleanor, Mary Alice. What can I get you ladies today?"

They looked at each other, then back at Lena. In unison, they answered, "The usual."

Lena nodded then glanced back at Dax. "You need a refill, darling? Or a fresh pastry?"

"I'm fine, thanks." As soon as Lena left, Dax swirled the coffee in his cup. "I appreciate you ladies meeting with me on a Saturday morning."

"Our pleasure," Eleanor said with a broad smile.

She ran her fingers over her necklace in a slow, seductive manner. Dear God, the woman was seventy-five if she was a day, but if he wasn't mistaken, she was flirting with him.

Mary Alice, the short, frail lady, wore too much makeup, but at least she didn't look at him like she wanted to eat him for dessert. The frown on her face made him wonder if he'd get much out of her. As if she could read his mind, she raised her hand.

"Yes?" Dax asked.

"It's not fair," she announced with authority.

He'd play her game. "What's not fair, Mary Alice?" That her friend hadn't shown up in days?

"They took Sadie, and I wanted to be the one." Mary Alice glanced at Margaret then at Eleanor.

"Excuse me?" he asked. Mary Alice might be battier than Margaret.

"Don't you know anything about alien technology? They do sexual experiments on humans, and I wanted to see what it was like to be taken, probed, and experimented on. They return you in one piece without harm, or so I've read." Her lips pinched together as she folded her arms over her chest.

Dax didn't know how to respond. Half of him wanted to burst out laughing, and the other half wanted someone to beam him out of there. He realized a little too late that he should have insisted on going with Jessie this morning instead of meeting with these ladies, but to be fair, Margaret had hired him to find Sadie, so here he was.

Time to bring the topic back into the real world. "I'd like to know where you women were when you saw these magical lights Margaret reported to the sheriff."

Margaret raised a brow at the word *magical* then cleared her throat. "We were on my front porch when we seen the lights, which were clear as day. The mine is only a mile away. We built our house nearby because my dear husband, Charley," she sniffed when she said his name, "used to own the Nash mines. When he died three years ago, I had to sell the business to Robert Catchman." Her lips turned into a sneer. "That crook ran the business into the ground and did it on purpose to spite Charley's memory. How he benefited, I don't know."

"Margaret," Eleanor chided. "The lights? Tell him about the lights."

"Oh, right. Of course." She turned back to Dax. "As I started to say, we seen these lights near the mine and wondered what was going on. Normally, it's black as coal in my part of town, so lights are something of a curiosity. The four of us drove out there, waited in the car, and watched." She folded her hands on her lap as though she was finished with her explanation.

"And?" Dax prompted.

"Well, the lights started moving every which direction for about ten minutes then disappeared."

"So you didn't see a ship descend or anything?" Not that Dax expected her to say yes, but with these women, nothing would surprise him.

"No, only the lights."

At least she wasn't totally senile. Dax took a sip of his now cool coffee. "Where was Sadie when all this was going on?"

Mary Alice leaned forward. "She was with us the whole time, that is until she decided to have a look-see for herself." From her expression, he could tell she didn't approve.

The women had told him Sadie had come home safe that night. "Go on."

Eleanor placed a hand on Mary Alice's arm. Guess she wanted to be the one to finish the story. "Sadie couldn't help herself." She shot a glare at Mary Alice, who then tossed Eleanor a disgusted look. "Sadie got out of the car against our wishes and made her way closer to the mine, but we kept our headlights trained on her. That's when she found the spectacles the aliens wore."

Dax didn't know whether to tell them the goggles were military issue, but he then decided it wouldn't do any good to disillusion them.

"None of you saw Sadie again after that night?" he asked.

They all shook their heads.

"Ladies, Sheriff DuPree implied Sadie might have gone off on a cruise or traveled across the country."

"Not without telling us," Margaret said sharply.

"So what's your theory about what happened to Sadie?" he said to no one in particular. *Please don't say aliens took her.*

Mary Alice slapped the table. "We already told you. The aliens took her."

Right—the sexually oriented aliens. He had finished off his coffee just as Lena came over with another freshly brewed pot, along with some tea. She dropped off the drinks as the ladies began speculating about Sadie, acting as though *he* was some invisible alien.

Fine by him. He listened with one ear while his gaze wandered over to where Jessie sat. She was facing him and he'd never seen her look so happy, and an emotion he refused to identify warmed his belly. Dax quickly shifted his attention to Jessie's booth mate.

A broad-shouldered man in a leather jacket sat across from her. Jessie laughed and leaned forward, not acting like the stiff, professional woman she'd presented to him. From the way she was tilting her head, she was flirting with the man, and Dax's fingers clasped the cup tighter. Her interaction wasn't like any interrogation he'd ever seen. No, this was personal.

"So what's your next move, Mr. Mitchell?" Eleanor asked, jerking him out of his fantasy viewing.

He straightened and refocused his attention back to the ladies. "If she had been taken by the aliens, there's not much I can do. If she wasn't, then I'll have to investigate. Margaret said Sadie was a seamstress. I'll see if I can get a list of her clients and ask if any of them saw her the day she disappeared."

Eleanor sipped her tea and made a face. She dumped in a ton

of sugar, stirred some more, and sipped again. "Much better. Mr. Mitchell, the person Sadie last worked for was Roberta Barton. Sadie was making curtains for her. I'd start with her if I were you," Eleanor said.

"Thanks." He made a note in his cell.

They seemed convinced he could find this Roberta woman without any more help from them and began chatting. While he sipped on his coffee and mentally mapped out his next move, Dax watched Jessie. He didn't need to be subtle as the woman paid him no mind.

No question about it. Jessie knew this man and liked him too. The guy could be a boyfriend, yet Dax didn't remember her mentioning she was dating anyone. Then again, he hadn't been there long enough for her to tell him anything about her personal life.

Who was he kidding? If he stayed a year, the highly professional Jessie Nash wouldn't tell him squat. She looked up and caught him staring, and just like that her smile disappeared.

He sank back against his seat. Now she probably thought he was some kind of creep. "Excuse me, ladies. I have work to do." He opened his wallet, whipped out a five-dollar bill, and dropped the money on the table. His empty stomach be damned.

As he stalked out, Dax could almost feel Jessie's gaze bore a hole right through him. Christ. He hoped he hadn't messed things up too badly with all his glances.

***

Jessie didn't know how to react to Dax's less than friendly stare. He'd seemed nice enough when they first met, but she'd never asked Nana how she found him. Knowing her grandmother, Nana might have seen an ad and believed his tales of greatness.

Jessie planned to run Dax Mitchell through the National Criminal Database to see if he had a record, and she could only hope he wasn't some criminal who'd come to take advantage of

Nana. Dax had suggested someone might have lured Jessie out of the house to harm her grandmother, but surely *he* wasn't thinking of doing that. They had no money and nothing worth taking. And to think he'd spent the night under their roof, where anything could have happened. Of course, nothing did, but that was beside the point.

"Jess, you okay?" Brian asked, placing a warm, callused palm on her hand. "You seemed off in space somewhere."

"Sorry. I can't seem to keep Clinton's death off my mind." *Good catch, Jess.* Next time she might not be so lucky. She pulled her hand from under his and pushed the image of Dax away.

Focus. She took a better look at Brian Richards, finding it hard to believe it had been ten years since she'd last seen him. He'd changed a lot and not necessarily for the better. Back then his hair had been long and shiny. Now, he wore it cut close to the scalp—military style—and had a few streaks of gray at the temple. The beard only served to make him look older, and the lines that shot out from around his eyes and mouth gave him a dangerous look, exactly how she used to like her men—until she'd wised up. To think he was only twenty-nine. He looked ten years older.

Back in high school, she'd dreamed of being with Brian for good, until he'd turned into a jerk his senior year. That was when she decided she'd had enough of the out of control man-boy.

"Can I refresh your tea?" Lena held the plastic pitcher over Jessie's half-filled glass.

"Why not?" she said even though she didn't plan on staying much longer.

"Any for you, Brian?" Lena waved a hot pot of steaming coffee, the aroma of warm beans almost making Jessie wish she'd ordered a cup.

When he held a hand over his drink, Lena smiled then went back to her other customers.

Jess studied Brian, and a sliver of guilt surfaced. To be fair, Brian was not at fault for his father's death. He'd found his dad hitting his younger brother and had gone ballistic on his father. Brian had landed a punch, and the drunken man had slipped, knocked his head on the corner of the coffee table, and died less than an hour later. His mom was devastated, but she'd convinced the authorities it had been an accident.

Jessie had felt so sorry for Brian at the time but then worried his father's violence might be passed onto Brian and to his kids. It hurt like hell when she told him goodbye, but she had her standards. When he'd said he wanted to leave Kerry for good right after high school, she sent him off with a fond farewell.

"I gotta say, Jess, you're looking mighty fine."

"Huh? Oh, thank you." She wiped her mouth with the rough paper napkin, not wanting to discuss how either of them had aged. "So, when did you get into town?"

"Three days ago. I didn't stop by because I heard about your grandmother's friend's disappearance and figured you'd be too busy to socialize. I didn't find out about DuPree's death until this morning. Man, Jess, what's happening to our little town?"

She leaned back against the soft, leather booth and shook her head. "I wish I knew. Speaking of disappearing, have you ever heard from George?"

"No." Jessie thought she saw a flash of fear cross his face, but it left so quickly she figured she'd been mistaken. "My brother walked out on the family what, fourteen years ago, and never looked back, lucky son of a bitch."

His attitude was a cover up. His older brother's leaving had hurt him.

Brian smiled. "So, is there anything I can do to help with your case load?" His hardness evaporated faster than sweat in winter.

This was the side of Brian she'd always liked—personable, eager, and charming. "Not really."

One eyebrow lifted up. "You sure? You are alone in the office." She shook her head. "Well, let me know if you think of anything."

"I will."

"So what have you been up to?" he asked.

"Work, work, and more work. Nana hired an outsider to find Sadie, and I'm trying to find out who killed Clinton."

Brian wrapped his hands around his coffee mug. "You got any leads?"

"Not yet." Brian had to realize she'd never leak information about an ongoing investigation.

"I've been thinking a lot about you." He looked up and her heart skipped a beat.

"Y-you have?" *Don't go there.* Brian was a bad boy, and someone who would try to control her. He was just the kind of man she didn't need.

Her mind skipped to Dax Mitchell again, who wasn't much better. She'd seen how he'd tried to take over the investigation as if she was some stupid hick. Nope. She'd keep her distance from him too.

"Yes, a lot. We had good times together, you know." Brian went on. "Real good times. Do you remember riding on the back of my bike? Or how about the time we went hiking and got lost?"

She laughed then took a sip of her lemony iced tea. "How could I forget?"

Jessie didn't want to remember those times though, at least not now. That was in the past, and she wanted to live in the present. "So tell me what you've been doing since you left. I know you reenlisted. How did that go?" No one seemed to know what had happened to Brian after his mom passed. Many thought he'd been killed in battle.

"I did one more tour then left the service for good."

She almost spit out her drink. "You left? Man, I pegged you for a lifer. What happened?" She dabbed her napkin on her chin.

His eyes turned cold for a moment, and then he shrugged. "Does there have to be a reason?"

Given it appeared to be a sore subject, she decided to drop it for now, but she'd do some digging later. "No. Then what did you do?"

He drained the rest of his coffee, though he didn't act as though he enjoyed the taste. "Worked construction in Tampa for a while. I know this is hard to believe, but I actually began to miss Kerry. The never ending heat down there and the lack of seasons finally got to me." He looked up at the ceiling for a moment. "Funny, I couldn't wait to get out of this town the moment I turned eighteen, but here I am, back for a job."

A squeal stopped her from probing further. Jessie looked up to find Lena hugging some tall blonde. The two separated, and Jessie's heart sped up.

It couldn't be, could it?

CHAPTER FOUR

Jessie twisted in the booth and faced Brian. "Is that Amanda Simmons?" If so, her best friend from high school sure had changed.

Brian nearly dropped his cup on the table. "Jesus H. Christ. It sure as hell is. Wow, she looks amazing."

Jessie laughed. The man was more fickle than any woman she'd known. She leaned back, certain Lena would drag the newcomer over any second. Sure enough, Lena turned and pointed at her. Seeing Amanda again almost erased the sadness that had saddled her all day.

Her friend strutted over, wearing a too short skirt and an obscenely low cut top. How Amanda even walked in those three-inch heels, Jessie didn't know. A few men whistled as she passed by their tables and she waggled her fingers at them. Jessie couldn't blame the men. Kerry wasn't a place that attracted women, especially hot ones.

Amanda had cut her long, blonde hair really short, but on her the style looked good. Jessie had never bothered to cut her hair in a particular style, and her no-upkeep do suited her fine.

Jessie slid out of the booth, and Amanda threw her arms around her in a huge bear hug. Uncomfortable with the closeness, Jessie was about to step back when Amanda held her at arm's length and ran her gaze up and down.

"Why Jessie Nash, look at you all dressed up in that uniform. I swear, girl, if it weren't for your long hair, you could pass for a boy. I need to take you shopping and get you gussied up. It's so good to see you." Amanda's gaze dropped to Jessie's ring finger. "Just as I suspected."

Former best friend or not, don't even think about going there. Jessie slipped her left hand behind her back. She had no intention of explaining to a girl, or rather a woman, why she hadn't married. She had that debate with Nana almost every friggin' night.

Jessie glanced to the booth where Dax had been sitting. If only Kerry had men like him, she'd be married in a heartbeat. Not to him specifically, since he was too controlling and too much the I-am-man type, but to some sensitive man who looked like him.

Jessie remembered her manners. "Amanda, do you rememb—"

Another shriek. "Ohmigod, is that you, Brian, underneath that scruffy beard?"

"Sure as shit is." He stood, wrapped his arms around Amanda's waist, and spun her, just like old times.

Jessie swore red underpants peeked out from under Amanda's skirt.

"Boy, oh, boy, do you look great," Brian said. "When did you blow into town?"

"'Bout four days ago."

"Same here."

Jessie sat down and scooted to the end of the booth while she waited for the two old friends to finish their out-of-control reunion. When they both slid in, Jessie realized she was a tad hurt. "Amanda, why didn't you let me know you were back in town?" Brian had already explained his delayed appearance.

Amanda slapped a hand on Jessie's wrist and squeezed. "Yeah, about that. I've been meaning to stop by, but I've been busy getting Momma situated. You might have heard she's not doing all that well, which was why I had to come home in the first place."

Jessie had heard her mother had been diagnosed with liver problems. Drinking was a bitch on the system. "I'm sorry she's so bad. Do you have a minute to catch up or do you have to get back to her?"

"I'm good. A friend is staying with her this afternoon."

Brian leaned forward with a gleam in his eye. "Say girls, you all know what's happening in three weeks, don't you?"

"No." Jessie hadn't a clue.

"I do." Amanda winked at Brian then flashed a big smile at Jessie.

Jessie shook her head. "What? Tell me." *I'm so not dying to know.*

"I can't believe you, Jessie Nash," Brian said. "It's only our tenth high school reunion. What say we all drive over together to Calvert and have a blast."

Brian had been the star athlete in high school while she'd been the geek. What he'd seen in her back then, she'd never know. "I'll pass."

The last thing she wanted to do was talk about the good ole days and how much their lives sucked because they'd done squat since high school. She didn't get over to Calvert much since only a small portion of their graduation class even came from Kerry.

Amanda nudged her. "Come on, Jess. I'm going. I wouldn't miss it for the world."

Really? Sure Amanda had been homecoming queen, but she never tried to be the most popular kid. Despite looking great, she had a mind too. "Look, I haven't seen many of the kids since we graduated." Nor had she wanted to.

Amanda winked at Brian. "Let me work on her. She'll change her mind."

Right. And the town's road would be sprinkled with diamonds.

***

Dax was stumped. He'd found Roberta Barton all right, but he wasn't so sure her information would lead him anywhere.

Roberta handed him a cup of steaming coffee. "Sugar's on the table in the little, flowered bowl there. I don't have any cream, so I hope that's all right."

"No problem." He needed to wait for the coffee to cool. "How would you describe Sadie's mood when she was here? Was she anxious, excited or what?" He slipped off his sweater since she kept the place stifling hot.

"Hmm. A, B, or C. I'll take B for one hundred," she giggled, acting ten instead of in her late sixties. "Excited."

"Did she say about what?"

Her brows furrowed. "Well, the aliens of course. Wouldn't you be if you'd found evidence they existed?"

He inwardly groaned at the mention of aliens again. The local theater must have shown some Roswell documentary, and the old ladies had bought into the conspiracy theory.

"Perhaps. How about telling me what you know about her disappearance, and start at the beginning." Dax took a sip of the coffee and it nearly burned his tongue. Yowza. Well, at least the drink was strong, and he needed the caffeine to help him stay awake in her heated home.

"She came by last Tuesday to measure my windows. I'd found the cutest blue and white check material at Wilson's Fabric House that I wanted her to use," she said waving a hand, "but I'm sure you don't want to hear about my home decorating plans. Anyway, that was the last time I saw her." Roberta sniffled then dabbed her eyes with a lacy handkerchief.

"I thought you said she sounded excited."

"She did when she told me about the goggles she'd found, and that she wanted to go back and see if she could find a piece of metal from the spaceship or something else alien. She was big into souvenirs."

Dax didn't want to go down that path. "Let's suppose, for argument's sake, she arrived home safely that night. Can you think of anywhere she might have gone the next day?"

Roberta closed her eyes. She remained still for so long, he thought she might have fallen asleep. Then her eyelids popped open. "Well, there was this man in town the week before Sadie left us. He rode in on some fancy schmancy motorcycle."

That sounded like a potential lead. "Can you describe him?"

"Oh, yes. He was youngish—maybe sixty-five, with really thick, white hair. He was sexy as hell." Roberta fanned herself.

Kerry must have done something to the water supply to make everyone want to get laid.

"Did you see Sadie and this man together?" he asked after nearly scalding his tongue on the coffee for the second time.

"Sure did. I could tell Sadie took a real liking to him. The Sunday before she disappeared, there was a church social. We always have a social on the third Sunday of the month. Could her man dance or what? He had Sadie doing the tango, and my, oh, my, they were attached at the hip most of the night. Why, I wouldn't be surprised if she hopped on the back of his bike and high-tailed it out of town."

Now he was getting some place. "Do you know this man's name?" Dax pulled out his phone to take down the information. He didn't want to bring up the fact that her friend probably wouldn't have measured Roberta's windows if she'd planned to leave town the next day though. This strange man could have abducted Sadie, although Dax saw no reason to wait a week after the dance to take her.

"Sadie called him Sexy Sam. She never mentioned his last name."

"I'll ask around and see if anyone can ID him. Do you know where he was staying?"

"Why with Sadie, of course."

Of course. He needed to get out of this crazy-as-a-bat town.

"Thank you for your time. If you think of anything else, I'm staying over at the Nash place."

She smiled. "Oh, don't I know it."

Great. He didn't need rumors spread about him. What he did need was a drink—a really strong, cold drink, and The Coal Mine Bar was just the place. He might even find out more about Sadie Palmer's new adventure from some of the locals. If that lead failed, he'd tackle Clinton DuPree's disappearance.

Fortunately, Roberta lived less than a mile from town, and he was at the bar in no time. Dax pushed open the heavy wooden door to relative darkness, and it took a moment for his vision to adjust. The place smelled of stale beer, sweat, and rotten wood— a stench worse than the first time he'd been there. Not that a bar ought to smell like some spa, but this place was foul. Maybe that's why it was called the Coal Mine Bar since it was like a fetid hole five hundred feet underground.

Dax scanned the insides. Only two other men were there, each with a drink in front of him, deep in conversation. Dax wouldn't disturb them unless he needed to.

A huskily built bartender was polishing the wooden counter with a clean, white rag, and since the stools looked safe enough to sit on, Dax took a seat. "Hi, I'm Dax Mitchell, a private invest—"

"I know who you are. Brad told me to expect you."

The town was smaller than he'd thought. "And you are?"

The bartender looked annoyed. "Bruno Quattrone, the owner."

"I'd like to ask you some questions about Sadie Palmer."

The bartender turned his back and lined up the liquor bottles behind him—bottles that were perfectly straight to begin with. Dax waited. It was what he did well.

Finally, Bruno turned around. "Sadie didn't come in here, so I don't know anything about her disappearance."

Dax believed Mr. Gruff. "Then what can you tell me about the sheriff's disappearance?"

His jaw clenched and his eyes squinted, as though he were in pain. "I wish I could help you there. I told Jessie everything I know, which was nothing." This time, the man came off as sincere instead of inconvenienced.

"Do you know if the sheriff had any enemies?"

Bruno laughed, but the sound held no joy. "Everyone in this town has enemies, mostly because everyone has a secret or two."

"What would the sheriff's secret be?"

Bruno shook his head. "If I knew, it wouldn't be a secret, now would it, Einstein?" The guy had a point.

A new customer rolled in and Bruno moved to the end of the bar to take his order. Dax swiveled around trying to figure out his next move. It was probably time to head to where Sadie had been seen last. He spun back to motion for Bruno, needing not only a drink but directions to the mine. The guy either was ignoring him or he didn't see him wave his arms. After not getting the man's attention for a good two minutes, Dax spoke up. "Hey, bartender."

The owner turned. "Name's Bruno. Do you have a short memory problem?"

His mom should have named him Pit Bull or Viper, but Bruno wasn't a bad second choice. Dax decided to play nice. "Bruno, can I ask you something?" There—nice as could be.

The man looked disgusted, but then excused himself from the other customer and ambled over. "Yeah?"

"Can you give me directions to the mine?"

"Whatcha want to go there for? It's been closed for a year." Bruno tossed his towel into the bar sink.

Dax held his tongue. "I know, but Sadie Palmer was last seen there."

Bruno's shoulders relaxed. "Oh, sure." He turned to his right and faced the front door. "Take Main Street 'till you come to Orchard Avenue." Bruno pointed with his right hand. "Take a right and go maybe three or four miles. Stanford Street is at the end, so when you reach it, hang another right. You can't miss the place. Lots of Do Not Enter signs."

"Thanks."

Just as Dax was leaving, the door swung open and nearly hit him in the face. Three dusty men, all looking like they'd just gotten off work at the cement plant, plowed in. From the smiles on their faces, they were good friends. Dax missed that sort of friendship, but P.I.'s were meant to work alone.

As he stepped outside, he realized he'd never received that longed-for drink, but at this late hour, he couldn't afford to stall. Maybe when he returned to town, he'd enjoy a cold brew. He checked the sky, noting the sun was close to setting, and calculated he had a half hour until dark. He would head to the mine, look around for a dropped handkerchief, a heel mark, or anything to show where Sadie might have been the night she disappeared, then head on over to The Sugar Shack for a bite to eat.

Worse case, he'd find some alien metal and go on a national tour. *Late Night, here I come.* Okay, so he'd lost his ever-loving mind. According to Mary Alice, alien technology could do things to a person, and he was close to being a believer.

With fantasy time over, Dax climbed into his truck and took off. Orchard Avenue was paved for the first two miles before turning to dirt. Dense forest lined both sides of the road, and boulders, some the size of an eleven-man football team, sat on the edge of the forest. Thick trees blocked out the last rays of the day.

Maybe coming this late hadn't been such a good idea. He probably should have waited until morning when the sun was shining and the trees weren't hovering over him like the specter of death.

Get a grip. He wasn't trapped in a mine elevator, and he wasn't hearing his father's last screams or feeling the heat of fire singe his feet after the methane gas exploded below. He was safe. Yet the panic still clawed at his gut every time he was in a small, dark

space. The woods at night might be in the wide open, but the
rush of anxiety still claimed him. So far, no amount of therapy
had helped.

Dax hummed and tapped the wheel to get his mind off the
dark, hoping to stop the impending panic from ripping out his
guts and making him wish he were dead.

Light peeked through the leaves at random intervals, and he
could see for a few seconds at a time, which helped reduce the
stress and lower his blood pressure. Once he reached the mine,
he planned to keep his headlights on, which meant he had
nothing to worry about.

Willing to take the jostling for the sake of time, Dax sped up.
His struts squeaked, proving once more he should buy a new
truck, but he'd grown fond of this one.

After another mile, the trees thinned. At the end, he hung a
right, and a terraced hillside appeared. Four wooden structures,
complete with a tall silo were pressed against a large mound of
dirt that some might call a small mountain. In front sat the
mine. A large *No Trespassing* sign was leaning halfway over,
looking as if the metal post had been run over by a car or some
piece of heavy machinery.

Pop. Ping.

What the hell was that? He looked around, straining his
senses to hear where the noise had come from when his car
jerked to the left, forcing him to fight for control. His tire hit a
pothole, and he flew upward, smashing his head on the cab ceiling. "Shit."

He let up on the gas pedal and slammed on his brakes. When
he brought the truck to a halt, he jumped out to check the
damage. Wind whipped his hair and sent a chill straight to his
bones. He stepped around to the passenger's side only to find his
tire was flat and the rim bent. That sucked. He knelt down and
ran a finger along the warm rubber, his heart nearly stopping
when he felt a familiar shape of metal lodged deep in the tire.

A bullet.

A pissing sound near his foot drew his attention, and then the smell of gas hit him. His gaze shot to the rear of the truck to where a second bullet had creased the side panel. When he ran a hand under the gas tank, liquid was streaming out. "You've got to be kidding me."

The beginnings of fear bubbled in his gut until anger took over. Dax stood and scanned the area, looking for the bastard who'd crippled him. He had to guess there was someone or something at the mine he shouldn't see. Whether the warning shot had to do with Sadie or Clinton, he couldn't hazard a guess.

Then reality sunk in. The shooter was still out there. Dax raced to the driver's side and ducked down. He didn't need to be pickings for some sharp shooter. He listened harder this time, trying to spot his location. Tree limbs banged against each other like dry bones, a bird chirped, and a squirrel raced up a tree, but that was all. No one was shouting for him to leave the area, and no one was running through the forest trying to get away.

Despite his training, Dax couldn't locate anyone. It was as if the man had dropped in from outer space. While Dax had a gun in the glove compartment, he couldn't hit what he couldn't see.

He hadn't passed any vehicle on the road nor spotted any car parked nearby. Because no one could have known he'd be there, the shooter might not have been targeting him personally. The town could have some sicko who lived nearby who took the *No Trespassing* sign to heart, though Dax couldn't see him spending his days waiting with a scope to his eye for the occasional trespasser. On the other hand, Bruno the bartender could have called ahead to say some out of towner was asking questions.

The Nash's used to own the mine, but Margaret had sold it to someone else. Batman? Catman? He'd have to ask her again.

Christ, he didn't need this. Shooting out a tire took amazing training, and if the man had wanted Dax dead, he'd be dead. Stranding Dax there made even less sense as he might think to seek shelter at the mine—exactly where the shooter probably didn't want Dax to go.

The sun's warmth was slowly disappearing, and with it, its light. Shooter or no shooter, Dax wasn't going to stay there any longer. He opened the driver's side door and slithered in, not wanting to expose his body to another shot. He opened the glove compartment and found his one and only flashlight, having handed his other one to Jessie last night. He grabbed his gun and shoved it in his side holster.

Waiting was not an option. Without gas, this truck wasn't going anywhere and given his cell phone didn't have any reception, he had no choice but to hightail it back to town. The only trouble was, would the shooter be close behind?

CHAPTER FIVE

After Jessie left Amanda and Brian bonding at the restaurant, her day went downhill from there. No sooner had she stepped from the café than she received a call from Harper Barton about a gas station theft. The owner said someone stole one hundred and fifty gallons of gas, but that he had some super-duper sophisticated camera trained on the pump. All she needed to do was watch the video, identify the thief, and make the arrest. Easy.

Too bad when she arrived, she discovered that someone had shot the lens out of his precious camera, and that Harold hadn't even watched the footage. Even spookier, when Harold replayed the part up to the shooting, the camera didn't pick up the person's image. All they heard was this loud popping noise, followed by the tinkling of glass hitting the pavement. With a dead-on shot, the person had to be in front of the camera—only he wasn't.

If she hadn't watched the footage herself, she wouldn't have believed it. The story just might qualify for *Ripley's Believe It Or Not*, especially since Harold kept a spotlight focused on the tanks twenty-four seven.

Jessie had even tried to duplicate the shot by standing five feet back from the camera and aiming her revolver at the lens.

Even pretending to take a shot, her hands shook enough to make hitting the two-inch lens unlikely.

As far as she was concerned, the only person who had the talent to do the job was a military marksman, and Jessie didn't know anyone like that in Kerry. The perpetrator could have been a passerby, but then the camera would have picked up the car driving in.

Something strange was happening to this town, and she wished like hell she knew what it was. She'd been with the department seven years, going on eight, and nothing like this had ever happened before. They had the usual domestic violence and drunks getting into fights, especially on a Sunday night, but not murder and theft.

Jessie refused to buy into Nana's alien theory. As for other beliefs, global warming affected the weather, but it didn't kill people or rob them.

That was when she decided Clinton had indeed been murdered, and that this wasn't some hoax, as the I-know-so-much private eye, Mitchell, had first suggested.

What she couldn't figure out was who had Clinton pissed off enough to want him dead? He'd arrested close to half the men in this town at one time or another, but she couldn't think of a single soul who didn't deserve the punishment. Then again, the guilty party might not share her definition of deserving. Thinking she might be headed down the wrong path, she went back to the office to check Clinton's desk drawer for some answers.

So here she sat, at his desk, completely confused. She'd found receipts for a generator, one for a large screen TV, and another for a tractor. The problem was Clinton DuPree didn't need a tractor for a lawn that was but fifty feet across, so what the hell was going on? She needed to figure this out fast before someone else was hurt. As much as she didn't want to admit it, it looked like Clinton was on the take, or worse, he could be blackmailing someone. If he had been, her list of suspects just shot up to around six hundred—the town's small population. Okay, maybe five hundred, since not every person in Kerry had a secret worthy of blackmail.

Her boss had lived a simple life. She'd driven by his house plenty of times and had even dropped him off a time or two, but she'd never been inside his home, so she couldn't know that for sure. She'd assumed it was a typical bachelor pad complete with cheap furniture that didn't match. From the outside, his house needed a lot of TLC in the form of a paint job and some landscaping that included weed killer. She was having a hard time believing that the man her father had recommended to take over the sheriff's seat was a cheat. But even the best were fooled sometimes.

Her eyes blurred, and she gulped down the rest of her cold coffee. She sure could use a break, but right now she couldn't afford to rest. She still had to look into yesterday's food raid at the Kerry supermarket and prayed this crime spree would stop.

Jessie picked up the crinkled piece of paper on which she'd scribbled the details of the incident. The manager had called yesterday, saying someone had walked off in broad daylight with a few caseloads of food in their grocery cart that was worth about four hundred bucks. She would have thought that a worker, a shopper, or even the manager himself would have noticed who'd skipped out without paying. Clearly, people walked around with blinders on.

Then there was Sadie's disappearance she still had to deal with. True, Dax Mitchell was working on the case, but she'd promised Nana she'd help too. As busy as she was, Jessie had found the time to speak with both of Sadie's neighbors on her way home from the gas station fiasco and before she'd discovered Clinton's double life, but those two women had been of no help. One was deaf and the other nearly blind. What she wouldn't give for a reliable witness. Hell, what she really needed was a clone.

"Hello?"

Jessie jerked and shot a hand to her chest. "Amanda, you scared the crap out of me. Why are you dressed up like a police officer?" Goodbye hooker, hello cop. Although Amanda carried off the look like no one else could.

"Sorry, darling, didn't mean to frighten you." She pulled up a chair, scraping the legs against the wooden floor and sat down. "I've come to ask you a favor, or actually, to *do* you a favor." Amanda brushed off some imaginary lint from her neatly pressed sleeve.

"What would that be? I assume it has to do with the uniform. Or is this a Halloween costume."

"No. I want a job."

With the crazy way today was going, all Jessie could do was laugh. She tried to remember if the costume shop down the street had many sheriff uniforms.

Amanda's eyes squinted and her mouth turned into a pout. "What's so funny?"

"Are you telling me that uniform is for real?" Her sleeve had a Georgia Sheriff's Department logo on it, but Jessie couldn't picture Amanda making an arrest. Hell, if she found two men robbing a store, she'd probably ask if they wanted to make it a threesome. No, Amanda Simmons and cop did not go together. Not unless the cop asked her to go for a joy ride or give him a blowjob. As soon as that thought crossed her mind, Jessie was ashamed of herself. Her rotten attitude was due to the stress.

Her friend crossed her legs and leaned back in the chair. "Absolutely it's real, darling, and I was damned good at my job when I worked in Georgia for two years. I have references if you don't believe me."

Amanda's story wouldn't have surprised her any more if she'd told Jessie that Nana had killed Clinton DuPree. "I don't know what to say."

"Try saying yes. You're swamped, aren't you?"

"That's an understatement."

Amanda threw her a satisfied grin. "There ya go. You need

help, and I need a job. When can I start?" She slapped a palm on the desk with a resounding thump.

Jessie jumped again. "I'm not sure ab—"

"Listen. I won't take no for an answer. I have a criminology degree from the University of Georgia, which was followed by a four-year stint in the Navy. After I got out, I worked at the Sheriff's Department in Macon for two years." She slipped her hand in her purse and produced documented copies of what she'd claimed.

Jessie studied them. "I had no idea." Amanda was bright and always had an interest in law enforcement, but she never thought she'd pursue her dream.

"If I don't work out after two weeks, fire me." She pulled a nail file from her purse and sanded down her pinky finger.

Dear God, Amanda had turned into a girlie-girl. How was that possible, given her career path? Back in high school she used to be more of a jock than a walking ad for a cosmetics company. Jessie wasn't even sure she could relate to this new person.

An authoritative knock sounded on her door. Without waiting for an invitation, Mayor Bob Kreplick and Peter Lucas, the President of the Bank of Kerry, marched in. *My, my.* Two dignitaries were coming to her lowly hovel. Maybe the aliens had disturbed the atmosphere as Nana claimed.

"Gentlemen, to what do I owe this honor?"

They stared at Amanda then back at her. "May we talk in private?"

Amanda stood. "I can take a hint." She twirled around to face the door and wiggled her fingers goodbye. "Later, gator."

Jessie was about to protest her friend's casual attitude, but Amanda held up her hand. Now wasn't the right time to pick this fight. As soon as her friend slipped out the door, the two men sat down opposite her.

"We have a proposition for you."

***

Dax's leg throbbed like a bitch with every step. To control the pain, he had to drag his foot, instead of putting his full weight on it. Once the ache turned tolerable, he jogged until the throbbing started again. Drag, jog, drag, jog. It got old real fast, but he had to reach Jessie and warn her about the shooter. It was possible the person trying to stop him didn't want anyone—including Jessie—to learn what happened to Sadie.

When he couldn't take another step, Dax rested his back against a tree and slammed his fist against the sharp bark at his weak leg. As fresh waves of sweet smelling pine and alder wafted toward him, he pushed aside his fatigue and began to move again, though he didn't remember four miles being this far. It seemed like he'd jogged or dragged for ten miles already.

The sky had turned dark and small animals kept scurrying in the underbrush. With all the racket they were making, he'd never be able to hear a person approach.

He swung his light back and forth to make sure no one was hiding behind a tree lying in wait for him. On the next pass, a pair of glowing eyes looked back at him and he stilled. Then the baby deer twitched its ears, and Dax relaxed. His imagination was out of control. He inhaled deeply and took a moment to marvel at the animal's beauty, but the spell was broken a second later when the deer jetted off, disappearing into the dense foliage.

It suddenly occurred to him that perhaps a hunter and not some psycho had nailed his tire and tank while trying to kill a deer. Regardless of who had shot up his truck, Dax had to forge on. Expecting the worst, he zigzagged to make it more difficult for someone to hit him. The evasive action came second nature to him, but it expended a lot of energy. He stayed close to the forest edge just in case a car happened to drive down this hardly-ever-used road. Assuming the person didn't look like a killer, he'd flag him down.

He did a mental head slap. It wasn't like he could tell a killer by his looks. God, he hated what was happening to his mind. The darkness was making him crazy.

He'd spent two years disarming land mines in Iraq and remained calm under stress. Facing a little darkness shouldn't cause him to panic, but it did.

A flash of lightning lit up the sky, and while his face burned cold from the wind, his body was hot from the exertion. He hoped it didn't rain because the flashlight might die if it became too wet.

Move.

Dax continued, counting his steps, trying to take his mind off the darkness. With his gaze on the beam hitting the leaves and rocks, he turned his thoughts to something more pleasant: Jessie. He pictured her sitting on the sofa, all snuggled up in a blanket, drinking hot cocoa, looking sexy and warm. He closed his eyes for a second to picture her face smiling up at him, but then he had to use his imagination since she'd mostly shown him a tense, uptight look. Only once had he'd seen her softer side.

Thinking of Jessie instead of where he was going, he tripped. The next thing he knew, he was face down on the cold, wet leaves, and his flashlight had slipped from his fingers. A crack sounded, and the light disappeared.

Oh, shit. *Please no.* Blackness closed in around him, squeezing the breath from his lungs. His instincts kicked in, telling him to find the light. As he pushed up to his knees, the rain came down in earnest, and Dax patted the ground, frantically trying to locate his precious beacon. The moon peeked from behind a break in the heavy clouds just enough to allow him to spot his much-needed light. He grabbed it then flipped the *On* switch but nothing happened.

No. No. No. It couldn't be.

He slapped the body of the light against his palm, hoping the batteries or the bulb had been dislodged in the fall, but it failed to turn on. His heart sped up and air slipped down his throat in a thin trickle. His palms sweated.

My fears are irrational. My fears are irrational. My fears are irrational. He kept repeating his mantra, but the calm didn't materialize. Instead, a sharp ache swirled hard in his gut.

Push the fear aside, as my shrink would say. I just need to walk until I reach town.

Yes. I can do that.

To help calm him, he pictured Jessie once more alive and happy. With teeth gritted, Dax moved to the paved road, self-loathing nearly making him cave. He'd give anything to stop the demons from attacking his mind and ruining his life, but so far nothing ever helped.

An engine roared in the distance, and he ducked back behind a tree, grimacing at the intense ache that raced up his thigh. A pair of headlights swung around the corner and headed straight toward him.

Was it a savior or a killer?

CHAPTER SIX

The Mayor tugged on his jacket lapels. "I apologize for stopping in so late, Ms. Nash, but the City Council's meeting this afternoon ran late." He glanced at Mr. Lucas and acted as if he needed his permission to continue. "We were wondering if you would consider the job as sheriff." He cleared his throat. "Until we find a replacement for Clinton, that is."

Replacement? "You want me to be a *temporary* sheriff?" She almost knocked over the coffee cup on her desk. "I think... no, I deserve to be permanent sheriff, just like my father and his father before him." Pleased she hadn't stuttered, she continued. "I've worked hard for the last seven years to serve the good people of Kerry." Not that these fat cats ever noticed.

Both men looked at each other as if she'd lost her mind. "But you're a *woman*."

Her mouth dropped open and anger grabbed hold of her, threatening to twist off her head. "You've got to be kid-kidding me. I could sue you for saying that." She didn't care if they fired her on the spot.

"Is that a fact?"

"Yes." She leaned forward and steepled her fingers like Clinton used to do. "Tell me. What does me being female have to do with the position of sheriff? I've broken up brawls by myself, handled the weekend drunks, and solved quite a few crimes in my time." She glared at the Mayor. "Why I even stopped your cousin from beating the crap out of his wife, or don't you remember?"

The Mayor held up a hand, his face turning pink. "Now let's not get defensive, dearie. You know what we meant."

Patronizing prick. "What will it take to make you realize I can do the job?" After her dad died, she'd carried on the Nash name of law enforcers. It was what she was bred to do and what she loved. She'd seen too much of the superior male attitude to bend to their will.

Both men looked at each other. "We aren't in a position to discuss this right now."

Smart of them to keep their mouths shut, but their attitude pissed her off. Jessie was tempted to walk out, but she loved her job too much to throw it away. These sons of bitches had no idea what it took to keep order in this town. "You do realize that you're going to have a hard time finding anyone who would even want the job as sheriff."

"Oh, I don't know about that."

A sliver of panic shot straight to her gut. Surely, they didn't already have a replacement in mind. Jessie put on her straight face, the one Nana always claimed could help her clean up at poker.

"If you want to replace me so badly, go ahead. But how do you think the Barton gas station job will get solved without my help? Or the grocery store theft? Or Sadie Palmer's disappearance for that matter, not to mention Clinton's possible death?" She was shouting by the time she got to the end of her litany. "And all of this has happened in the last three days. So fine, find someone willing to take this crappy job."

They'd probably can her on the spot, but she was spitting mad right now and didn't give a damn.

"You misunderstood us. We want you to keep your job as

deputy. It's just that we think a... well, someone with more experience should be sheriff."

That was crap. She had nearly eight years of experience under Clinton's mentorship, not to mention all the stories she'd heard growing up being around her father and grandfather. What they meant was that they wanted some good ole boy they could twist around their fat little fingers. She stared at them both.

The Mayor held up a hand. "I will admit it will take the City Council some time to find a replacement, but I'm a reasonable man." Mayor Kreplick stroked his chin and straightened his already neat tie.

Kreplick leaned over to Peter Lucas once more and whispered something, but with his head turned, Jessie couldn't read his lips. She hoped they were discussing the impending lawsuit she'd flung in their faces.

He turned back to her. "Okay, here's what we're willing to do. If you can solve all those *issues* you mentioned before we find a suitable replacement, the job's yours."

The smirk on his face told her he didn't believe she had a chance in hell of being successful.

"Let me see if I have this right. If I find a missing person, capture a killer, and locate two thieves, I can be sheriff for good?"

"Yes."

Great. Now all she needed was a Superman cape. No, make that a Wonder Woman belt.

These two goons didn't know Jessie Nash. They'd thrown down the gauntlet, and she planned to win. "Fine, but I'll need help."

They looked at each other again, acting as if they couldn't make a decision on their own. What a bunch of wimps. "Where are we supposed to find this help, if as you claim, no one wants to work here?"

"I have a friend who's applied for the position as my deputy and comes highly recommended." Jessie figured she would read the recs right after as she called the Macon Sheriff's Department.

"Not that new man in town, is it?" He looked hopeful.

"No." Though Dax would be a fine addition to the force, despite his need for control.

"Well, then." The Mayor stood and Mr. Lucas followed. "We'll give you three weeks, but not a day more."

"Three we—" He'd said she had until they found a replacement.

They were out the door before she finished her second word. Well, wasn't that peachy. But hey, if God created the world in seven days, she ought to be able to solve all the mysteries in the town in twenty-one.

Jessie prayed God wasn't a multi-tasking woman.

**

Headlights blasted Dax in the face, and he darted to the other side of the tree before sliding to the wet ground. A car engine idled not ten feet from him, their lights blinding him. Damn.

"Oh, yoo-hoo," sang out a distinctly female voice that he recognized as Ms. Mary Alice's—the woman looking for alien love.

Relief washed through him, though he'd have been happier if it had been Jessie out searching for him. Dax stood and limped toward the car. The wind and rain had soaked his sweater to the bone, causing him to shiver. Margaret Nash rolled down the driver's side window halfway. "Why Dax Mitchell, what are you doing out here in the rain? You could catch your death of cold."

"It's a long story. Can you give me a lift back to town?"

"Why of course. Hop in the back."

Dax opened the rear door and spotted Roberta, the one who needed new curtains, along with Mary Alice. Riding shotgun was

Eleanor, the one who'd flirted with him. On second thought, he might be safer with the killer.

"Move over, Roberta," Mary Alice said, swatting her friend's thigh. "Can't you see Mr. Mitchell's leg's bothering him? He needs room."

He didn't want to get Margaret's seat wet, but he saw no towel of any kind to sit on. "Mrs. Nash, not that I'm not grateful for being rescued, but what are you ladies doing way out here?"

"Looking for Sadie, of course. And please, call me Margaret."

Her seatmate twisted around. "You can call me Eleanor, or Ellie for short." She batted her eyelashes at him.

Oh, boy. "I don't know for sure, but Jessie might be in danger, so could we get going? I'll answer all your questions once I'm sure she's safe."

Margaret turned around in her seat. "Jessie's in danger? Whatever from?"

"I'm not sure, but we need to leave now." He did not intend to scare the bejesus out these harmless women by mentioning a shooter was on the loose.

Margaret must have sensed his urgency because she put the car in reverse, did a three-point turn and nearly hit a tree in the process. She then floored it, sending gravel in every direction. The woman was a terror on the road, but he could kiss her right now.

In less than ten minutes, they arrived at the sheriff's office, and the moment he spotted Jessie's cruiser, the knot in his stomach loosened.

Dax couldn't wait to get away from these ladies and see if Jessie was okay. The minute Margaret slowed, Dax jumped out, and raced for the office door, throwing a "Thanks, ladies," over his shoulder.

This time when he went up the steps, he took all three at once. Leg pain be damned.

***

The door to Jessie's office flew open and her heart did a somersault. Now what did the Mayor want? She looked up. "Dax? Ohmigod, what happened?"

Jessie jumped up from her office chair and raced around her desk. He was soaked through and through, his pants were streaked with dirt, and his brows were pinched as though he was in pain. But damn, the man never looked finer.

He held up both hands. "I'm fine. Just a little wet."

"Sit down. You must be freezing. Can I get you a cup of coffee?" The poor man looked like he'd go hypothermic any minute. She wanted to strip him naked and rub her body all over his to warm him up.

Stop it, Jessie. Get ahold of yourself.

"Coffee. Yes. That would be great." His teeth chattered.

"What happened?" She touched the glass carafe to make sure the coffee was still hot, but found it lukewarm. She flipped the switch to *On* and waited with her back to him, her mind reeling.

"I went to check out the mine area where Sadie was last seen, and apparently, I got a little too close. Someone shot out my tire and put a hole in my gas tank."

She spun around. "Someone shot up your truck?"

"Yeah, and I had to walk back. Got about a couple of miles when your grandmother stopped and picked me up."

"Nana was near the mine?"

"Yes, your Nana, along with her quilting group were trying to do a little detective work on their own."

Jess couldn't help but smile at the image of Nana quilting. "She plays bridge. She'd never have the patience to make a quilt."

"It doesn't matter. She was with her friends."

"Did she say what she was doing out there?"

"Looking for Sadie."

This couldn't continue. "I'll speak with her." Her grandmother's interference could get her killed.

"Jessie, listen." His strangled cry cut straight through her. "I think you might be in danger."

She turned back to the coffee maker to hide her shaking hands. "Why would you think that?" She poured the cup of coffee and carried the drink to Dax.

He took a sip, and his shoulders relaxed. Holding the cup in one hand, he leaned forward and placed his elbows on his knees. "Someone obviously doesn't want me snooping, and I'm fairly sure once you start asking questions, they'll come after you too."

"Criminals never like it when they think we're onto them."

"I won't have your death on my hands."

His sudden bitterness—or was it fear—startled her. "You're exaggerating. You're a stranger here. I'm sure that's why you got the warning shots, assuming they really were warning shots and not just some hunter or—" She stiffened. "Oh, shit."

"What?" Dax started to stand.

She reached out a hand. "No. Sit. You said someone shot out a tire and hit your gas tank, right?" She took a step back and bumped into her desk.

"Yes."

"While you were moving?"

"Hell, yes, I was moving."

"Then I think we're all in trouble."

CHAPTER SEVEN

"Let me get you a towel. You're dripping wet," Jessie said.

She didn't care if the water puddled on the floor, Dax would catch cold if he didn't dry off. From the file cabinet against the wall, she retrieved a towel that was used for when she, Clinton, or someone else were ever caught in the rain. Without thinking, she stepped in front of him and placed it over his shoulders, and then began to rub him dry.

When he smiled, she realized that she was leaning over, her breasts in his face. She stood. "Sorry."

His smile broadened. "Don't be."

The man did something to her insides. He made her feel warm, cozy, and feminine. But now wasn't the time to let down her guard. If she allowed his good looks to get to her, she'd be crawling into his bed and forgetting all about finding Sadie or Clinton's killer. "Ah, would you like some aspirin or anything?"

When he had rushed in, his limp had seemed worse than usual. Before he could answer, she dashed back to her desk and pulled open the drawer. From inside, she found her bottle and extracted two pills. Just like Nana used to do, she strode over and held open her palm. "Take these."

"Yes, ma'am." Dax swallowed both pills. "You were telling me about the gas station heist?"

Happy to be on more familiar ground, Jessie told him about the camera lens being shot out at Barton's gas station, along with the fact that there had been no evidence of a shooter. When she went to take a sip of coffee, her cup was dry.

He looked off to the right, as if putting the pieces together. "I think we may have stepped into something bigger than the disappearance of your grandmother's friend and the death of the sheriff."

"Bigger?" She didn't buy his theory. "This is Kerry, West Virginia, with a population of under a thousand. It's not Baltimore." Jessie fixed herself another cup of hot coffee. Dax hadn't finished his yet.

"Watch it, sis. Don't start knocking my town, now," Dax said with humor in his voice.

Normally, she would have smiled at his attempt at levity, but her mind was racing faster than a spun barrel on a revolver. Jessie took a few sips of the bitter brew. "How could something sinister be going on right under our noses? I'm sure there's a logical explanation, but I don't think it involves a mega plot to take over the world."

Dax stared at her for a moment then took another drink. His hands still shook from the cold. "Maybe not."

They didn't need to be discussing Armageddon while Dax caught pneumonia. "Right now, you need to get out of those wet clothes." The quick flash of a naked Dax materialized, and she had to push the lust away. "Come on, I'm finished here for tonight. Let me drive you home."

He smiled and she didn't like that every time he looked at her, her hormones did the happy dance. Other men paid attention to her, like Bruno and Brian, yet she didn't sit up and take notice of them.

Dax stood. "Does your plan include food?"

He looked so forlorn she had to smile. "Food I got. Let's go."

***

The hot shower ranked up there with a cold brew on a summer day. The throbbing in Dax's thigh had calmed a bit, but he'd be sore tomorrow. After he changed into something warm, he followed his nose downstairs where a feast lay before him. God bless Margaret.

Without any fanfare, he dug in and enjoyed the dinner. They'd already agreed that Jessie would wait until later before chastising her grandmother about driving out to the mine. "I have to say that was one fine meal, Margaret."

"Why, thank you." The light in the dining room was a bit too dim to be sure, but he thought she blushed.

Jessie wiped her delicate mouth with a napkin and threw it on top of her empty plate. "It was wonderful, Nana. Thank you, but now I have to do my rounds at the cement plant. I'll be back in less than an hour." She scooted her chair from the table and stood.

"I'll go with you." He wasn't about to let Jessie wander around alone until he figured out who'd shot at him.

A defensive look flared again—lips in a thin line and shoulders back. "You don't need to. I imagine you're tired and exhausted. Why don't you rest? You can help me best by looking for Sadie tomorrow."

Dax laughed.

"What's so funny?"

"You. You act as though I'm trying to take over your job; trust me, I'm not. Think of me as a tiger, always on alert, always on the move." He curled his fingers and pretended to claw at her, needing to convince her to take him along. "Sitting still, waiting for you to come back, is not my style."

She looked hopeful. "You sure?"

"Yes. I've been in a lot worse shape and survived."

She hesitated then did that cute thing where she looked up at the ceiling. "Fine, but we do as *I* say."

From the way her lips quirked up for a moment, she was fighting a smile. "No problem. You're the boss." He gave her his best salute. "Give me a sec while I grab my gun."

Margaret sucked in a breath. "You plan to shoot someone?"

Jessie stepped over to where Margaret was seated and kissed her grandmother on the cheek. "Only if we have to."

"I do feel better with Dax along. Besides, I'm paying him, so you might as well use him."

Dax wasn't sure if he liked the word *use*, but hell, if it got Jessie to let him tag along, she could say what she wished. Something about being around Jessie calmed his inner demons.

When Jessie looked up at him and smiled, Dax thought he'd never seen anything prettier. He dashed up to his bedroom, retrieved his gun, and then returned.

She faced him. "Did you bring anything else warm to wear? Your sweater's still wet."

"Aw, you care." He hoped that was true.

She lightly punched him. "Never said that."

"Uh-huh."

Margaret waved a hand. "I thought you two were heading to the cement plant."

"We are!" Jessie said.

"If you're going, I better lend Dax one of your granddaddy's sweaters. Just you wait a minute and I'll get one."

Dax was about to protest, but she seemed so set on helping, he didn't have the heart to tell her he could have snatched the heavy jacket he'd brought.

A moment later she returned with something that looked like it belonged to a Harvard professor. Margaret held up a brown, button-down cardigan with leather patches at the elbows. He glanced at Jessie who was obviously trying not to laugh.

It looked warm, and warm was what counted. Dax slipped his arms into the heavy wool sweater that smelled of mothballs and whose sleeves didn't reach his wrists by a good two inches, but he could tell his wearing it meant the world to Margaret. "Thank you. It's perfect."

She beamed. "You look so much like Charley, I swear." She sniffed. "Don't you two stay out late."

"Nana, this isn't a date. We'll be back in an hour."

Margaret made a shooing motion. "Remember, the sooner you go, the sooner you'll be home."

Dax smiled then turned to Jessie. "My flashlight broke while I was in the woods. Do you still have the one I lent you yesterday?" He held his breath.

"Sure." She shot him a puzzled look, but he didn't intend to discuss his deep-seated issues with her—not now, not ever.

Jessie dug through her carry all and pulled out his lifesaver. After making sure it worked, he followed her out.

He didn't quite understand why she needed to inspect the plant every night, but he'd follow her wherever she went. She might not think danger was lurking, but he didn't want to take any chances.

The drive out to the plant took them through town and past a small housing development. He'd seen the construction project when he'd first arrived but hadn't realized how far away it actually was.

Once the town's light disappeared from view, they headed down a dark, narrow road where trees were holding hands across the pavement. It might be pretty in the daytime, but right now, the scene was making him queasy—like right before a panic attack started.

God, he didn't need this. He refused to break down in front of Jessie, not wanting her to see what a mess he really was. It would kill him if she saw him drop to his knees and fight for his next breath for no apparent reason. His rational side knew his claustrophobia was all in his head, and he wished like hell he could just get over his fear.

He coughed to cover his unease. "So, do you know of a good repair shop that can fix a gas tank?"

She glanced over at him, looking as if she wanted to ask him about why he seemed so nervous. "Walter's Repair Shop is the only place in town that does any kind of body work."

A body shop. Good. He needed to think about getting his truck fixed and not on how dark the sky had grown. "How long do you think he'll take?" He prayed she'd say less than a week.

"If Walter has to order a part, there's no telling when you'll get your truck back. It could take a few weeks."

He dropped his head against the seat, and as she rounded a corner, the plant loomed in front of them. Dax clasped the heavy light in his hands as Jessie pulled to a stop. The place looked bigger close up. "You ever find any problems on your rounds?" He didn't need to be here any longer than necessary.

"Other than a bunch of mischievous kids, no." She pushed open the driver's side door. "Come on. If you take the south side, I'll take the north. We can be finished in no time."

Dax inhaled, trying to act casual, but he feared he wouldn't be successful. He slipped out of the cruiser and into the night. Fortunately, he was able to keep his back to her to ensure she wouldn't notice the panic that was surely crossing his face. He gripped the flashlight, determined not to drop the damned thing again.

Wind whistled through the trees and leaves rustled along the ground. Out of habit, he blew out a breath to test for the cold. Yup, frost was in the air tonight. Dax swept his light along the building's perimeter, careful to avoid the cement bricks and lumber carelessly strewn on the ground.

First, he checked inside the cranes' cabs before working his way to the back of the building. As he scoped out the area, his light caught something red—a color that didn't belong among the gray walls and brown wooden beams.

As he approached the tractor, a piece of fabric that looked like silk, flapped in the wind, partly attached to the seat. "Hey, Jessie. I think I found something," he shouted.

A moment later, her light rounded the corner, and he was

surprised by his sense of relief that no evil spirit had whisked her away. *You're an idiot, Mitchell. Crazy thoughts coming out of nowhere are not a good sign.* No one was out there but them.

"What did you find?"

He fingered the soft material. "What do you make of this?"

She aimed her light on the fabric. "Not exactly something a man would wear, or a woman in construction for that matter."

Dax didn't like it. "Why don't you bag the evidence while I take another look around."

"Like I carry forensic stuff with me?" She held up a hand. "Never mind. I'll store the scrap someplace safe."

Dax appreciated her helpful attitude. He then mentally marked off the surrounding area in a grid pattern and began looking for signs of a struggle or a woman's footprint, anything to indicate a female had been there.

As he scoped out the place, his mind jumped to Sadie, even though the mine was miles from there. If only he had some idea what happened to her, he'd know how to better proceed.

Twenty minutes later, he'd covered every inch of the place but found nothing else. The only area left to search was the forest bordering the building site, and the dark woods was the last place he wanted to go.

Bats, snakes, and rabid animals didn't bother him, nor did jumping out of a perfectly good airplane or disarming a bomb, but standing around in the dark haunted him.

Jessie slipped next to him. "I checked inside, and nothing's been disturbed. You find anything else?"

"No, but tomorrow morning we should look in the woods."

She smiled, grabbed his arm, and dragged him forward. "No time like the present."

He dug his heels in. "We can't see anything at night with only a quarter moon to light the way."

"The moon's practically full." She waved her flashlight. "Besides, that's what God made these puppies for." She took off. "I just want to take a quick look," she called over her shoulder.

Dax raced after her—or at least he did his best imitation of racing, given his leg was acting up again. "There must be hundreds of acres in there. We could get lost."

She spun around and flashed her light on his chest. "Why, Dax Mitchell. Are you afraid of the dark?"

His chest constricted at being caught. Shit. "Certainly not. Let's go." Those were the hardest words he'd said in a long time.

He tried to convince himself he could do this. The last thing he wanted was to look like a fool when his imaginary demons were ripping the air from his lungs. His ego pushed him forward, but he let Jessie lead. Her light, together with his, helped ease the pressure on his chest.

A few minutes later, Jessie stopped and ran a finger along a broken branch. "See here? Something caused this to break. The ends are still green."

Given the break was shoulder height he doubted a deer had caused the crack. Most likely, the offender had been human.

They moved farther into the black forest, and with each step, Dax's breaths became more labored. He was about to swallow his pride and tell her he couldn't go on when his light caught something peeking out from under a leaf. He knelt down and wiped away the detritus. "Jessie?"

She turned and rushed back. "What is it?"

He picked up the metal object and rubbed off the dirt with his thumb. "A woman's button, and from the looks of its ornateness, if that's a word, I'm guessing it belonged to someone older."

She knelt beside him. "No rust on it either, which means it must be a recent addition. Good find. Let's keep going."

Dax was surprised her words of praise brought more air into his body. He might as well follow her since he was already in hell.

When something rustled off to his left, he swung his light in a large arc, and shot his beam in the direction of the sound. "Psst."

She paused and joined her light with his. A raccoon and two

babies froze in their combined beams, and he almost laughed at his relief.

"They're adorable," Jessie said, "but hardly the hardcore criminal we're looking for."

"Let's hope we don't meet anyone sinister tonight." Not that he couldn't handle himself in a fight, but he wanted to do battle under better conditions—like when the sun was up.

Jessie continued along the path that was full of small rocks and roots until they came to their umpteenth fork. "Which way do you think we should go?" she asked, looking around.

"You're the boss."

She nodded and chose the path to the right. They'd traveled a good ten minutes when she stepped off to the side and ducked under a large rhododendron tree whose branches cascaded to the ground. "Ah, Dax?"

"What is it?"

"I might have found a body."

CHAPTER EIGHT

Dax pushed aside the half-bare mountain laurel branches to expose a mound of dirt, sticks, and leaves that was about the length of a body. His heart sank. Poor Jessie was going to be devastated if this was someone she knew.

He was still haunted by the sight of his first body. It had taken him days, and a lot of luck, to locate the ten-year old buried in a field in rural Maryland. Only an autopsy provided the identity of the boy who'd been tortured, carelessly tossed in a shallow grave, and eaten by bugs. The thought of what happened to him still made Dax sick.

He blinked, and the raw image in front of him brought back fresh anger. It didn't matter the bastard who'd brutalized the boy had been caught and executed; his death didn't bring the son back to the grieving parents.

As Jessie started to bend down, Dax took hold of her arm and gently drew her away from the grave. "I don't think you need to see what's under there."

"Do you think it's S-Sadie?" Her voice cracked.

"That or the sheriff, but I don't think red was his color."

Jessie glared up at him. He'd tried to bring a little levity into a very grave situation, no pun intended, but apparently she wasn't ready for that kind of humor. Too many years on the Baltimore force had hardened him.

"I have to go b-b-back to the station and g-get a shovel. We need to dig her up." The wind couldn't seem to leave Jessie alone, forcing her to push her hair out of her face. "It's all my fault," she choked out.

Her emotions seemed to be running away from her—not that he blamed her.

"You had nothing to do with her death. Besides, we don't even know this is Sadie." She moved in the direction of the cruiser. "Come on. We have to call the Medical Examiner."

He wanted to refocus her grief away from the emotional to the practical. Dax didn't add that they'd need some helpers to transport the body the mile to the car, as well as some much-needed strong coffee. Lots of extra light was a given.

The wind shot through his wool sweater, and Jessie rubbed her hands up and down the sleeves of her nylon jacket. He itched to share his body heat, but he bet she'd balk if he touched her. He wished he understood why Jessie acted as if showing grief would make her less of a law enforcement agent.

Forget it. He wouldn't be here long enough to follow through if he did get her to loosen up. Besides, Jessie deserved better than a washed up homicide detective with a bum leg who couldn't stand being in the dark without panic ripping his soul in two.

As though a hoard of terrorists were after her, she suddenly took off through the woods toward the crest of the hill. He rushed after her and a stab of leg pain nearly felled him to his knees. Dax straightened and drew in a deep breath. He had to push on, had to get out of the forest, and had to make sure Jessie stayed safe.

When she reached the trailhead, she turned around and flashed her light on the path between them. "Dax, I'm so sorry, I wasn't thinking. I should have waited for you."

He waved her on. "I'll catch up." He didn't need her sympathy, or anyone else's. It wasn't her fault he'd missed locating the damned land mine. If he hadn't been in such a hurry to get out of the area by nightfall, he would have found the explosive device, and Evan would still be alive.

Jessie disappeared down the hill, and only the faint glow of her flashlight illuminated the tree limbs. Fuck. Why did he have to show her that scrap of red material? If only he'd kept his mouth shut and suggested they come back tomorrow morning, he wouldn't be here in the dark. But he was, and he couldn't do a damn thing about it. As his captain used to preach, once a ball started downhill, there was no choice but to follow it.

Fifteen minutes later, Dax reached the cruiser where he slipped across the seat from Jessie. The relief from the wind and cold relaxed the tension in his chest. "You okay?" he asked.

"What do you think?" she said, drumming her fingers on the steering wheel.

The sarcasm cut off his reply. Before he even got a chance to fasten his seatbelt, Jessie peeled away from the construction site, acting like demons were chasing her. He certainly could relate to those. He even had names for his—Mr. Dark and Mr. Guilt.

Not needing to add to her anxieties by chatting about the dead, Dax kept quiet as Jessie traveled down the long, eerie road. He understood that her mind would be sifting through all the possibilities, accepting some, tossing away others. She'd be asking if the body was Sadie's, Clinton DuPree's, or belonged to some vagrant.

Less than twenty minutes later, they pulled in front of Jessie's station. To his surprise, the main road was stacked with cars, and he wondered what the big attraction was. When he pushed open the door, music filtered from the bar down the street, answering his question.

Jessie jumped out of the cruiser, slammed the door, and raced up the three steps, acting as if he hadn't come along. Easing his leg out of the car, he winced then carefully climbed the steps, needing the handrail tonight. Jessie was already on the phone when he walked inside.

"At the cement p-pl-plant... Right. I'll meet you there... No, I'll bring a shovel... okay, bye."

Jessie rubbed her stomach then rushed over to Clinton's desk. "That was Doc

Whitmore. He's meeting us there." She whipped open a squeaky, wooden drawer, and pulled out the digital camera then tugged open a second drawer. "We had a Polaroid, but I can't seem to find it, though now that I think about it, I don't think Clinton was able to find film for it anymore. Dammit." She pointed to a dented, four-drawer file cabinet. "Our forensic kit is in there."

"I'll get it."

He removed the large metal box that took up one entire drawer and set the kit on Clinton's now clean desk. Inside were vials, latex gloves, cotton balls, swabs, tweezers, lifting tape, and other assorted paraphernalia that he'd need to process the scene. The kit was neatly organized and looked like it had hardly been used.

He then checked a second drawer and found something more important—a large flashlight. To make sure the batteries still worked, he flicked it *On* then *Off*.

Jessie called someone else and seemed to be on hold quite a while. This town really needed cell reception. She kept her back to Dax as she wore a path between the entrance and her desk. The woman sure could log some hours on the pacing circuit.

"Tom, thank God I got a hold of you. It's Jessie. I need your help. I found a gravesite over by the new cement plant." She went on to explain the need for two workers and one single-wheeled gurney to transport the body through the woods. She hung up and her shoulders slumped. "I can't believe this."

"Can't believe what?"

"That Sadie could be dead." She ran a hand through her hair, but the curls sprang back—soft ones that he bet smelled like springtime. "I warned Nana and her friends not to go out anywhere alone, but they wouldn't listen. I should have been more insistent." She shook her head. "They are the most stubborn women I know."

He stepped over to her. "We can't control what others do."

Jessie turned away and a little part of him ached from disappointment.

She wrapped her arms around her chest. "A small part of my brain knows I'm not at fault, but my heart tells me I could have done something more."

"Hey, come here," Dax said. She looked up at him, pain filling her eyes. Without asking permission, Dax gathered her in his arms and held her tight, absorbing all of her goodness.

He expected her to pull away, but she placed her palms on his chest and her head on his shoulder. A few seconds later, she cleared her throat and leaned back. She looked off to the side, as if she had been embarrassed to accept his warmth. "Thanks. I need to make some, um, coffee."

She stepped over to the coffee maker and tapped the side, probably to see if it was warm, then flipped the switch.

Dax stepped behind her. "Don't beat yourself up. You'll need all your strength before the night is through. As I said, we don't know the body in the grave is Sadie's."

"I can only pray it's not."

"Why don't you find the shovel, and I'll take care of the coffee," he offered.

She gave him a brief smile. "Thanks."

Poor Jessie. She was too much of an I-won't-let-anyone-help me type of woman for her own good. From what her grandmother told him, both Jessie's dad and Margaret's husband had been sheriff, and Jessie always felt pressure to live up to the Nash name. It was a tall order in a town where women weren't always given an equal chance.

She returned with the shovel a moment later. "I need to let Nana know not to expect us back anytime soon."

"I bet she'd appreciate it."

Jessie was rather curt on the phone, but he understood her need not to let Margaret ask any questions.

Ten minutes later, with a coffee mug to go, they were back on the road, heading into the darkness. When they arrived, the medical examiner's station wagon was at the plant, with his engine running, brights on.

Jessie sucked in a large, audible breath. "I really don't want to do this."

Dax placed a hand on her arm. "You don't have to. I'm sure Doc Whitmore and I can process the scene." *I don't mind losing my breath and feeling like I'm about to die, but for you, Jessie, I'll handle it.*

She shook her head. "No, I have to see this through."

In truth, he'd expected nothing less from her, and his admiration grew. Jessie was the type to keep going despite all adversity. His dad and the service had drilled that same attitude into him. He guessed they had more in common than he'd originally thought.

"I understand."

"Remember, I'm in charge."

"Got it." He'd let her have the needed control, for now.

Jessie scooted out of the cruiser, opened the trunk, and then banged the lid shut.

He slipped out. "Let me carry the shovel." He didn't mind playing flunky for one night if it would help Jessie cope.

She handed it to him then grabbed the forensic kit from the back seat along with a roll of orange tape. He hoped she planned to mark the trail. She stepped up to the Medical Examiner's wagon, and his door opened. Doc Whitmore stepped out, his white hair and thick glasses making the man look close to the grave himself. Not a charitable thought, but right now, he wasn't in a good mood.

"You ready?" Jessie asked Dax.

"Let's do it."

The three of them headed into the too dark forest, and he prayed he could keep his demons at bay for another few hours. The trees blocked the moon's rays, causing his lungs to cut off his breath once more. Trying to focus on anything but his fears, Dax kept an eye on the aging doctor to make sure the elderly man didn't slip. Tons of rocks and fallen branches could trip even the most nimble footed.

Dax carried the shovel in one hand and his larger-than-life light in the other. With all three flashlights aimed at the forest floor, his overwhelming loss of control gave way to ordinary anxiety, which he could handle in small doses, though it took concentration to put one foot in front of the other.

The wind seemed to have picked up, carrying with it the strong aroma of pine and wet leaves. He did love the forest—just not at night. Their boots made enough crunching noises to be heard a mile away, which caused the animals to scurry. They had to rest a few times on the short trip up the steep hill, as Doc wasn't in the best of shape, but Dax said nothing as Jessie pretended to need the rest more than Doc.

Once they reached the ridge, Jessie flashed her light around. "Here's the broken tree branch I found before, so I know we're heading in the right direction." She hung a piece of orange tape from the limb to mark their route.

After a while, Dax lost track of all the bends, twists, and forks, which was why he was thankful Jessie was placing the tape at every turn. The last thing he needed was to be wandering around anymore than necessary.

He surveyed the area. "I guess we should have marked our trail the first time, but from the disturbed leaves I can tell we went this way." A small pile of wet leaves appeared off to the side. "Hey, this is where I found the button that may have belonged to Sadie." His pulse sped up at his good luck.

"You still got that button, son?"

Dax patted his pocket. "Yes, sir."

They went deeper into the woods where spider webs slapped

Dax in the face. Fast spinning buggers since they weren't there when he and Jessie first arrived. He hoped they were still on the right path.

"There." Jessie shown her light on the big laurel tree fifty feet ahead.

When Dax reached the area, he pushed aside the branches and spotlighted the grave. Thank God, nothing had been disturbed. For a split second, he thought they might have had a repeat performance of the disappearing corpse.

He turned back to Jessie. "We forgot our coffee mugs. Damn. Would you mind going back and getting them?" The twenty minute one-way trip would keep her away for a good while.

She set down the kit. "I know your game plan, Mitchell. You think with me out of the way, I won't see the body. Well, it won't work. I'll be back before you finish unearthing the corpse. Save me a seat."

"Will do." He liked her spunk.

She pointed a finger at him. "I'm only leaving because I have to wait for the men with the gurney and show them the way."

He'd momentarily forgotten about them. "Don't forget the coffee when you come back."

She turned and gave him the finger over her shoulder, which actually pleased him. Anger was better than depression, or God forbid, tears.

From what she'd told him on the ride over, the attendants were at a hospital some forty minutes away. Maybe he could take care of the body before she returned with the men.

Dax held the camera out to the medical examiner. "You want to do the honors, or should I?"

Dr. Whitmore waved a hand at the grave. "Be my guest."

Dax spent several minutes photographing the grave as well as the surrounding area. A couple of times, the medical examiner asked him to take some specific shot, and he obliged. "I'll come back tomorrow and snap some more photos of the surrounding area," Dax said. "Daylight can often pick up something the camera misses at night."

"Good thinking."

Dax stuffed the camera into his sweater pocket. "If you could aim the light on the grave," Dax said, "I'll start digging."

The doc placed a hand on Dax's shoulder. "Be careful, now. We don't want to damage the body. It's hard enough to do the autopsy; even more so if you put shovel marks in the flesh."

"Don't worry. I've been through the drill a few times."

Dax carefully dug around the edge of the shallow gravesite, and within minutes, two fingers emerged from the earth. "Shine the light closer," Dax said. A dark, gnarled forefinger flapped in the wind.

"You think it's Sadie Palmer?" Doc asked.

"Hard to tell. Decomp does strange things to a body, but you already know that."

Dax continued to peel away the dirt until the smell of gases made him move back for a moment. He pressed on, as he wanted to finish before Jessie returned. Dax pulled on a pair of latex gloves and dropped to his knees. Using his fingers, he pushed the dirt away from the body's face.

The rustling of leaves, along with voices, told him Jessie and her help would be there in less than a minute. When he finished unearthing the darkened face, he looked up at Doc. "Well?"

CHAPTER NINE

Doc held the light steady over the corpse's face. "That's Sadie, all right. Dear Lord in Heaven, have mercy on her soul." He made a sign of the cross.

"Dax?" Jessie rushed up to him, her voice sounding like she was drowning.

He jumped up and held her at arm's length, shielding her view of the body. "Jessie, I'm so sorry. I'm afraid it's Sadie."

"Ohmigod, no." She tried to step around him, but he blocked her path. "I can't believe it. I mean, I can b-believe it, but I don't want it to be true. Are you sure?"

"Doc identified her."

Her lips firmed, a clear sign she was fighting for control. "How did she die?"

He debated sugar coating the cause of death, but Jessie would be angry when she found out the truth. The bullet had penetrated the skull and lodged in her cheek. "A shot to the back of the head."

She gasped then bent over a few inches acting as if someone had punched her in the stomach. "Here's your damned coffee." She shoved the mug at his chest, but he recognized her anger wasn't directed at him.

"I'll take over, sir." One of the attendants slipped the shovel from Dax's fingers.

"Thank you." He turned back to Jessie. "Why don't I walk you to the car while these men finish up here?" In her emotional state, she'd only get in the way.

She straightened, shot him a focused glare, and then pushed past him to step to the edge of the grave. A strangled cry left her lips, and for a moment, he thought she might become sick viewing the body, but she didn't.

Instead, she clenched her hands and whipped back around. "I don't know how they do things in Baltimore, but in Kerry, it's my duty to stay until Sadie is safely in the medical examiner's van."

He gave her a two-fingered salute. It had been a mistake to treat Jessie with anything less than total equality. She was a fine officer. "Understood."

Dax moved out of the workers' way, lifted the lid off the hot coffee, and guzzled it. Damn if it didn't lack that needed kick he was looking for. He took a sniff but detected no aroma. However, on a cold evening, he couldn't be picky.

"Excuse me, Jess," one of the attendants said. "We need to move the gurney closer to the body."

"Jessie, stand by me," Dax said.

She moved, but it was to the other side of the grave. Perhaps he'd been too patronizing. Hell, he couldn't help it. He was used to giving orders, being in control, and looking out for everyone.

It took close to half an hour for the two attendants to place the body into the bag and ready the gurney to transport to the van. Except for the scuffling of feet, both human and animal, along with the occasional squeaky wheel, the team marched in silence along the path. Maneuvering down the rocks took skill, but the two attendants handled the chore well. Doc was a bit shaky going down, but Dax couldn't tell if it was his age or from being upset over Sadie's death.

When they arrived back at the plant, Jessie went into her deputy mode, directing the men on how they should do their job until one of the attendants took her aside. Dax couldn't hear what was said, but from her rigid posture, she didn't like what he told her.

Jessie then began her pacing ritual while the men finished up with Sadie. After Dax cleaned the shovel the best he could and dropped it in the cruiser's trunk, he pried the field kit from her fingers. She was holding the damned kit so close to her chest he'd have thought she had a million dollars' worth of diamonds in there.

In the time it took to dig up Sadie, a fog bank had rolled in, blocking the light from the moon. If he believed in vampires and werewolves, he'd be convinced they'd surely be on the prowl right now. Hell, he could almost hear them baying in the wind.

Dax stowed the kit in the back and then snagged Jessie's car keys so he could turn on the cruiser's headlights. The moment the area flooded with light, his shoulders relaxed and his breathing evened out.

When Doc Whitmore and the men had Sadie safely stored inside the medical wagon, he took off. The two men from the hospital followed a minute later, leaving cement dust in their wake.

With her hand blocking the headlight's glare, Jessie watched the team depart, looking like a child who'd been separated from her mother. Dax stepped toward her, debating whether to offer comfort but decided his embrace wouldn't be welcome—not this time anyway.

Red glowing taillights eased around the bend and disappeared. Goodbye, Sadie. He wished he'd have met her under better circumstances, but such was life, or rather death.

After being outside for several hours, he was almost immune to the chill that had seeped into his lungs. Odd, he never did like the cold, but tonight he was dead inside and out and barely felt it.

Dax brushed the grime off his pants, kicked the mud from

the bottom of his shoes, and then slipped back into the passenger's seat, letting Jessie deal with the trauma in her own way.

A moment later, she ripped open the driver's side door and jumped in. Clearly, she was battling her inner demons and probably losing. Despite their talk at the station, she still acted as though Sadie's murder was her fault somehow. From experience, nothing he could say would change her mind, so he kept quiet, letting her work through the pain.

Jessie threw the car in reverse with a little too much gusto, backed up, and raced out of there. No cars were on the road, yet she took a curve so fast two wheels lifted off the pavement for a second, forcing him to grab onto the dashboard.

"Ah, Jessie. No one's chasing us." It wasn't subtle.

She slowed. "Sorry. I just wanted to get away from there."

"I can't blame you."

Jessie was halfway to town before she spoke again. "Sadie's death is going to kill Nana, you know."

She sounded composed, but deep inside she had to be hurting. "I figured. You know, one of the reasons I left the force and went into private investigation was because telling someone a family member was dead, ranked up there with someone shoving a gun in my face." Not the whole truth, but part, anyway.

She half-smiled. "Thank you."

At least he hadn't made the situation worse. For him, he considered it a small victory.

"Before we go home," she said. "I want to do my rounds at the bar. Do you mind?"

She took being an officer of the law to the extreme, but he figured by checking on the bar, she could avoid telling Margaret about Sadie for a bit longer. In a way, he wished she would break down, as it might help release the anger from her system. "Are you there to check up on the locals or do you plan to have a drink?" He hoped the latter.

Not answering, she gripped the wheel tighter.

***

As Jessie drove back to town, a wave of depression almost made her stop and vomit on the roadside, but she swallowed hard to keep down the bile. She still couldn't believe Sadie was dead. She'd suspected something bad might have happened to Nana's friend, but she'd wanted to believe Sadie would come breezing back into town with some wild adventure story, like she had so many times before.

This news would break Nana's heart, just as hers was breaking now.

Jessie glanced over at Dax. He was staring out the side window, seemingly off in his own world. Working in a big city like he did, seeing a dead body was probably no biggie, and she wondered what encountering corpses on a regular basis did to the soul—crush it or make him immune to any caring?

She set aside the horror and concentrated on the road. As they neared town, the traffic picked up, and she sighed. Saturday night was in full swing, and she definitely wasn't in the mood to deal with any drunks, but keeping her routine would help her regain some control.

She circled past the bar and returned to the south end of town. "Do you mind if we park at my office and walk the few blocks to the Coal Mine?" Not that she had a choice as the parking spaces in between were taken.

"I'm game."

She thought she saw him wince. Darn. She should probably drop him off in front of the bar given how badly he had been limping, but she bet he wouldn't appreciate being treated as an invalid. If it had been her, she wouldn't have wanted special treatment.

Jessie pulled to the curb in front of her office, cut the engine, and stepped out. Fresh, cold air woke her up and helped ease the ache in her belly. Jessie tried to brush off the dried dirt and grass stains from her pants, but she didn't succeed. Her beige slacks were now ruined. She hoped people wouldn't take one look at her and think she'd had sex in the forest with Dax—on her knees.

For a brief moment of escapism, Jessie let her mind drift far away from the horror of the night. She bet Dax would be smokin' hot in the bed department—not that she'd ever find out. Any man with his body and strong hands would surely be amazing at—

"You ever go to the bar just to relax and visit with friends or even enjoy a dance or two?" he asked.

"Huh? Oh, the b-bar. Not really. Clinton and I took turns checking on the place, especially on weekends, since we needed to make sure no one became too out of hand or too drunk to drive home. I didn't go very often just to have fun."

"I see."

That made her sound so lame, but having fun was expensive. *Be honest.* Fine. It might be that she was afraid to let anyone or anything in. Her desire to live up to the Nash name required all her dedication, though of late she had wondered at what expense?

They walked in silence the rest of the way to the bar. Jessie usually enjoyed looking in the bookstore window and in the small craft shop, but tonight, nothing interested her. Dax's face remained tense as he held open the door to the Coal Mine Bar. Perhaps seeing Sadie's body had upset him more than she'd realized.

"Thank you," she said as she stepped past him.

Body heat and the stench of spilled beer slammed into her the moment she crossed the threshold. Too many people were in here tonight. If the fire chief stopped by, half the town would be out on their asses.

Familiar country music blared from the jukebox. As the couples swung their butts around on the tiny dance floor, a twinge of regret grabbed her. Deep down inside, she wanted a dance partner for life, but to let go like that could alter her too much.

Dax moved behind her. "The place is packed."

Jessie turned and looked up at him, happy to be talking about facts instead of emotion. "It's always like this on a Saturday night. There's not much else to do in Kerry but drink. You should have seen it before the mine closed. I swear there was often a line a mile long to get in here."

He dropped his gaze and seemed to focus on her face. "Impressive. This actually puts Baltimore to shame."

Jessie could feel her cheeks burn. Her uncharacteristic reaction to this man was upsetting. She blinked a few times to clear her head, and then looked back at the crowd, hoping, in some small way, she'd have to spend her time using her deputy skills instead of sitting near Dax for the next hour while she mourned Sadie's loss. Being this close to him took her way out of her comfort zone.

Damn if all the booths and tables weren't taken. "You mind sitting at the bar?" Jessie yelled over the noise.

"Not at all."

Two adjacent seats were free, and that in and of itself was a rarity. She was happy they'd found a spot until she realized their arms would touch, and she'd be able to watch the planes of his jaw move in a sexy way, which would send her thoughts where they shouldn't go.

What had gotten into her tonight? Sadie was dead, which meant her thoughts should only be on her friend and what this would do to Nana—not on being comforted by a man she barely knew. This was not the place to think about total abandon.

As they wove their way through the crowd, a high-pitched laugh caught her attention. She turned and stopped. "Lena?"

Good Lord. The woman's husband had dumped her less than two weeks ago, and here she was out on a date in full makeup, hair actually curled, and a low cut top that covered barely a third of her breasts. The outfit took rebounding to a new level. Jessie had to admit the woman had guts. At least Lena wasn't sitting home feeling sorry for herself like Jessie would have been, but her situation had been different. She'd dumped her last boyfriend instead of the other way around.

Her friend rushed over, looking wasted. "Jessie! Don't you ever rest?"

"Actually, I'm here to relax." No way would she say she wanted to drown her sorrows. The town didn't need to learn about Sadie's death so soon.

Lena touched Dax's arm. "I remember you from the café." She let go and turned back to Jessie. "You got something to tell me, honey?" Lena looked up at Dax then back to Jessie and winked.

Oh, boy. This was the last conversation she needed, especially with Dax standing right next to her.

As if he read her mind, Dax leaned close to her ear. "I'll snag those two seats at the bar for us."

Us, as in a couple. It had a nice ring, but it was definitely not in the direction she planned to go. "Okay."

To move past her, he placed a hand on the small of her back, and his touch sent heat through her shirt. She needed to have her head examined. The man was here to do a job—one that was finished as of an hour ago. He'd be gone as soon as Walt repaired his car.

Lena clasped Jessie's hand and squeezed. "You've been holding out on me, Jess."

She withdrew her fingers from her friend's grasp and crossed her arms. Details would only lead to other questions. "Dax is helping with an investigation, that's all."

"So it's Dax now, is it?" She giggled. "Whoops. Where are my manners? Jessie, this is Seth Walker. He's new in town." The man had sidled up next to Lena the moment Dax left.

Nice looking guy, military fit body, and short-cropped hair. As they shook hands, she made a mental note to keep an eye on him "Welcome to Kerry, Seth."

If he was in the military perhaps he had some marksman skills—enough to shoot out a tire and a camera lens. If the noise from the bar hadn't been so loud, she might have questioned him.

"Thanks."

"Well," Lena said, "Don't keep that hunk of yours waiting too long. Good men don't come by very often." She turned back to her date and looked all googly-eyed at him.

Jessie let the lovebirds enjoy each other's company as she headed back to Dax. On the way, a good half dozen people insisted on speaking with her, offering their condolences regarding Clinton's disappearance. Thank goodness they didn't know about Sadie. She could only take so much sympathy at once. Breaking down in front of everyone would surely get back to the mayor and kill any chance of her making sheriff.

To push aside all the bad thoughts that were scrambling her brain, she focused on wonderful things, like blooming gardenias, rainbows over waterfalls, and Dax's remarkable profile. *Stop it.* She didn't need to be staring at his Roman nose, strong chin, and his thick, dark hair. She quickly added his muscular body to the list of things she didn't need to be thinking about.

Dax wasn't looking at her when she slid onto the stool next to him. In fact, he didn't even seem to notice she'd arrived. He was definitely lost in thought, and she wondered what had captured his attention.

Bruno rushed over. "Evening, Jess. What can I get you?" He smiled as he always did when she stopped by. The man was eternally hopeful.

She noticed Dax had nothing in front of him, so she touched his arm to get his attention, and powerful muscles bulged under his long sleeved shirt. "You don't want a drink?"

He turned to her as though startled. "Yeah, I do." Dax nodded to Bruno. "But getting service around here ain't easy." He furrowed his brows.

Whoa. She hadn't seen him lose his cool before.

Tension jumped to Bruno's face faster than a spreading wild-fire. "Can't you see I've been busy?"

Jessie held her breath. The last thing she needed was a bar fight, especially between these two. Bruno must be upset because she was sitting with Dax, but he needed to get over the fact she didn't want to go out with him.

"I'll have a Guinness," Dax said relaxing back against the chair.

Relieved he hadn't made a scene, she wrinkled her nose. "Ale's too bitter for me. I'll have a scotch on the rocks—and make it a double."

Bruno's eyes widened. "Are you sure? You've never ordered anything stronger than a beer."

"Tonight's different."

"Okay, you're the boss."

Dax turned his seat toward her. "I'm sorry about Sadie."

Before she could answer, Bruno returned. "Here ya go." He set down the drinks. "I'll put these on your *date's* tab."

The man definitely had unresolved issues. She'd have to set him straight when she wasn't with Dax. Too exhausted to squabble over the check, she let it slide for now. Tomorrow, she'd slip Dax some cash.

He peered into his beer, looking sad, distant, and quite trou-bled. She wanted to reach out and touch him, but she couldn't handle any more problems tonight. He then swiveled around and faced her, opened his mouth then shut it. She figured he wanted to talk about what had happened, but she didn't—or rather she couldn't. Thinking about Sadie's withered skin made her gag. God, it had been so awful.

Jessie grabbed the tall tumbler. To hell with it. Tonight, she needed to drink. It wasn't everyday she found her grandmother's best friend brutally murdered.

She was halfway through her scotch when a hand reached out and tipped the glass downward.

"Easy there. I thought you didn't have to rush home?" Dax said.

Damn him. "I don't. Just leave me alone, will ya?" She turned her shoulder to the side. She shouldn't have snapped at him, but she was barely holding it together. Hopefully, he understood that she was hurting and not angry at him.

Jessie polished off the rest of her scotch, not caring that she was drinking it too fast. She needed to blot out seeing the body that had been limp, discolored, and lifeless. She hiccupped and slapped a hand over her mouth. If Nana were here, she would be horrified to see Jessie drunk, especially while in uniform.

She motioned for another scotch. When Bruno didn't magically appear, she turned around and faced the crowd, searching for him.

People moved and mingled, and she finally spotted the owner leaning over Seth, Lena's date. Bruno looked ready to kick some ass, and she tensed. The owner usually tried to please his customers, not antagonize them. Then she remembered the man with Lena was a newcomer, and Bruno didn't do well with them. When he finally moved back to the bar, she motioned him over. "Something wrong?"

"Hell, yes. That guy with Lena? He's supposed to be working tonight, not socializing with the clientele. He doesn't get paid to get women in the sack."

Too much information for her, though if Bruno had hired Seth, he must have checked his references. "Okay. May I have another, please?" She waved her glass.

He looked at her hard then moved his gaze to Dax whose fingers wiggled. Too bad she couldn't tell what kind of hand signal he was giving Bruno. The last thing she needed was his controlling behavior tonight.

A moment later, another double scotch arrived. Well, maybe he'd indicated he'd be the designated driver. Someone had to make sure they arrived home safely, and tonight Jessie wasn't sure she was capable.

She was mostly through her next drink, when Dax leaned over and whispered in her ear, causing her senses to explode. "Would you like to dance?" he asked in a slow, sexy way that had her pulse racing. For the briefest moment, she forgot where they'd spent the last few hours.

She moved her head to see if he was kidding and their lips nearly collided. "D-dance? I don-don't dance. And how can you ask me to enjoy myself when Sadie's dead?"

He took her hand, and she didn't pull away since his warmth calmed her.

"Would Sadie want you to sit around and mourn, or enjoy yourself?"

That was an unfair question. Of all the people she knew, Sadie loved to party the most. "The woman liked nothing more than to dance." A pleasant memory surfaced and the briefest of smiles lifted her lips. "She sure could run circles around the best of them."

"Dancing will take your mind off the pain. Trust me."

Dax tapped his leg then stood. Before she could protest, he had her on her feet and was pulling her through the crowd. Dear Lord, she felt like she was back in high school with Brian at their first dance. She thought she'd erased that from her memory banks, but apparently, she hadn't.

A Clint Black melody ended and an even slower song began. She started to make an excuse as to why this wasn't a good idea, but her lips wouldn't move. Her feet weren't doing such a good job either. Without warning, Dax wrapped a strong arm around her waist and was clasping her right hand in his. Her breasts were plastered against his amazingly hard chest, causing her pulse to race and parts of her body she long thought dead to wake up.

For some reason, the security of his arms did more for her than all the scotch she'd had. She thought she heard someone snicker, but she didn't want to look at anyone but him. Dax was glancing down at her with a dreamy look on his face too. It was as though he was remembering something from the past. Soon, the slow, sensual music made her muscles relax, and the alcohol forced her mind to block out the scene in the woods.

"You okay?" he asked.

She looked up and saw two heads resting on his broad shoulders. "Sure."

Had it not been for the crush of people, and Dax's strong arms around her, she might have dropped to the ground since her knees were having trouble holding her up.

Oh, shit. She was actually drunk. Jessie couldn't even remember the last time she had so much alcohol in such a short period of time.

She reached up and touched his cheek. "Your face feels like sandpaper. Did you know that?" She prayed her words didn't sound as slurred to him as they did to her.

He grabbed her hand and slid it around his neck. "That happens sometimes."

"I think I've had too much to drink."

He smiled. "Don't worry. I'll watch out for you."

"No, I really am drunk. I think it's time we head to bed."

CHAPTER TEN

Several people whistled as Dax half dragged Jessie out of the Coal Mine Bar. She stumbled on the entrance mat, but he caught her before she fell. Poor thing. Her reputation did not need this kind of scrutiny.

The moment they stepped outside, his ears stopped ringing from the blaring music, and the cold wind evaporated the sweat from his forehead.

Jessie stood up straighter and grabbed his arm. The fresh air seemed to have woken her up. "Ohmigod, if the City Council thinks I can't handle my liquor, I'm toast. Did you know those ba-astards gave me only three weeks to solve four crimes? Or was it five?" She shook her head. "I'll be damned if I can remember. We partly solved one tonight, so that should count for something."

"What are you talking about?"

"The City Council doesn't want me to be sheriff. They want a stinking *man*."

He refrained from chuckling. "You're kidding." He had a hard time believing anyone in the twenty-first century would say that. If those men had been in Baltimore and mentioned the reason she couldn't have the position was because of her sex,

they'd have had a lawsuit waiting for them before they got back
to their office.

Dax walked with his arm around Jessie's waist, but she didn't
seem to notice how much he was holding her up, touching her,
enjoying the—

"I wish I were kidding," she said, her words a little slurred.
"Can you believe it? They said if I wanted the job, I had to p-
prove myself." The fear and depression in her voice made him
ache for her.

When they reached her cruiser, Dax took the car keys
dangling from her fingers, opened the passenger side door, and
eased her in. He couldn't wait to take her away from prying eyes.

After making sure she was buckled up, he took off. He'd
barely reached the edge of town when her soft snores filled the
cab. He was quite impressed that in all her grief, she'd actually
fallen asleep. The alcohol and stress must have done her in.

Fortunately, he remembered the way to her house, but
locating her hidden, dark drive was another matter. She needed
lights at the entrance to help guide people in as he missed her
drive twice.

Once he found it, he wove his way along the dirt road, the
front porch light glowing like a beacon. The inside, however, was
pitch black, which was probably a good thing. Margaret wouldn't
have to see Jessie drunk or be able to question her on what she'd
found at the cement plant.

He shook her shoulder. "Jessie?"

She groaned, opened her eyes, and smiled. "Hi."

Dax came around to the passenger's side. "Let's get you
inside."

He helped her out even though she swatted his hands away.
"I can walk just fine."

O-kay. He followed behind in case she stumbled while
admiring her nice ass. She managed to make it up the porch
steps all right but then couldn't open the front door—a door

that wasn't even locked. He made a mental note to speak with Margaret tomorrow about security.

After letting them in, Dax wrapped an arm around Jessie's waist again. This time when she swatted his arm, he ignored her. "You want some coffee?" he asked. "It might sober you up."

"Coffee? Hell no. It'll keep me up. I want to sleep forever and maybe when I wake up, Sadie will come back to town."

He hoped she didn't believe that fairytale. Denial was common, but if she thought the dead would rise again, she was delusional. Then again, she was drunk.

Somehow he managed to get her up the stairs and to her bedroom without incident. "Can you take it from here?" he asked. The last thing he needed was to have to undress her, see her perky naked breasts, soft round hips, and long trim legs.

Stop it.

Before he had a chance to step out, Jessie threw her arms around his neck and kissed him. Whoa! Every male instinct jumped to attention and her soft lips and dreamy eyes made him lose all control as he walked her backward and pressed her against the wall. When she ground her pelvis into his erection, she felt so good, so right, so incredible that he didn't want to stop.

Then as if his hand had a mind of its own, he slipped a palm over her plump breast, and she sucked in a breath and widened her eyes. Not believing it was even possible, she moved closer, and when she eased her tongue through his slightly parted lips, need exploded through him.

Then, dammit, that stupid little man inside his head told him to step away. Jessie was drunk, grieving, and unaware of what she was doing to him.

"Good night, Jessie." She'd regret the action tomorrow if he let her get carried away. She was upset, and this was probably her way of coping.

"Goodnight? Oh. Right. Goodnight." She reached up to

touch his face, but he stopped her in time. His level of nobility couldn't take any more temptation.

Guilt slammed into him at her forlorn expression, but damn, he didn't want to hurt her. She couldn't know that if she'd touched him again, he'd have to give in, and Jessie wasn't the type to have casual sex. If a man made love to her, she'd consider them a death-do-us-part couple, and Dax was anything but a steady man with way too many issues.

***

When the aroma of freshly brewed coffee filled the room, Jessie opened her eyes and pushed up on her elbows. "What are you doing here?" she asked, immediately pulling the crocheted afghan over her chest. No man had been in her bedroom before —other than Doc—and Dax last night, and even then he'd only made it in a few feet.

Dax waved a tray. "I come bearing breakfast."

The pain behind her eyes pounded, stabbed, punched, and squeezed her head. Now she remembered why she rarely drank. Besides losing control, alcohol gave her a wicked migraine, but hopefully, the caffeine would help.

Jessie rubbed her temples, but the ache didn't ease. She remembered awakening around three in the morning from the nightmare of seeing Sadie's body covered in dirt. The lack of sleep and the strain of learning about her death caused the tension to wring all function from her brain.

"Thank you, but you shouldn't be in here." She grabbed the coffee mug off the tray and took a sip. "Ah, just the way I like it, thank you." She leaned over the steaming liquid and inhaled the wonderful rich bean scent. Heat from the steam eased the throbbing around her eyes. "Absolute heaven."

"After that kiss you gave me, I figured I was given an open invitation to be in here." He smiled broadly as he placed her breakfast tray on her bed. While the buttered toast tempted her, the scrambled eggs did not.

The man was clearly out of his mind. "What kiss?"

He threw her an exaggerated frown. "At your bedroom door last night. You were a little tipsy, I admit, but *you* threw your arms around my neck and kissed *me*. Trust me, I didn't imagine it."

She had a vague recollection of Dax pressing her back against the wall. His lips. His heat. His whole body pulsating against her. *Ohmigod.* "I'm sorry. I was too drunk to know what I was doing."

The cheer on his face disappeared faster than water on a hot griddle.

"You'd had all of two drinks."

"Two doubles. That's like four regular ones, Mr. Mathematician." Damn. Being snarky was unattractive at best, but she was off balance whenever she was near him.

He winced. "I know, but even with that amount in your system, you would have known what you were doing, but I understand next day remorse. You don't have to worry, it won't happen again." Dax spun on his heels and disappeared, though from the small chuckle and the slight shake of his head, he wasn't too pissed.

She had hurt his feelings though, and that upset her, but she wasn't going to give him liberties when his time in Kerry was days from ending. At the thought of him leaving, along with the poor way she'd just handled herself, an unexpected sadness swept through her.

She set the coffee on her nightstand next to her bed and dropped her head back on the pillow. Eyes closed, she slapped a forearm over her face and the images came flooding back, enabling her to recreate the scene from last night in her mind's eye. If she'd kissed him, why had *he* pulled away? She would have remembered telling him no.

Maybe he just wasn't attracted to her, despite being able to make her feel all warm and safe inside, something no other man had succeeded in doing. He'd made her feel... *Call a spade a spade, Jess.* Horny. She wanted him. Hell, if he hadn't stepped away, she bet she would have dragged him to the bed and made incredible love to him, but it wasn't to be. She'd been a fool to think there might have been something between her and the tall, dark stranger, but as he said, it would never happen again. Bottom line, Dax Mitchell was off-limits.

If by some chance, she was misinterpreting his actions, and he really did want her, it was too late now. He'd be leaving soon —if not tomorrow, he would when his truck was repaired.

She could almost hear Sadie cursing her, convincing her life was too short to walk away from the sexiest man Jessie had ever known.

Shut up, Sadie.

Her stomach complained about the lack of food, and as she sat up to take a bite of toast, realization slammed into her. This morning she'd have to tell Nana about the oh-so-wrong murder, and what little appetite she had disappeared. One thing was sure. She would find out who did this terrible crime if it was the last thing she did.

***

Jessie slapped the wheel. "I shouldn't have listened to Nana and just left her to grieve on her own."

Seeing Jessie upset tore Dax up. He'd been by her side when she told Margaret the grim news. While Jessie's grandmother seemed to be working hard to keep it together for Jessie's sake, he wouldn't be surprised to hear she'd broken down later.

"Your grandmother's in good hands. All her friends are giving her their support. You heard her. She wants us to find who committed this atrocity, and you know the drill: for every hour that goes by, the chances of finding the killer goes down—way down."

"I know." Jessie bit down on her lower lip. "I wish I had a clue where to begin."

"Kerry hasn't had a murder in a lot of years, right?"

She glanced at him. "My father said a local butcher was killed in '88. Apparently he was cheating people on their meat purchases."

"Not exactly a documentary waiting to happen," he mumbled. She glared at him, and he regretted saying that out loud. "Sorry. All I'm saying is that for your town to have two, count 'em, two murders in such a short time, something isn't right. I think whoever took a shot at my truck is connected to one, if not both, of these crimes."

"I think you may be right. If we find out who shot at you, we'll find our killer."

"*Might* find our killer, not *will*."

"I know. It's wishful thinking," she said.

This morning, they'd returned to where they'd found Sadie's body so he could photograph the scene during the day, but they didn't find any additional evidence. While he'd suggested she stay in the cruiser while he snapped the pictures, Jessie had insisted she go with him. Once they finished with that chore, they decided to check out the mine to see if Sadie had discovered something there.

They rode in silence until she turned down Orchard Avenue toward the mine. "Shit. I forgot to call Walter about towing your truck."

"Let's first see if it's still there."

"No one would steal your truck. Kerry isn't—" She looked over at him. "Never mind. I forgot about the gas station heist and the grocery store theft." She shook her head. "Why did all this have to happen on my shift?" She shrugged. "Bad karma, I guess."

"Or else someone is trying to make sure you don't get the sheriff's position."

Her eyes widened. "You think the City Council is trying—"

He snickered. "I wasn't serious. People don't commit murder to keep someone out of office."

"I'm not so sure."

The paved road turned to dirt, and they bounced every time she hit a rut. Like his truck, the cruiser's shocks needed a major overhaul, but he understood money didn't flow in a town without jobs.

As they neared the mine, he let out a long breath. "There she is." Good. As soon as the gas tank and rim were fixed—and they solved two murders—he could leave town. Only he wasn't anxious to go. He doubted that one kiss would make him want to hang around as he wasn't the waiting type, but something seemed to be reeling him in, and it sure as hell wasn't the aliens.

Jessie pulled to a stop behind his truck, and he jumped out to stretch his sore leg. Dax then scanned the area. During the day, the place looked amazingly peaceful in comparison to the frightening way it had turned into at night. Birds chirped, the wind gently blew the tree branches, and the smell of pine and rich soil filled the air. At night, the forest had been a nightmare.

"Aren't you going to check out the damage?" she asked.

"In a minute. I'm enjoying the scenery. Is that okay?"

"Sure. It is pretty here. I just wished I could enjoy it."

Jessie probably had a hard night and an even harder morning. He wished he could help her get over the rough spots in her life, but he'd be gone soon, and it wouldn't be fair to her—or to him—to get involved.

He limped over to the passenger side and crouched in front of the tire. Jessie came up behind him, and he glanced up. "The bullet's still there."

Her brows pinched. "Why wouldn't it be?"

"Think about it. The bullet is evidence in a crime. I wouldn't have been surprised if the guy came back and removed it, though the one in the gas tank would have required taking half the truck apart and might not have been worth his effort." Or else the shooter didn't believe Jessie would follow through with a seemingly small crime in comparison to two murders. "We should check the caliber and striation marks against the one found at Barton's gas station. I'll be curious to see if they match," he said.

"I agree. While you work on getting out the bullet, I'm going to have a look around," she said.

"Be careful."

After rifling through the toolkit he kept locked in the back of his truck, he grabbed the needle nosed pliers and plucked the bullet from the tire. Pocketing the evidence, he hobbled over to where Jessie was snooping. The mine's multiple wooden structures seemed wobbly, but he figured the rails and elevator shafts had to be in better shape if the place only closed last year. Not that it mattered. He'd never go down in a mine again. His last experience, twenty-five years ago, had nearly cost him his life.

Jessie tugged on the large padlock that led into the mine. "Still holds."

"Good." Small footprints were scattered along the ground. "Looks like Sadie might have been here. Why do you think anyone would have cared enough to kill her?"

She shrugged. "I don't see any evidence of anything illegal going on here that she might have discovered, and certainly nothing to deserve being murdered over."

"What kind of illegal things are we talking about?"

"Moonshine, for one." Jessie stepped away from the main entrance and walked around to the side. "Hey Dax, what do you think made those drag marks?"

He checked them out. "The better question is, who made them?"

CHAPTER ELEVEN

Dax studied the markings in the sandy soil that ended at the main entrance. "Looks like someone dragged a couple of large crates through here. Do you think we should go down there to check it out?"

Of course, the *we* meant Jessie. He'd never go down into the dark shaft—ever, but he figured Jessie wouldn't mind, given her grandfather used to own the place until three years ago. She'd probably spent half her childhood down there.

"We can't get in *legally*, but I can ask Mr. Catchman if he wouldn't mind us taking a peek."

She'd be doing the looking alone.

Too bad cell phones didn't work here or they could have called the owner and saved themselves a return trip. This lack of service was starting to irritate him. He'd forgotten how the luxury of having instant communication sped up crime solving. If he'd known, and had the money, he would have rented a satellite phone for the week since those worked anywhere.

"Well, there's nothing else here to give us a clue as to Sadie's murder," Jessie said, defeat written all over her face.

"I'll have to agree with you."

He headed back to his truck, gathered his tools that were probably worth more than his ten-year old vehicle, and placed the toolbox next to the cruiser. He then waited for Jessie to pop the trunk.

Instead of returning, she stood at the entrance staring at the padlock. Wind blew her hair and billowed her shirt. It would have been such a pretty sight had it not been ruined by her sad stance.

"Come on, Jessie. We have more work to do," he shouted.

She dropped her hand from the lock and headed his way. "I know. I'll come back tomorrow since I don't want to be away from Nana any longer."

***

The warm, soothing shower had relieved some of Jessie's tension, but watching Nana and her friends pretend to play bridge renewed the knots in her shoulders.

They all looked so sad and were surely missing their friend. Jessie missed Sadie just as much since she'd been like an aunt to her.

Dax looked rather miserable too, sitting in the upholstered, flowered chair opposite her. Poor guy was flipping through a magazine without looking at the pages. Guess *Helpful Hints To Cooking* wouldn't make his bestseller list any time soon. Jessie had told him she wasn't sure she could handle these grieving women by herself, so he said he'd keep her company. Dax Mitchell was definitely a nice guy.

A fresh plate of her favorite dessert sat on the coffee table within arm's reach, and as much as she loved the smell of home-made chocolate chip cookies, tonight her appetite had flown out the window, along with her enthusiasm for doing anything but sitting.

She didn't even want to think about what to do with the

boatload of food in the kitchen. Half the town must have emptied their refrigerators, along with The Sugar Shack, who'd donated more than a week's worth of food. Nana and she wouldn't have to cook for a long time.

Mary Alice tossed her cards on the table. "I fold."

Eleanor, her partner, laid her hand gently on the corduroy tablecloth. "You don't *fold* in bridge. You pass. Come on, Mary Alice. Sadie would want us to move on."

"I know, but it's so hard. To think we'll never see her again." She turned to Dax and sniffled. "Did you see any evidence the aliens did this to her?"

For the first time in two days, Jessie's heart lightened. Good old Mary Alice. She lived for love—even if that love did come in the form of an alien.

Dax's mouth half opened before he shut it. "No. The markings definitely indicated her killer was of the human variety."

"Oh, thank you." She almost looked angelic.

Roberta held her cards close to her face. "I bid five clubs."

Nana, her partner, looked disgusted. "We can't make five clubs."

"But you bid two no trump to my two clubs. Are you saying you lied about what you had?"

"No, but, aww hell. I'm not in the mood to play anymore either. How can I concentrate knowing Sadie is looking down from above?" She tossed her cards in the middle of the table.

"I agree." Eleanor said.

"Me too." That came from Mary Alice.

"Well shit." Roberta sighed. "I finally have a twenty-four point hand and you all toss in your cards. Margaret, I'm taking the small slam." She marked the score down on the pad. "I'm sure we would have bid and made that."

"That's cheating," Eleanor piped up. She turned to Nana. "Can she do that?"

Jessie had had enough of the bickering. "Ladies, please. We're all stressed tonight. How about if you put the cards away and I fix you a nightcap?"

As if they were children promised candy if they behaved, they promptly shut up. Jessie looked to the heavens. *If you're up there, Sadie, thank you.*

Jessie brought two bottles in from the dining room liquor cabinet—one a Scotch and the other gin. Dax stepped next to her and lifted the bottles from her hands. "Here, let me help."

His musky aftershave sent a flutter through her stomach, which was the last thing she needed. "That's okay, I'll do it." She wished her body didn't turn traitor every time he came near.

"I have to keep busy and can't sit another moment," he whispered. "The cooking mag isn't doing it for me."

He was a good sport. "I really appreciate your support."

"You're welcome." He tilted her chin with one finger, and his amazing warm, brown eyes nearly made her forget her grief.

Jessie pulled away, quickly grabbed four glasses, and placed them on the credenza. Dax poured the liquor while she readied the mixers.

"Listen, Jessie. You do realize as soon as Walter gets me on the road, I'm out of here? Unless you need me to help with the crimes, that is."

Dax tapped the liquor bottle on the rim of the glass and looked at her, waiting for an answer.

"I do. Need you, that is." In more ways than one.

***

Jessie pointed to Barton's smashed security camera. "Take a look at the lens."

Dax walked around, checking the apparatus from all angles. "Someone had a damned fine aim." The camera sat on a pole, ten feet above the ground, pointing directly at the two gas pumps. "Barton got a ladder?"

"Probably," Jessie said. "I can ask him."

Dax probably shouldn't have offered to stay in town, but being here for another few weeks to help Jessie solve Kerry's crimes wasn't the worse thing he could do. She needed his help, and it was possible someone might come after her.

Money didn't grow on trees, which meant he should be back in Baltimore taking on more jobs, but doing nothing while he waited for his truck to get fixed wasn't his style either. Hell, if he stayed, he might even get to sample those luscious lips again.

As she headed to the convenience store, she swung her butt right then left enticing him. She sure caught his attention.

A minute later a burly man with a mustache, wearing a red plaid shirt and worn jeans, walked out with Jessie and pointed around back.

She continued on to Dax. "Barton will be here in a minute."

By the time Dax retrieved his needle nosed pliers from the trunk of the cruiser, the man had returned with the ladder.

The owner unfolded the metal legs that sent out a loud, grating sound and placed the creaky ladder under the camera. "Here ya go."

Jessie introduced them and they shook hands. Harold nodded. "I'll go back in if you two don't need me."

"Go ahead. Wouldn't want you to keep the customers wait-ing," Jessie said with a smile.

"What customers?"

Jessie chuckled and shooed him away. From what she'd told him, Kerry only had two gas stations, and given this one was farther out of town than the other one, Dax was surprised Harold stayed in business at all.

Dax climbed the ladder and inspected the damage done by the bullet. "This is unbelievable. Whoever took the shot hit the lens dead on. He must have had a laser site on his weapon. No one's that good without the help."

"Can you get the bullet out?"

"I'll try, but it's lodged in there pretty tight." Dax tugged and twisted until finally it broke free. "Gotcha."

A white Ford Taurus pulled up to the pump, and the driver rolled down the window. "So there you are. Jess, did you forget this was my first day?"

Jessie's eyes widened. "Oh, Amanda. I'm so sorry. I...I kind of got wrapped up in this case."

The blonde pulled the car onto a grassy area, parked, and then strutted over to the camera pole and looked up. "Hi, I'm Amanda Simmons, Jessie's new deputy."

He glanced at Jessie for an explanation, but she was still focused on her new hire. Guess taking on Amanda had slipped her mind, because otherwise Jessie would have asked her new recruit to help rather than him. Technically, he'd offered, but if she had a reason for withholding the information, he hoped she'd tell him.

Jessie stepped between Amanda and his ladder, acting almost protective.

"This is Dax Mitchell. He's a private investigator from Baltimore who came to find Sadie."

"Oh, really? Then I guess you're almost done in Kerry, Mr. Mitchell." Amanda struck a pose that he guessed she thought was sexy. Even in a uniform, she looked... well, cheap.

"Pretty close." News of Sadie's death sure traveled fast. For some reason, he didn't feel the need to mention he'd promised to stay a bit longer.

"Here's the bullet." He climbed down the ladder and handed the evidence to Jessie.

"Thanks. I'll put it in the evidence bag I have in the cruiser," she said.

She was halfway to the car when a gunshot sounded. He jerked around, searching for the source but spotted no one. Feet pounding on the pavement caught his attention. Amanda was sprinting toward the store, so he tore his gaze back to Jessie. Face bleached white, she looked frozen in time, as if the shot had paralyzed her with fear.

"Jessie, get down!" Dax shouted as he sped over to her, his leg screaming in pain. Either she didn't hear him yell, or her mind had blanked. Needing her to get out of harm's way, he grabbed her by the waist and half carried, half dragged her the ten feet to the cruiser. Her legs gave way just as he eased her to the ground.

Her eyes widened. "I think I've been shot."

CHAPTER TWELVE

Dax's heart nearly stopped at the thought of Jessie being injured. "Where does it hurt?" He prayed her condition wasn't life threatening. The horror of losing someone he cared about blasted him.

"M-my l-l-leg." Jessie grabbed her calf, and blood seeped through her pants.

He let out a long held breath. She'd be okay. He'd make sure of it. While the wound would hurt like a bitch for a while, she'd live—unless help didn't arrive in time. "Hold on. I need to make sure we're safe before I move you."

With his gun in hand, he looked out from behind the cruiser but detected no movement nor did he see any vehicle off in the distance. The shooter seemed to have evaporated into thin air just like at the mine.

He returned his attention to helping Jessie.

Amanda peeked her head out from inside the store. "Is it clear?"

"I hope so," Dax called back to her. "Call 911 and tell them an officer's down."

Jessie grabbed his arm. "Have her call Doc. It'll be f-faster. Harold will have the number."

He relayed the instructions to Amanda when then disappeared inside.

Dax leaned over Jessie. "I need something to stem the flow of blood."

She grabbed his arm. "Don't leave me."

He didn't intend to. Carrying her inside would make him a target, but he had to chance it. "Wrap your arm around my neck."

She did as he asked, and he slipped his arms under her legs. His leg protested as he stood, and as much as he enjoyed holding her, reaching the convenient store in one piece would be a challenge. With Jessie snug in his arms, Dax took off, zigzagging toward the store, ignoring the stabbing in his hip. Their luck held and no more shots were fired.

Once inside, he set her down away from the window. "Stay here. I need to look for medical supplies."

Harold hurried over. "What do you need?"

"Towels—clean ones—gauze, antiseptic. Anything to take care of a wound until the doctor arrives." The bullet could have clipped an artery. If Jessie bled to death, he'd never forgive himself.

"I'll get what I have," Harold said.

"Hurry."

Amped up on adrenaline, Dax did a quick check outside to see if he could find the elusive shooter, but the man was a ghost. Just as Dax returned to Jessie's side, Harold lumbered over with enough supplies to put the Red Cross to shame.

"Here."

"Thanks. How about standing behind one of the racks and letting me know if you see anyone." He didn't need the owner hovering or the shooter planning a sneak attack.

"Will do."

Dax sorted through the supplies, constantly checking on her, not liking how her pulse was thready and her face pale. "I know you're hurting, but I need to check your injury."

Thankfully, Harold had included a pair of scissors. As carefully as he could, Dax sliced open Jessie's pant leg.

"Damn. That was my last good pair."

"It can't be helped." He snipped the material higher.

Jessie winced. "Ouch, careful."

"Sorry." Dax returned his focus to her injury and checked the path of the bullet. "An entry and exit wound. You're lucky."

"You call that lucky? I've got a gaping hole in my leg." From the slight humor in her voice, she was trying to keep up her spirits.

Amanda finally rushed over. "I called Doc, and he's on his way. What can I do?"

"You got a gun?" he asked.

She twisted and showed him the thirty-eight caliber Remington revolver on her hip. "Yup."

"Given the guy's been quiet for a while, you up for seeing if he left any trace?"

"Sure thing."

"Be careful. I don't need two wounded warriors."

"I'm good," she tossed back.

While he counted the minutes until the doctor arrived, he put on latex gloves and held a towel over both of her wounds.

"It stings," she said wincing.

"I know, but you'll be up and moving around in a week." He had no idea how long her recovery would take, but Jessie needed to believe her mobility would return in no time.

She grabbed his arm in a vice grip. "You don't understand. I don't have a week. My job is on the line."

He lifted her hand from his arm, and the blood flow returned to his wrist. "I do understand. And what's more, if you move, your recovery will take longer. Now relax."

Amanda traipsed back inside. "I didn't see anyone or anything."

Dax looked up at her. "Nothing? You didn't find an area

where the shooter might have been lying in wait?" Then again, she'd only been gone a few minutes.

"Oh. You mean like did I find matted down grass and a spent shell casing?"

"Yes." Amanda wasn't being as cooperative as he would have liked, but she might think he was out to take her job. Dax debated searching the area himself, but he didn't want to leave Jessie, and he doubted Amanda would take good enough care of her.

"If you want me to look again, I guess I can."

I guess I can? "Please do. Look for broken branches or anything to show how he got here. The man didn't hover above the ground. All that's out there is underbrush and tall grasses."

She popped a bubble. "Back in a sec."

Jessie moaned, and Dax eased up on the pressure. Harold came over and gave her a bottle of water. "You need fluids."

She reached up, sucked in a breath, and grabbed the drink. "Thanks."

While Dax stemmed the flow of blood, she obediently drank her fill. When she was finished, she set the bottle down. "Who do you think shot me? The same person who put out the camera?"

"If we can find the bullet from your wound, we can do a comparison, but the hole in your calf looks like a twenty-two, and the caliber of the ones I took out of my tire and the camera looked closer to a forty-five."

"Oh."

"As to who shot you, my money's on some psycho who has a vendetta against this town, and since you're the representative, tag you're it."

Amanda rushed back, this time having been gone much longer. "Good news. I think I found where the guy came from. I followed the path back to a forest road, and while it was hard to tell how old the tires tracks were, I think the guy must have driven to the edge of the open field and walked in."

"Good work. Now, I'm wondering how he knew we'd be here."

Amanda shrugged. "Beat's me. Can I do anything else for you, Jess?"

Jessie sat up straighter, her breathing more rapid and shallow, which concerned him.

"Since I'll be out of commission for a bit, how about checking out the grocery store theft," Jessie said between gritted teeth.

"Sure. What do you know about it?"

She gave Amanda the details.

"I'll stop by your house later on and let you know what I find."

Jessie needed her rest. "How about making it tomorrow?" Dax asked. "The store will survive another day without knowing who robbed them."

Amanda looked offended. "You take care, Jess. Don't worry about a thing. Little ole Amanda will make sure nobody messes with this town while you're down and out." She smiled as though she was happy to be the one in charge.

As soon as the new deputy took off, Doc's wagon rolled in. Carrying the proverbial black bag, he rushed over. "Jessie Nash. What have you done to yourself now?"

***

Staying in bed all day sucked. Jessie wanted to move about, search for clues, bring the bad people to justice, only she couldn't. To make matters worse, her stupid leg was killing her. Yes, the painkillers Doc prescribed worked wonders, and if she kept still, the ache was quite manageable, but doing nothing was driving her crazy. The only good thing to come of her injury was that Nana seemed to focus on Jessie's well-being and not so much on Sadie's death.

A knock sounded on her bedroom door—the sweetest sound she'd heard in hours. "Come in."

Dax stepped in with something wrapped in a napkin. "A birdie told me you loved chocolate chip cookies, and Margaret warmed up a few."

Jessie smiled. "I just might be able to keep these down, thank you." The medicine had upset her stomach, and she hadn't been able to eat lunch or dinner.

"How do you feel about company?"

"Company?" Spending time talking with Dax would be wonderful. "I'd love some."

"Then you'll have to make your way downstairs. That guy, *Bruno* is here. Unless you want him to come up here."

From his tone, he acted as if the man was a threat, even though she thought she'd made it clear at the bar that she felt nothing for him. Men with lots of body hair and tattoos on every inch of skin did nothing for her.

Thinking of skin, she wondered what a naked Dax would look like. She bet he'd have just the right amount of chest hair and certainly nothing covering his back. He was in the service so he might have a few tattoos, but they'd have meaning if he had them.

"Jessie, are you all right?"

"Yes." She had to stop daydreaming, but it did help ease the pain. She sat up, placed both feet on the floor, and winced as the blood rushed to the injured area. "You know, for something as small as a little hole, it sure can cause a lot of pain."

"Don't I know it." He looked around. "Where are the crutches Doc gave you?"

"Downstairs. I can't go up and down using them. I'll trip and fall."

He smiled and her insides lit up. "Then I'll just have to carry you."

Before she could tell him he'd do no such thing, she was in his strong arms. Too bad, when he'd carried her into the convenience store, she'd been in too much pain and shock to appreciate it.

As he walked across her room, her muscles relaxed. She might as well enjoy the ride and even pretend he was her white knight.

Oh, I've read way too many romance novels.

As he stepped through the doorway, Jessie leaned into him, but because she was focusing on how nice it felt to be in his arms and not where he was taking her, her foot banged against the doorframe, sending a sharp, jabbing pain up her calf.

"Ouch. Shit, that hurt."

"I'm sorry, but I can't really see where I'm going. You'll need to pay attention for the two of us." He smiled then slowed down as he carried her to the top of the stairwell. "You know, for a lady, you have a pretty foul mouth."

No one had dissed her before for swearing. After all, it was the twenty-first century. "It's a hazard of the job. I've had to consider myself one of the guys, and every one of them swears."

"Doesn't make it proper."

Proper, schmoper. "What are you saying?"

"Being feminine isn't a bad thing, you know."

He had to be kidding. She'd never been so insulted in her life. Just because she wore baggy pants and shirts a few sizes too large, it didn't mean she wasn't a woman.

Oh shit. Had Dax stopped kissing her at the door because he didn't think she was *feminine* enough? Amanda had said the same thing, not to mention that Nana harped on her every day to fix herself up. Perhaps she needed to consider some changes—just as soon as she earned the right to be sheriff.

Speaking of being sheriff, both sets of uniforms were now ruined. Wearing jeans would rub against the wound, meaning she might have to wear a dress. She bet that would freak him out. Actually, it might be fun to see if she could get Dax Mitchell to see her more than just a police officer. Of course, if she were successful in attracting him, she'd have to say goodbye all too soon.

Dax's brows pinched as he took his time going downstairs. She bet his leg was hurting him, but he didn't complain. Once they arrived in the living room, he set her on the sofa across from her guest.

"Hi, Bruno," Jessie said.

Nana came bustling out of the kitchen with a tray full of goodies. "Here you all go. It's so nice of you to stop by and see Jess. She's been antsy all day."

Bruno took a brownie and stuffed it into his mouth then moved next to her. Immediately, Jessie scooted back until she hit the sofa's arm. "Thanks for stopping by. Is Brad handling the bar tonight?"

"Yup. Just like he does every Monday night."

Could she say, awkward? Men didn't come calling on her very often, so she was out of practice.

Bruno looked up at Dax. "Mind getting me something to drink, buddy?"

Nana started to rise, but Dax held out his hand. "I'll get it," he said. "Jessie, you want something?"

"Hot tea would be wonderful, thank you."

Nana stood. "I'm going to watch a little TV in my room. I'll let you young people be alone. Goodnight."

As soon as Nana left, Bruno scooted closer if that was possible. "What do you know about this Dax Mitchell fellow?" he whispered once Dax disappeared into the kitchen.

"Dax?" Jessie had never heard such a ridiculous question. "What do you mean?"

"Just what it sounds like. The moment the man came into town, the proverbial shit hit the fan—two deaths, two robberies. Come on. Something's going on. I get vibes when I'm working that all is not right in Kerry."

Jessie was horrified. "Dax had nothing to do with any of those atrocities. As a matter of fact, I was with him when I was shot, and possibly the same person shot at him!" Thankfully, Dax was making enough noise in the kitchen that he wouldn't hear them.

"All I'm saying is do your research. Have you checked him out on your law enforcement websites? Isn't there a way for you to see if he has a criminal record?"

Her pulse sped up as her stomach filled with such unease that she almost vomited. "I can run a check on him, but I promise you, I'll find nothing."

"You've known the man for what? Less than a week?"

"Yes, but he didn't just drop in from Mars. Nana hired him."

"And your grandmother did an in-depth background check, including fingerprints?"

"Keep your voice down. Dax might hear you. You know very well that Nana did no such thing." She glanced at the kitchen door to make sure Dax wasn't about to come in. "I'll toss the same question back at you. Have you done a background check on your new man, Seth?"

His brows rose. "As a matter of fact, I checked all of his references. He's clean."

As if the object of their discussion was clairvoyant, he pushed open the kitchen door carrying two cups of hot steaming tea, preventing her from asking anything else about the new hire.

Dax set the drinks on the coffee table but said nothing. His glare told it all. He did not like Bruno being here.

Before either said a word, the doorbell rang.

"I'll get it," Dax said.

A moment later, Amanda breezed in. Gone was the cop uniform, and in its place was something suited for a ski resort— black stretch pants and a fluffy, fleece jacket.

"Jessie, how are you doing?" Amanda rushed over to her.

"As well as can be expected. I'm sore, but I'll live."

Amanda looked at Bruno and held out her hand. "Hi, I'm Amanda Simmons, Jessie's new deputy." Apparently, he was the one man she hadn't met.

"Bruno Quattrone. I own the Coal Mine Bar."

"Bruno, darling," Amanda said. "If you don't mind, I have police business to discuss with Jess. I know she'll be off to bed soon, but I wanted to share a few things with her."

Bruno looked pissed, but he stood and grabbed his jacket. "Remember what I asked you to check?"

"Got it." He was such a jerk.

Amanda took his place on the sofa and waited until the door closed. "What was his problem?"

"Who knows?"

With Dax standing there, she certainly couldn't tell Amanda what Bruno had suggested. "What brings you here that couldn't have waited until morning?"

"Waited until morning, huh? Are we angry I sent little old Bruno away?"

Jessie smiled. "Actually, no, you saved me."

"Good." Amanda opened her purse and removed several photos. "After I left the gas station, I wanted to see if I could find any clues to the sheriff's death, so I took the liberty of checking out his house."

"You broke into Clinton's place?"

She looked indignant. "It's not like I could have asked his permission. Just so you know I didn't break a window or anything. I know how to pick a lock."

She'd store that piece of information away for later. Jessie pointed to the pictures. "Okay, so what are those?"

Dax slipped onto the flowered chair across from them and leaned forward.

"I found these in Clinton's bedside table drawer." She handed the photos to Jessie. "I think our dear sheriff was killed by the man he was blackmailing."

Jessie flipped through them and sucked in an audible breath. "I can't believe this."

CHAPTER THIRTEEN

Dax held out his hand. "May I take a look?"

"Sure." Jessie handed him the first photo.

He glanced for only a second. "Not something I needed to see," he said and handed it back.

Worse porn had crossed his desk, but he hadn't expected to be shown such a photo in Kerry.

"Haven't you ever seen two men kiss before?" Amanda asked with a hint of a smile.

"They were doing a lot more than kissing. Who are these men?" Curiosity had the best of him.

"The one on the bottom is our mayor," Jessie explained in a surprisingly neutral tone. "The owner of the bare butt is the President of the Bank of Kerry. I have no problem with this, except both are married men."

Dax whistled. She bit her lip and looked away from the photos that were no doubt making her uncomfortable.

"Did anyone ever suspect they were involved?"

"Are you kidding?" Jessie said. "These men are the epitome of respectability. They're the ones who said they wanted a man to be sheriff. Now I know why."

Hidden agendas always sucked. He faced Amanda. "Besides

the fact you found these at the sheriff's house, do you have any evidence DuPree was blackmailing these men?"

"Not yet, but I'm not finished investigating," Jessie said. "No, wait a minute. I found receipts in Clinton's desk that were for a large screen TV, a tractor and a generator."

"Meaning what?" Dax asked.

"Big ticket items? Blackmail? They go hand in hand." She looked up at Amanda. "Did you see a big TV or a generator when you were at his house?"

"I didn't see either of those things," Amanda said, "but then again, I wasn't looking at his décor."

"Just because a guy spends some money, doesn't mean he's blackmailing someone," Dax said. He leaned back in the chair and switched his glance from Jessie to Amanda, and then back again. "For a crime, you need means, motive, and opportunity. Motive I get, but we don't even have a body, and until we do, these photos and those big ticket items mean squat."

"That's one man's opinion," Amanda said acting tough. "I want to speak to these men to see if DuPree approached them with the photos."

Jessie grabbed her arm. "Don't be stupid. If they killed Clinton, they could come after you."

She shrugged. "I can take care of myself."

"Amanda, please don't do anything until I'm feeling better." Jessie smiled. "You know how you could help me?"

"How?"

"Dax would you excuse us? We have some girl stuff to discuss."

He wasn't happy, but he went upstairs. Girl talk, indeed. For the life of him he couldn't fathom what that would be about.

***

Refusing to sit home another day, Jessie was thrilled to finally be back at work. Over Nana's protests, she'd convinced Dax to drive her to town. She had a lot of paperwork to do and could rest her leg sitting just as well as being in bed.

Dax admitted he didn't mind taking her, claiming he wanted to check on the progress of his truck repair. There would come a time when he was able to leave, and she wondered how long he'd stay. Murder investigations could drag on for months, or so she'd been told.

Once she fired up the office computer, the first thing she did was run Dax Mitchell's name through VICAP, the Violent Criminal Apprehension Program, as well as through the National Criminal Database to see if he had a record. She suspected Bruno's warning was made out of jealousy, but she wouldn't be a good officer if she didn't follow through on one of her constituent's suspicions.

The little processor clock ran and ran. *Come on.* A screen popped up that gave her the chance to type in Dax's name. After a few seconds, the search came up empty, and she looked up to the ceiling to say a silent prayer.

He'd mentioned something about being in Iraq, which was where he probably received his leg injury, but she didn't have access to any military databases.

To be thorough, though, or perhaps because she was plain nosy, she Googled Dax's name, and three newspaper articles appeared. That surprised her. She was a little uncertain if she even wanted to read any dirt on him, but hell, she'd come this far, so she might as well find out if there was anything to Bruno's claim.

Jessie took a sip of her freshly made coffee and began to read. The first article was dated three years ago. Apparently, Dax's fiancée, a fellow detective by the name of Laura Santiago, was involved in a drug sting gone bad. The Santiagos had received a ransom note stating if they wanted to see their daughter alive again, they had to convince the Baltimore Police to release Roberto Ramirez from custody and drop all charges, as well as pay one million dollars. Dax was quoted as saying the department was doing everything possible to bring Laura back alive.

The second article showed Dax by a gravesite, head bowed, looking years older. According to a police spokesperson, the department had refused to bend to the will of the terrorists, despite the Santiago's willingness to cough up the money. Because of their decision, the drug lords followed through with their threat and Laura's body was found a week later in an abandoned warehouse. She'd been executed, but the kingpin had not been apprehended.

Jessie's headache returned. Poor Dax. To lose a woman he loved in such a horrible manner would destroy anyone. No wonder he seemed like such a lost soul, and why he wasn't with someone now.

The sudden need to comfort him overwhelmed her. *Stop it, Jess. You'll only end up hurt when he returns to Baltimore.*

The third article, dated six months ago, showed Dax standing next to a six-year old girl who looked like she might be his daughter. Her heart pounded as she leaned closer to the computer and read further. The little girl had wandered off into the Maryland woods and wasn't heard from for days. Dax had followed the informational trail, as well as the literal one, and found her. She'd been abducted, but then was saved by some hermit. Dax was proclaimed a hero by both the press and the little girl's parents.

Her pride swelled. Stupid Bruno. Villain, indeed. Dax saved people, not slayed them.

A knock sounded on the office door, and Brian waltzed in, but she wasn't in the mood to socialize.

"Hey, Jess."

"Brian." She lowered her propped up leg to the ground, and blood rushed to her wound, sending stabbing spikes up her leg. Stupid bullet.

"I heard you were shot. How's the leg?"

He sounded friendly enough, but she could tell he wasn't

there to chitchat. "Sore, but I'll live." She checked her watch. "Shouldn't you be at work?"

He threw her a sheepish grin. "I haven't started my job at the cement plant yet. I've been busy fixing up the old homestead."

"So you're living in your old house? I thought your mom's place was rented."

"It had been, but the old geezer living there had to leave."

"I'm surprised I hadn't heard." Nana must becoming forgetful.

"His daughter took ill or something. It was actually good timing for me. I needed a place to stay, and it was *one* of the reasons why I chose to come back to Kerry."

He scanned her from head to toe, making her uncomfortable. He acted as though he wanted to pick up where they left off ten years ago, but she'd never date him again. "What can I do for you? Are you here to report a crime?" she asked in her most professional voice.

Brian pulled up a chair too close to her desk and sat down, forcing Jessie to scoot back.

"I was taking a break and wanted to see if you needed anything. I don't think I mentioned it but I served in the Military Police for a few years, so if you need any help with Clinton's murder or Sadie's, I'm your man. At least for the next few weeks until I start work."

She had to think how she could let him down gently. "I do appreciate the offer, but Dax and I are on the case, and Amanda is helping too."

He cocked a brow. "Dax and you?" His lips pressed firmly together. "I trust he's the big fella who's been hanging all over you?"

"Dax doesn't hang, nor are we an item. He helps me move about. We're just coworkers." Part of her—the insane part—wanted more.

"I hear differently."

She had to laugh at that. "Well, you heard wrong." She

tapped the screen. "I hate to be antisocial, but I have work to do, so if you wouldn't mind?"

He held up a hand. "Ask no more. You know where to find me. I'll stop back tomorrow to see if you've changed your mind, but don't worry, there are no strings attached. I don't move in on another man's woman." He shoved his chair back so hard, it almost tipped over. "Take care, Jess."

Before she could respond that she wasn't Dax's *woman*, he shot out the door, although as soon as she healed, she wouldn't mind snuggling up to the sexy P.I. for the time he was here. She was strong enough to keep her emotions at bay—or so she hoped.

Once the quiet returned, she went back to her computer. On a whim, she typed Brian Richards' name into VICAP, but nothing popped up either. For the sake of being thorough, she looked in the National Criminal Database.

After an interminable wait, several Brian Richards showed up, so she chose the one with the correct age and clicked okay to get a more detailed description of the crime. She got a hit.

As Jessie scanned this list, her palms sweated. *Brian, what have you done?*

His list of offenses surprised and depressed her. The two convenience store thefts didn't bother her, but the most recent crime did—one that was bad. Really bad.

"Hey," Amanda said, bouncing into the office.

Jessie's heart skipped a beat. "I wish you wouldn't startle me like that. Knock or something next time."

"Sorry." Amanda was carrying three large bags. "Wait until you see what I have for you."

"I didn't ask you to buy the store. I can't afford all that stuff." She could almost hear her bank account nosedive into the negative.

Jessie was about to protest when Amanda held up her hand. "Don't worry, I found good deals." She pulled out a long red, slinky dress with a low V-neck, and Jessie gasped. Next, her *friend* dragged out a pretty jeweled necklace and matching earrings.

"I'm not wearing all that jewelry. I'd look ridiculous. As for that dress, it's ob-ob-obscenely low cut."

"Listen, Jess, if you want to attract a man, you have to look like a woman, not one disguised as a man."

She refused to rise to the bait and argue the second assertion. "Who says I want to attract a man? I asked you to buy me some clothes I could wear that wouldn't rub against the wound on my leg, and that's all."

"A dress is just what you need. Anyway, I figured as long as I was shopping, I might as well buy you some makeup."

"Makeup? Sheriffs don't wear makeup. Dear Lord in Heaven, I'll feel totally out of place with goo all over my face."

"That's your problem. You don't consider yourself feminine, but I plan to change that." Amanda smiled and pulled out a fleece sweat suit. "Huh? You like?"

"Now you're talking."

"It's fitted, so you won't look like you're swimming in your clothes. The dress is for evening, the sweat suit is for lounging around, and these," Amanda said, holding up a few more items, "are for work."

The A-line jeans skirt and modest sweater she could do. "Thank you."

"Why don't you try something on?"

"Now?"

"Yes, now. Oh, I almost forgot. I bought you a pair of sneakers and some flats for the office and matching red pumps to go with the dress."

Jessie laughed. "It feels like Christmas."

"I bet it's been that long since you've treated yourself to anything new, am I right?"

"Too right."

Amanda set all the packages on her desk. "Try on the dress. I'm dying to see if it fits."

Her friend wouldn't leave her alone until she put on at least one outfit. Using her crutches, Jessie swung her way over to the bathroom, while Amanda carried the dress. Believing her friend would follow her in, Jessie turned and held up one hand. "I want to surprise you."

Before Amanda had the chance to protest, Jessie snatched the dress and jewelry before closing the door. Standing on one foot, she was able to change. The small wall mirror only gave her a glimpse of what she looked like, but she could tell she looked good. Too bad her boobs didn't fill out the dress as nicely as Amanda's or Lena's would, but there was little she could do about it.

Jessie slipped on the heels, but she drew the line at Amanda slathering makeup on her. She took a step and the pain in her leg eased. Interesting that the added height allowed her calf to relax a little.

When she hobbled out, Amanda sucked in a loud breath. "Now that's what I'm talking about. You look gorgeous, and those earrings are striking."

Jessie shook her head, and the cold, dangly steel caressed her face. She actually felt sexy.

"Now for the makeup," Amanda said as she routed through another bag.

Jessie held up her hand. "Let's not waste it. I'm just sitting here, so no one's going to see me."

"Dax will when he picks you up tonight."

Heat raced up her face. "Why should I care? He'll be leaving as soon as his truck is fixed." There was no use discussing his generous offer to stay. Amanda could help just as well.

"It'll be fun to get a rise out of him. Come on, let me do my girl thing."

As though they were back in high school, Jessie gave in and let Amanda line her eyes and lips, then fill-in with who knows what color. She felt like a poodle after a day at the doggie spa.

Amanda pulled out a compact mirror and held it up to Jessie. "What do you think?"

"Wow," said a low, sexy voice at the entrance.

Jessie jerked around.

"W-what are you d-doing here?"

CHAPTER FOURTEEN

Jessie blushed the prettiest shade of red, her cheeks matching her dress perfectly.

"I finished with Walt and came back to see if you wanted to go to lunch." Dax never expected to find someone this hot sitting in the sheriff's office. Her transformation made him tongue-tied.

Amanda smiled. "Yes, she'll go to lunch. It's a date."

"Am-an-da."

Dax stepped over to Jessie and her perfume made him even harder than he already was. "You are truly beautiful."

Jessie looked down at her shoes. "Thank you."

"I know it's a little early, but are you okay to eat?" He was only hungry for her, but he was willing to go now just to be near her.

She looked up at him. "I'm starving, actually." She turned to Amanda. "Thank you for the clothes. I appreciate everything you've done for me."

Amanda waved away the compliment. "What are friends for? It was fun dressing you up, just like we used to do in high school. Now go, and don't worry. I'll hold down the fort."

"I can't go to the restaurant looking like a... a vamp."

Dax laughed. "You look like a very sexy woman that any man in town would be proud to be with." He hoped he wasn't drooling when he told her how remarkable she looked.

She kept her gaze averted as she threw on her Pea coat—a too-big, worn Pea coat that definitely didn't go with the fancy dress and earrings, but he understood her need to stay warm.

Jessie fingered the lapels. "I guess I'll need a new coat if I plan to dress up again."

"I think you look cute," he said.

Jessie focused on the ground as she hobbled outside. Fortunately, The Sugar Shack was only a block away. While using her crutches appeared painful, driving her the one block had its drawbacks. Once he dropped her off, he'd have to return to the station to park, and she'd be alone for too long.

Dax purposely walked slowly so she wouldn't feel rushed. The wind had died down and the easy stroll made him feel as though they were on a real date. Unfortunately, the moment they walked inside the restaurant, the calm he'd experienced shattered.

Lena started screaming Jessie's name as she raced over to them. "I can't believe it. Jessie Nash, what did you do to yourself? You're gorgeous. You look so different, so good."

Every pair of male eyes swung in Jessie's direction—something he didn't like.

"Did I really look so bad before?"

Lena's face contorted. "Bad isn't the right word, maybe—"

"I get it. You sound like Nana." She chuckled. "Do you have a booth in the corner for us?"

Lena looked flustered, poor thing. "Absolutely."

As he and Jessie made their way to the back of the restaurant, several men whistled, and Dax couldn't help but glare at them. He wanted to wrap his arm around her waist to indicate the men needed to back off, but with the crutches, he couldn't get near enough to her.

When they reached the booth, Dax set her instruments of

torture on the floor then scooted in across from her. "So what have you been up to this morning?" He wanted to take the focus off her new appearance and onto a more comfortable topic.

"Before my fairy godmother came in and bestowed all the clothes on me, Brian Richards stopped by."

"Who's Brian?"

"He was the one I was sitting across from at the diner."

"What did he want?" He worked hard not to sound possessive.

She bit her lower lip, sending his thoughts below his waist. The cool air had dampened his lust for a moment, but now the urge was back.

"I'm not quite sure."

Her avoidance sent a message. "Are you two dating?" This time, he failed to keep the anger from his voice.

"No, not at all. And that's what made me a little suspicious about why he'd stopped by. We dated like ten years ago, but he's been gone forever."

No doubt he stopped by to check out his hot ex-girlfriend. The guy probably wanted to pick up where he left off, but if that were the case, Dax would have to set him straight. "Suspicious how?"

"He told me that given I'd been shot, he wanted to see if he could help with the investigation. He let me know that he'd been with the MP's in the service and thought he could lend a hand."

"Sounds like a reasonable request, although in truth, he probably just wanted a chance to get in your pants," Dax mumbled.

"Excuse me?"

There he went again, thinking out loud. "Sorry. What did you tell him?"

She didn't answer for a moment, which didn't bode well for him. Between her scowl and pursed lips, she looked as if she was about to tell him to fuck off but then thought better of it. "I told him you and I had everything under control."

Relieved he didn't have to deal with seeing Brian with Jessie every day, Dax leaned back against his seat. "Good." From the way her gaze bounced from her hands to the other customers, she was hiding something. "What aren't you telling me?"

She grimaced. "You see, of all the people from school, Brian was the most gung ho about the service, and he couldn't wait to get away from Kerry. He even falsified records to get his then sixteen-year-old brother into the Army. Brian had almost finished his second tour of duty when his brother was killed, and Brian claimed it was his fault for convincing Jimmy to enlist."

"And the purpose of this story is?" He wasn't interested in the life of her former lover.

"I'm getting to the point. After the funeral, Brian re-upped again. When he came back here last week he told me he was no longer in the service."

"So? I did two tours, and then left."

"Yeah, but I figured you left because of your leg injury."

"True. Go on."

"Once he left the office, I ran a check on him."

Lena rushed over. "I'm so sorry to keep you two waiting. It's been so crazy around here with the new cement plant hiring right and left. Our business is booming big time. Now what can I get you?"

Dax would have liked to have heard the rest of Jessie's story, but they did have to order. Not wanting to take the time to pour over the menu, he ordered something he knew they'd have. "A hamburger, medium rare, and a Coke."

"Me too, only I want an unsweetened iced tea," Jessie said.

"Fries with that order and everything on top?" Lena's hand hovered over her pad.

"Sure," they said in unison. Jessie smiled and he felt that rush of hormones run through him again.

"Got it." Lena hustled off, and Dax motioned for Jessie to continue.

"Well, I got to wondering why Brian had returned to Kerry. His father died his senior year in high school, his mom took her life after her youngest son was killed, and her oldest son, George, left town. There was nothing here for him, so I checked Brian out with the National Criminal Database and guess what I found?"

"What?" Dax tapped the spoon on the table.

"Don't be so impatient. Brian was arrested for stealing automatic weapons! Can you believe it? He didn't come back to Kerry any sooner because he was in jail."

Dax whistled and dropped the spoon on the table. "Are you thinking he had something to do with the murders?"

"I don't know. I'm just saying that someone who was with the MP's would know how to shoot, don't you think?"

"Certainly seems likely. Do you believe Brian shot you?"

Before she could answer, someone cleared his throat.

Jessie looked up and her face paled. "Mayor Kreplick."

Dax had to admit the Mayor looked quite different fully clothed. The image of the married man and the bank president in bed had turned his stomach. Cheating on a spouse was wrong, at least in his world it was.

"What can I d-do for yo-you?" Jessie asked.

The Mayor motioned toward the empty seat next to Dax. "May I? I won't take up much of your time."

Dax scooted over as far as he could, watching as a flash of fear crossed Jessie's face. This mayor held her whole life hostage, and that pissed him off.

"I wanted to know what you're doing to find Clinton's killer." He directed his comment only to Jessie.

Ah, the sixty-four thousand dollar question, though without the body, they couldn't be positive he was dead. Would she say she thought the Mayor, himself, had killed the man? She should claim she needed more time to prove it, but when Jessie opened her mouth, not a word came out.

Dax leaned forward on his elbows. "We have nothing, Mr. Mayor. Not a clue. And even if we did, we wouldn't be at liberty to divulge the information. It's a confidentiality thing. You must run into that all the time in your position."

Jessie looked at him as though he'd saved her, and a spurt of happiness shot through him.

"And who the hell do you think you are? I asked Ms. Nash."

Dax laughed. "And I'm answering." Bob Kreplick turned four shades of unhealthy pink. "Listen, when and if we find the killer, we promise you'll be the *first* to know."

Bob Kreplick jumped out of the booth and nearly knocked down Lena taking an order at the next table. He straightened his tie and brushed off the seat of his pants as if sitting with them had given him a disease. Asshole.

Mayor Kreplick turned to Jessie. "Having him around," he nodded to Dax, "changes nothing. You have less than three weeks to clean up this town or you're out of here."

"You said that I'd be deputy if—"

The Mayor lifted his nose in the air. "I recall no such discussion. Good day, Ms. Nash."

What an arrogant prick. The bell rang above the door, and as soon as Kreplick disappeared down the street, the noise level in the restaurant returned to normal, implying the whole place had been listening to the embarrassing exchange.

She glanced up at him, looking as though she'd lost her best friend. "Can he really threaten me like that?" She wrung her hands together.

His strong urge to reach across the table and take her hand surprised him. If he touched her, though, he might not stop at her hands. "The man's scared. He'll say anything to take the heat off himself."

"You think so?"

"Hell, yes."

Before he could calm her fears, Lena rushed back with their food, a bit out of breath. "So the big man came to talk. What did he want?" The gossip queen was practically drooling. From what Jessie had said, it was tell Lena, tell the town.

"He just wanted an update on the cases," Jessie said in a remarkably calm voice.

"Did you tell him?" Given the fact Lena was standing less than five feet away pouring one cup of coffee for five minutes, she must have heard nearly the whole damned conversation.

Jessie leaned forward and smiled ever so sweetly. "So, tell me about this new beau of yours."

Lena placed their food on the table, and the aroma from the juicy hamburger made his mouth salivate, but he waited for Lena to finish before he dug in.

Their waitress didn't seem to pick up on the change of topic, and if she did, she didn't let on. "He's divine. Seth is everything I've ever wanted in a man." She inhaled deeply, closed her eyes for a moment, and then let out a long sigh.

"What about Kevin?" Jessie turned to Dax. "That's Lena's husband."

His jaw clenched. He hadn't been aware Lena was cheating on her husband with that Seth guy.

"That's the best part," Lena said, "I received the divorce papers this morning." She glowed. "We're finished, and I couldn't be happier."

"That was a fast divorce." Jessie turned to Dax. "Her hubby enjoyed using Lena as a punching bag." She grabbed Lena's hand. "I'm glad he's out of your life."

In that case, good for her. Spousal abuse was the lowest form of pond scum, only slightly above murder.

"I wish you luck with Seth," Jessie said.

"Hey, Lena," Bill Peters shouted from across the restaurant.

"I gotta go," Lena said, still beaming. She scurried off to take care of her customer.

"You do have some characters in this town," Dax said.

"That's an understatement." She bit into her hamburger. "Mmm." Juice ran down her hands and she wiped away the liquid before it got on her ever-delicious dress. "So what's our next step?"

"You never answered me if you thought Brian could have shot you."

She finished chewing then wiped her mouth with the napkin. "I would have said absolutely no way before I checked his record. Now I'm not so sure."

"I say it's time we check out Clinton's place."

She took a sip of her ice tea. "Amanda already did."

"I know, but you said you found receipts for some big-ticket items, and I'd like to see if he has any other expensive items in his house that could add to the circumstantial evidence we have against the Mayor."

***

Jessie estimated Clinton's two-bedroom home to be no more than a thousand square feet. It had a small living room, a cramped dining room, and one bathroom, but a surprisingly spacious kitchen. From the looks of the ratty furniture, she wouldn't have guessed the man was on the take.

She spotted an old film camera on top of dining room table that had been missing from the office. She turned to Dax. "You know what I find strange?"

Dax was sifting through some papers on Clinton's desk. "What?"

"Clinton harped on never keeping anything at home that belonged to the police department. He said that even though we didn't have much crime in Kerry, we should keep everything at the office. And a rule was a rule, he'd say. Does that make any sense? I'm babbling, I know. The medication must be screwing with my thought processes."

"I totally understand. I was happy the digital camera was in the office the night you found out Clinton was supposedly dead."

She appreciated he believed Clinton might still be alive. "So why do you think this film one is here?"

Dax stopped searching and faced her. "I don't know. Maybe he couldn't return it because he got killed?"

She pointed a crutch at him, not liking how he suddenly changed his mind about her boss. "Sarcasm doesn't suit you. I know I'm not as smart as you, but you don't have to be—"

He jumped up from behind the desk and rushed over to her. "I'm sorry. I didn't mean to get testy." He rubbed her arms in a gentle, caring way, and her anger diffused as other body parts turned traitor. "It's just that I'm used to handling one crime at a time, not five."

Her mind raced. "Five?"

"The fifth being the crime against you." He nodded to her leg. Dax stepped back then stabbed a hand through his hair before straightening the mess he'd made on the desk.

"I'm betting if we find one criminal, we may have 'em all," she said.

Dax turned, and when he hooked his thumbs in his pockets, sex appeal leaked off him.

"Brian had no reason to kill the sheriff," he said. "He just arrived in town."

"True."

"Okay, let's assume Brian's innocent of this crime. Could the Mayor have killed Sadie and the sheriff, robbed a store, a gas station, and then shot you?"

Her calf was throbbing, forcing her to sit at the table. "When you put it like that, no. Kreplick and Sadie got along okay, and I always thought he and Clinton were close. Shows what I know."

"Do you know if the Mayor had been some kind of sharp shooter in the day?"

Jessie leaned her head against the back of the chair. "Anything but. He loved hunting, but I don't think he ever bagged a deer in his life."

"Then let's dig deeper. For now, we'll keep both the Mayor and Brian on our list."

She hated not knowing which way to turn. "Fine. I'll start with Clinton's bedroom."

"Okay."

Despite not knowing what she should be looking for, Jessie searched her boss's closets and drawers. She rubbed her upset stomach. Not only did the house have that nobody's-been-in-there smell, digging into her boss's personal effects was plain wrong. Nonetheless, she kept going.

After the twenty-minute search turned up nothing, she returned to the living room. "I can't find anything to link Clinton with blackmail—other than the pictures of the two men."

"Which we aren't even sure he took."

She hadn't thought of that angle. "Are you thinking someone showed the pictures to him for kicks, and Clinton confiscated the offending photos then tossed them in his side drawer for safe keeping?"

"It's possible. As long as we're guessing, either the Mayor's wife or Lucas's wife could have taken the pictures. Maybe they wanted Clinton to do something about the affair."

"Now that's something I would have never thought of."

He tapped the side of his head and smiled. "Work as a private investigator long enough and you see all sorts of sordid shit going on."

Jessie was glad she didn't work in a big city. The small town of Kerry suited her fine.

Dax picked up a trophy and studied the label. "Clinton used to ride in a rodeo?"

"Can you believe it?"

He put the object back down. "Did you find any suitcases in his bedroom?"

"Yes, why?"

"If none of his luggage had been there, I might have concluded he'd skipped town along with the theoretical black-mail money."

"You know, for a city boy, you're on the ball." Dax flashed her a megawatt smile and her heart pinged.

"Thanks."

She had to chuckle at his antics. The experts were right when they claimed laughter was the best antidote to depression. Jessie hobbled over to the sofa to rest her leg. "Speaking of skipping town, where do you suppose Clinton stashed his car?"

Dax's eyes widened, seemingly impressed with her observation. "It's not at the mine, the cement plant, here, or at the office. Maybe if we find it, we'll find Clinton."

"Do you think I should check every garage in town?"

He shook his head. "A killer wouldn't be that stupid."

"I should do a search of Kreplick's and Lucas's garages though. The arrogant S.O.B.s might think we'd never suspect either of them."

"By all means, check them out, but from personal experience, I think if either of them killed Clinton, he would have driven the car to a remote site and dumped the vehicle, hoping no one would notice Clinton's cruiser was missing for a while."

"Hard to hide a police vehicle."

"Good point." He held up a finger. "Oh, while you were in the bedroom, I looked out back but didn't find a lawn tractor."

"I didn't expect one." She looked around. "We didn't find a big screen TV in here either."

"Maybe his new purchases haven't been delivered yet."

"It's a possibility. I'll check the date on the receipts when we get back to the office."

Dax shuffled back to Clinton's desk and looked through his *Out* box. "Do you think you could get access to his bank account?"

Jessie stood and swung over to where Dax was searching. "Are you thinking we might find a few large deposits?"

He looked up at her and studied her. "Yes."

Dax was like her kryptonite. Every time she neared, some

internal change occurred, and she wasn't sure if that was good for her.

"It's w-worth a try, but I'm beginning to think Clinton was clean." God, she hated to stutter, but every time she became nervous—which she was right now—she couldn't form her words right.

"Given the bank president has a good reason to stall, we might run into some resistance. Even if we could get a warrant, which at the moment looks doubtful due to lack of evidence, he might falsify the information."

"Damn. I mean darn. This case is getting more complicated by the minute."

"Murder cases usually do."

Depression gave her a quick jab in the gut. "I guess I don't want to believe the man who mentored me would be capable of doing something so deceitful."

Dax nodded in sympathy. "Maybe he didn't. Stay put while I do one final check in the kitchen."

Jessie didn't object. She sat down in Clinton's chair and studied the dining room and living area. The refrigerator banged shut and the cabinet doors opened and closed.

He came back out with a hand on his hip. "If the man was blackmailing someone, he didn't have much in the way of food or expensive tastes. Hell, if I'd come into money, I'd have a freezer full of filet mignon and a liquor cabinet stocked with Chivas Regal."

"So what are you saying?"

"If he didn't take the photos himself and use them as black-mail, maybe someone planted the photos in Clinton's drawer or, as you said, he was merely the holder of the offensive pictures."

"If someone did plant them, we're back to square one unless we can think who would benefit from trying to misdirect us."

Dax's laugh held no humor. "Oh, I know who'd benefit."

"Who?"

"The killer."

***

After an unsuccessful search at Clinton's house, Dax and Jessie drove back to the office where she placed a call to Mr. Catchman, the mine owner, hoping he'd give them permission to search his land. Those drag marks didn't get there by accident, though she didn't really expect to find anything inside the closed down mine either, but it never hurt to cover all of her bases.

Dax sat at Clinton's office desk looking for something while she tapped her pencil on her desk. "Answer, dammit."

Dax looked up at her and she slumped against the seat. She forgot that ladies didn't swear. She pulled the V-neck closer together. Women wearing hooker dresses weren't fit to investigate crimes. Amanda should be shot.

"This is Wayne Catchman."

"Mr. Catchman."

"I am out of town until November fifth. Please leave a message at the beep."

Jessie hated messages, but she asked him to call her back the moment he was able. She'd just hung up when her phone rang. Man that was fast.

"Sheriff Nash." She liked the sound of her new title.

"This is Deputy Morris over in Hardy County. We found an abandoned vehicle registered to the Kerry Sheriff's Department."

Her muscles weakened and her breath caught. She glanced up at Dax who'd stilled. "Where's the cruiser now?" He gave her directions to the vehicle's location, and Jessie jotted them down, her shaky hand making her letters almost illegible. "Thank you. I'm a little short-handed right now, so I can't be certain when I can make it over, but I'll call before I come if that's all right."

"No problem." He gave her his number. "If you can't make it tonight, I can meet you tomorrow just as easily."

"Thank you." She hung up.

Dax came over to her desk and leaned a hip on the edge. "Clinton's car?"

She nodded. "He's really dead isn't he?"

"It's looking like it."

Jessie refused to break down. She didn't have the time. "Maybe you and Amanda can drive over and pick up the car. It's a good forty-five minutes away."

He tucked a strand of her hair behind her ear, and his touch sent a shiver of need to her groin. *Stop reacting.* Maybe the dress was having a cosmic effect on her senses.

"I don't want to leave you alone," he said. "We'll go together."

She glanced at her watch. "Let's make it tomorrow if that's okay. Hobbling around on crutches has tuckered me out, and by the time we get there and come back it'll be dark. Besides, I don't want Nana to be home alone any longer than necessary."

"You won't get any argument from me." Dax stood. "Are you sure you put the receipts back in Clinton's top drawer?"

"Yes, I'm sure."

"Well, they aren't there now."

CHAPTER FIFTEEN

Dax didn't expect to discover a hell of a lot by following Mayor Kreplick or the bank president, Peter Lucas, but he had to satisfy that voice in his head that told him something wasn't right with the whole blackmail theory. To him, Amanda and Jessie's concept had too many holes.

He wasn't happy about leaving her, but Jessie should be safe with her sharp shooting Nana by her side. He had to chuckle at the image of the old lady practicing her rifle skills, but there was little question Margaret Nash was no ordinary woman.

Once Dax dropped Jessie at home, he returned to town and parked the cruiser in front of the office, figuring that following a suspect in a police vehicle would never work. He might as well use a bullhorn and announce he was right behind him.

Jessie had locked up the office after they'd returned from Clinton's house, and he felt fairly certain no one would be stupid enough to break in, especially with an official vehicle in front. But hey, stranger things had happened since he'd come to Kerry.

Dax chose Peter Lucas to tail because banker's hours were more predictable, and because he had no idea about the Mayor's schedule. Besides, find one, catch the other.

Across the street from the bank was the Western Wear shop.

He entered and pretended to browse through the selection of cowboy boots and hats while keeping an eye on the stately bank. He hoped Peter Lucas wasn't the type to stay too late past the close of business or Dax might be walking away with a new but unwanted wardrobe.

He tried on a few pairs of boots to make his stakeout appear legit, but there was no way he'd be caught dead in anything made of snakeskin. A cowboy he was not. The salesman was good though. He had to give the guy credit, but Dax never did cotton to Stetsons or big belt buckles. Unfortunately for the clerk, he wouldn't be making a sale off him today.

At precisely four thirty-three, the object of his tail, Mr. Peter Lucas, exited the bank. Dressed in a neatly tailored blue pinstriped suit, the man looked downright dapper.

He turned to the salesman. "I want to think over my choices and perhaps I'll be back tomorrow."

"I'll be here," the clerk said with a smile.

Dax slipped outside, turned left, and waited in the alley between the Western Wear shop and the hardware store to see where Mr. Lucas would go. His destination happened to be The Sugar Shack. It seemed as if the whole town did their business there. Whoever owned the place had to be richer than sin.

A block farther south of the shop, the Mayor popped out of a building. Could be a coincidence, but Dax didn't believe in them. Walking briskly, Kreplick crossed the street, traveled three blocks to The Sugar Shack, and ducked inside. Hmm. They certainly weren't going to have a clandestine meeting in there with every gossipmonger looking on.

Dax would have to wait for them to come out, but he wanted to be ready when they did. It wasn't like he could waltz in and have a meal since the Mayor would probably drill him again.

If he wanted to follow them when they came out, he'd need better transportation—and that meant picking up his vehicle at Walt's garage. He made it there in less than ten minutes.

"Hey, Dax. You come for your truck?"

He'd stopped by before and learned the repairs would be done by this morning. "Yes, but do me a favor?"

"Sure."

"Don't tell Jessie my truck's fixed, or anyone else for that matter."

"No problem. Jessie told me you were a big time private eye. You investigatin' someone?"

"You could say that. How much do I owe you?" Dax asked as Walt tossed him the keys.

The old man scratched his head. "Well, the parts were a might expensive, and I did have to put a rush on it. Four hundred should cover it."

Dax whistled. That would really strap him for cash. He flipped through his bills, silently counting his stash. "I only have two hundred on me. You take credit?"

Walt shook his head. "Nope. Can't afford the fees."

He wasn't surprised. "Can I get you the rest after I go to the bank tomorrow?" His emergency funds could be wired there.

Walt waved a dismissive hand. "Sure. Jessie won't let you run out on a debt."

"No, she wouldn't."

As Walt took Dax's money, he looked at him with a sly smile. "Let me give you a piece of advice, young man. If you're hot on Jessie, you'd better be careful."

A quick shot of panic made his throat dry. Surely there wasn't an ex-husband hanging around. "What do you mean?"

"Jessie's like a daughter to me, and I wouldn't want to have to take you down a peg or two if you hurt her any."

Dax relaxed and smiled. The whole town was protective of the cute sheriff—all except for the Mayor and a phantom shooter. "I'll do my best to see that won't happen." He managed to say that with a straight face.

Walt smiled and when Dax jumped in his truck, he saw the man had filled up his tank. Now that was a right friendly thing to do.

As he pulled out of Walt's garage, he caught sight of Brian walking out of the small grocery store a block away, laden with a ton of groceries. Now *he* would be a far more interesting tail than the Mayor or the banker any day.

Dax pulled over and leaned back against the seat, waiting for Brian to settle into his vehicle. The guy didn't look right or left as he placed the bags in the truck's bed. He either was feeding an army or planning to stay holed up in his house for a while.

Once he finished loading his groceries, Brian took off down the road and stayed well below the speed limit. While there were many explanations for the man's caution, the most obvious was that he didn't want to be stopped for speeding because he had something in his truck worth hiding.

Dax followed at a distance. Given the few roads in Kerry, Brian would be easy to keep in view. The sad part was the guy didn't seem to have a clue that Dax was behind him. Even stranger was that Brian didn't act like someone who'd been in the military police. He should have checked his rear view mirror every few minutes, especially if he had something he didn't want someone to find.

Instead of being careful, Brian bounced up and down in his cab as though he was listening to some hip-hop station, enjoying the day. He hoped for Jessie's sake that her former boyfriend was clean. Once more, he questioned his own motives for following him. He told himself that the guy had done time for stealing arms, and with all the unresolved crimes in town, Brian just might be guilty of something.

Liar, liar.

Fine. Dax wanted to follow Brian to make sure that when Dax went back to Baltimore, Jessie's ex wouldn't be a threat to her. Dax had grown fond of the cute little sheriff.

He followed a half-mile behind for about five miles, but it didn't take a genius to guess where Brian was headed. The only house in sight was a rundown two-story wooden structure on top of a hill, far away from any neighbors. Jessie had mentioned that Brian's parents had died and left him the old homestead.

The sun was slowly setting and Dax cursed his timing. He'd only planned on seeing what the two lovers were up to, not tail Brian, but hey, when opportunity knocked, he had to answer.

Dax slowed down then pulled onto the berm as Brian continued up the long road to his house. From his vantage point, Dax could see the truck climb the hill, disappear, and then reappear again as he wound around the curves. He'd give Brian a few minutes to get into his house, and then he'd take a look at what he was up to. Not that he expected to find Brian sitting in front of the fire, cleaning his AK-47 assault rifle or anything, but one could never be sure.

Lights went on in Brian's house one after the other. Using his high-powered binoculars, Dax watched him step out a side door and head for a large detached garage with a smile on his face.

Time to get a closer look. Dax jumped back in his truck and eased up the hill, recognizing that he couldn't get too close or Brian might spot him. When he was about five hundred feet from the house, Dax once again pulled to the side and parked under a large oak tree.

The sky was turning darker now, forcing Dax to keep vigilant about the time. He should have another thirty minutes of light, but just in case, he grabbed his flashlight, checked to see it worked, and headed up the hill along the tree line.

As he neared, a door squeaked open, and Brian walked from the detached garage back to his house. Given he'd parked his truck outside, the garage might be full of junk.

As Dax neared, a strong smell of cat urine assaulted him, and he froze. He was pretty sure the stench didn't come from animals, not unless Brian had about twenty or more creatures hold up somewhere. He'd bet his P.I. license the smell resulted from a meth lab, and his gut almost revolted.

Maybe that's why Brian had come back to Kerry. His house,

or rather his parents' house, was isolated—the perfect location to cook up some illegal substance without getting caught.

If Dax could get a good look in the guy's trash, he bet he'd find a shit load of cold tablets, Drano cans, or bronchodilators. Jessie was going to be royally pissed when she learned what Brian was up to, but first, he needed to be certain of the crime before he hauled her up there to arrest him.

If Brian had any of his assault rifles from his heist, they'd need plenty of backup to take him down. Hopefully, another town could lend a hand. If he had his way, Jessie would stay at the office while Amanda and a few other officers made the arrest, but he was pretty sure Jessie wouldn't go for it.

As he snuck up to the garage, Brian's stereo blasted through the house walls, convincing him Brian wouldn't hear him. Dax shone his light through the garage window. Bingo. The lab wasn't big, but it looked sufficient to cook up enough drugs to keep half the teenage population high. He snapped a picture with his cell, but the quality was too poor because of the bad lighting.

On a long table, he spotted two antifreeze containers, a metal can of paint thinner, several hot plates, and lots of glass beakers. For the shortest moment of time, he wondered if he should ride down the hill and pretend he'd seen nothing, but then realized he couldn't do that. Honor, duty, and all that bull-shit were too ingrained in him.

Besides, Dax couldn't let Brian run around free only to chase after Jessie once Dax returned to Baltimore. A strong ache speared his gut, and he recognized something was happening between them that shouldn't, but he seemed powerless to stop it.

The house door squeaked open again. Shit, Brian was coming back, which meant it was time to disappear.

CHAPTER SIXTEEN

By the time Dax parked his truck down the street from Walt's then drove the cruiser back to Jessie's, he was beat—more emotionally than physically. He pushed open the front door to Jessie's house, and the wonderful rich aromas poured out of the kitchen. Because he hadn't eaten anything since lunch, he was starving.

Margaret's Cadillac sat in front, yet when he peeked around the entrance into the living room, no one appeared to be home. Then Jessie's laugh made him stop in mid stride. She and Margaret were in the kitchen. He walked over to the swinging door, and as he placed a palm on the doorjamb, he hesitated. He wanted to think about the best way to break the news of Brian's crime.

"Thanks for dinner, Nana. I don't think I've eaten that much in days." Jessie's voice came through the door clearly.

"Don't thank me, thank Shirley Hoffsteder. She made the chicken casserole."

For the next minute, the only sound was the clinking of knives and forks against China plates.

"Nana, what do you think about going to Irene's Beauty

parlor tomorrow and treating ourselves to a new hairdo? And maybe even a facial and a manicure?"

His groin tightened, not sure how much more he could handle of the new Jessie. The low cut red dress that hugged her curvy body had already tested his resolve. Add in a new hairdo and he might break.

"I'd love that, dear, but it'll be so expensive. It's why I haven't had a facial in years."

Dax smiled at the easy conversation. He missed having someone to exchange ideas with, feel comfortable around, and just plain enjoy.

"I know, but with all the stuff that's been going on, I think you and I deserve to pamper ourselves for once."

"You're right."

He bet Jessie was suggesting the spa day, not for herself, but to help take her grandmother's mind off the recent tragedy. Not wanting to interrupt their bonding moment, he leaned his back against the wall and soaked in the moment of family love.

"Good. Tomorrow morning, Dax and I need to drive over to Hardy County to pick up something, but when I get back we'll get beautified."

Time to go in.

"Speaking of Dax, I want to hear all about you two," Margaret said, her comment stopping him cold.

"Dax? What's there to tell?" Jessie coughed, though he couldn't tell if it was because she had to or if it was to cover up her discomfort. "He's been... a big help to me with the investigation. Without him, I'm not sure I'd have found Sadie."

Her testimony sounded very matter of fact, as if he was nothing more than the hired help.

"Do you think of him in the same way you thought of Clinton?"

Dax held his breath, wondering the same thing. That little person inside his head told him to stop eavesdropping. "Shut up," he mouthed.

"Nana, you know as well as I do that Clinton was over twenty years older than me and was more of a father figure than anything. Besides, he had a big beer belly, whereas I bet Dax has abs to die for."

Abs to die for, huh? He couldn't help but suck in his gut. Maybe he'd have to find a way to take off his shirt and show her. "Given all those arm muscles, I bet he has a six pack. So how would you describe your relationship with Dax?"

The resulting silence nearly killed him. Come on. *Say Dax is the most remarkable man I've ever met.*

"Well, Dax is a lot smarter than Clinton, but both were fine officers."

Praise, yes, but not what he wanted to hear.

"I know all that," Margaret said. "I mean, tell me about the romance I've seen written all over both of your faces. Have you jumped his bones yet?"

Yes, the romance. Wait a sec. Romance? He'd kissed her once. Or rather, she'd kissed him, and while he'd thought of the exchange as romantic, he hadn't been sure she had.

"Nana!"

"What? With such a fine specimen as Mr. Mitchell, I would have thought you'd be dreaming about him, wanting to touch those big, bulging muscles. I'd kill to run my fingers through his thick, soft hair, wouldn't you? Don't tell me you don't find him too sexy for his jeans?"

Dax almost blew it by laughing out loud.

"Oh, Nana, you miss Grandpa, don't you? Ever since he died, you've had a one-track mind on sex."

"That's beside the point. Dax Mitchell is one fine catch and you should think about setting a trap for him."

"A trap? Maybe that's how they did it in your day but not mine. I really do appreciate you caring for my well-being, but Dax won't be staying around forever. Have you forgotten he lives in a different state?"

"What do you take me for? Don't answer that. Besides, there's no law that says he has to go back to Maryland."

He wished he could stay, but he had a life in Baltimore, although the more he thought about it, the lonelier that life appeared.

"If Dax remained in Kerry, what would he do for a living? Construction is out with his bad leg."

That was what he wanted to know.

"Why law enforcement, of course."

"What, as my deputy?" Jessie asked. "He'd never work for me. We'd butt heads at every turn."

Dax had to agree, though the experiment would be an interesting one.

"It wouldn't be the first time a man worked for a woman you know."

"Nana, Dax isn't the type of man to deal with a woman as his boss, though the idea of telling him what to do does appeal to me. I can see it now. He'd be on his knees with *me* in control. Hmm. Or maybe I should just tie him up."

"I think it's a wonderful idea. I wish I had a man to do that to."

Jessie laughed. Dax didn't. Tie him up indeed. He'd tie her up was what would happen. Spread eagle, he'd lick her until she couldn't stand it anymore, then he'd—

"Well, then you could work for him," Margaret said.

Now we're talking.

"I've worked too hard to be anything but the boss."

Aw. Even if he were in charge? He had more experience than Jessie. Dax stilled. He'd lost his ever-loving mind. He had no plans of staying in Kerry.

"With an attitude like yours, it's no wonder you haven't landed a man."

"That's old fashioned thinking," Jessie said.

"Fine. So if you feel that strongly about him, move to Baltimore. You could get a job with the Baltimore Sheriff's department."

He had no idea she felt strongly about him. His pride surged, until he realized Jessie would never leave her grandmother. If she ever did, she'd hate it in the big city. Hell, there were days when he did too.

"Na-na! Who said anything about feeling strongly about him? And you know I'd never leave you."

Dax wasn't sure he wanted to listen to the rest of the conversation now that Jessie's talk wasn't exactly ego boosting. The squeak of her chair indicated she was getting up.

"You're a fool, Jessie Nash. Good men like Dax Mitchell don't come prancing into town every day." Margaret's voice grew louder as though Jessie were heading for the door.

Before she barreled out, he pushed open the door and nearly ran into her. "Hi, ladies." He kept his voice light, huffing a little as if he'd just come in.

"Hi," they said in unison. Jessie's eyes widened and Margaret just beamed.

Dax followed Jessie back to the table. He limped over and pulled out a chair.

"What's wrong?" Jessie asked.

She was one perceptive woman. "Tired is all." He decided it was better if Margaret didn't hear how his afternoon had panned out.

"Dax, you must be starving." Margaret stood and opened the refrigerator. "I'll just warm up your plate."

"Bless you, Margaret." With her back to them, Dax mouthed he had something to tell Jessie.

"Nana? Dax and I need to do some sheriffing stuff. Can you bring his dinner into the living room?"

"Why of course, dear." She turned back to Dax. "Do you want a Coke?"

"Yes, thank you."

Jessie had changed out of her incredible dress, but the skirt and snug top had turned him on the second he saw her. As they moved into the living room, Dax had to laugh. The two of them were quite a pair. She hobbled, and he limped.

Once they were seated on the sofa, she glanced at the kitchen door then turned back to him. "So what did you learn?" she asked.

He decided to start at the beginning and break the news about Brian later. "I saw Peter Lucas and Mayor Kreplick together."

She brightened. "And?"

"They left work around four thirty and met at The Sugar Shack."

She snapped her fingers. "That's right. It's Tuesday. The Mayor meets with the City Council every Tuesday. I'm sorry I didn't remember sooner."

"That's all right." Nana came out of the kitchen carrying a large tray, and Dax jumped up. "Here, let me help."

"Why, thank you." She batted her eyelashes. "You are such a gentleman. Jess, Kerry doesn't have men as nice as Dax here, do we?"

Oh, God. Matchmaker, matchmaker, make me a match. He didn't need any help from Margaret.

"No, Nana, they don't," she said. "Now, if you could excuse us, we have work to do."

"I'll just head to my room then. If my loud television bothers you, let me know. Of course, I'll probably fall asleep in a few minutes and won't hear anything you two do." She smiled then winked.

He swallowed his laugh. Did she really believe they wouldn't see through her act? "Yes, ma'am."

Jessie turned a pretty shade of pink as he sat back down next to her. He took a bite of a delicious chicken casserole and washed the food down with a much-needed Coke. "Now where was I? Oh, yeah. As I was waiting for the Mayor to finish his meeting, guess who I saw coming out of a grocery store?"

"Who?"

"Brian."

"Well, he does have to eat."

"I know, but I decided to follow him anyway."

"You did what? He might have a criminal record, but he's served his time and deserves peace." Her defensive attitude implied she still cared for him.

He spent the next few minutes explaining his logic, and she fortunately seemed to buy it. Of course, he left out the part about wanting to make sure Brian wasn't a threat to her once Dax left town.

"Tell me the rest," she said.

"To be thorough, I looked in his garage and found something."

"What?"

"He has a meth lab in there." Dax leaned back waiting for her to blow up at him again. He would have shown her the picture he took, but it came out mostly black.

She rolled her eyes. "Brian would never be so stupid. He was recently released from jail. Besides, he never did drugs in high school."

"You don't believe me?"

"What I think is that you're jealous."

That was rich. It didn't matter if he were. "I know what I saw. Besides, ten years is a long time. The war can turn the most innocent person to drugs."

She bit down on her lower lip. "Did that happen to you?"

Dax bristled, until he realized her question was logical. He swallowed his anger and answered in a civil tone. "I experimented, sure. When my leg was injured, Oxycodone was the only way to get through the day, but I'm clean now."

Her jaw tightened and her breaths came heavy. "Are you sure you saw a meth lab? Could it have been some chemistry experiment? Brian was always big into science."

Dax explained about the urine smell, the paraphernalia in the garage, and finally how meth was made. "Yes, I'm sure. Before I worked homicide, I did vice. I know my meth."

She dragged a hand down her face. "I don't need this. Not now."

He took her hand. When she didn't pull back, he moved closer until her perfume turned his insides to mush. "At the very least, we need to bring him in for questioning."

She leaned her head back against the sofa and closed her eyes. He wanted to kiss those delectable lips again, but he wouldn't. The timing wasn't right.

"Fine." She sat up. "Do you think you, me, and Amanda can handle Brian?"

"I wouldn't take that chance. I'd ask for help from another town if I were you."

She blew out a breath. "Sometimes I hate this job. I guess I could call in a few favors."

CHAPTER SEVENTEEN

Jessie had been able to borrow two deputies from Stanport, the next town over, to help with the bust. If Brian had any firepower, she didn't want to be caught without backup.

Deputies John Williams and Quentin LoRe met with her, Amanda, and Dax at the office to go over how to bring Brian in without incident. After thirty minutes of debate, she felt as if she'd been in a military meeting to discuss how to take down an army of insurgents.

"Guys, this isn't some Pentagon operation," Jessie said. "We go up to Brian's place, knock on the door, and ask him to come with us."

Dax looked at her as though she were crazy. "The man just got out of jail, and you think he'll go nicely? I won't let you put yourself in that kind of danger. We can't be sure he won't go ballistic on us."

He might be right, but she'd had enough of his he-man attitude. "It's my town and I'm the sheriff. For how long, I don't know, but I say we ask nicely first. I have no problem with John and Quentin covering the back of the house, and Amanda staying in the cruiser ready to take chase should Brian bolt, but we're not going in with our guns raised. Do I make myself clear?"

"Yes," all but Dax said in unison.

"Fine," he responded, "but anything goes even the slightest bit wrong, we do it my way." He tapped his chest.

My way. Please. "Nothing's going to happen, you'll see." Her voice shook, and she prayed she was right.

They went over the routine once more before taking off. Amanda drove separately in case she needed to go after Brian. Dax insisted on driving since he claimed her leg wasn't up to braking fast enough. What he really meant was that he wanted to be the one to handle any high-speed chase.

He said nothing for the first five miles then glanced over at her. "Are you upset?"

Was he referring to the fact that Brian was about to be arrested or that Dax was acting as if he were in charge? "What kind of question is that? Of course I'm upset. Brian was a friend, and even if he weren't, I don't like drug dealers in my town."

"Did you love him?"

Jessie couldn't believe he'd asked that question. "What the hell does that have to do with anything?"

His lips thinned. "Did you?"

"I had a crush on him in high school and we dated for a while, but after his father died, we broke up. Brian became too violent for me." She didn't think it appropriate to discuss that the father beat Brian's brother or the manner of the father's death.

"So what makes you think he's not still violent?"

Brian's brother is dead. "Good question."

With all the other crap on her plate, she didn't need Dax questioning her. Though if Brian were guilty of all the murders and thefts, she'd prance up to the Mayor and his lover and throw her success in their faces. But that wouldn't happen without a lot of evidence, which at the moment they didn't have.

Dax said nothing more as they traveled up the mountain to Brian's house. If Mr. Meth happened to be looking out his window, he'd spot the brigade and know something was going down. She could only hope he was too absorbed in doing his thing to notice.

Dax stopped a half-mile from the house, stuck his hand out the window, and motioned the other two vehicles to pull over.

Quentin came alongside and John rolled down his window. "Are we hiking in from here?"

"Yes," Dax said, "but keep along the forest line and out of sight. When you're in position, we'll drive on up."

Amanda, who'd pulled up behind, came over a moment later, and tapped her hand against the revolver at her hip. "I'm ready."

"Good. The second we're inside, Amanda, you park around the bend and wait."

"Got it," she said.

Jessie leaned across the seat, and all three looked at her with questioning faces. "Remember, it's my bust."

"Okay, but Dax's instructions seem the best way."

"Right," Quentin acknowledged.

She had to agree. The two deputies parked, and then ducked into the woods before making their way up to Brian's, while she, Dax, and Amanda waited behind.

"You know," Jessie said, "Brian could have shot the sheriff, especially if Clinton got wind of the meth lab, but why kill Sadie? It makes no sense."

"Maybe she overheard Brian mention something about drugs and threatened to go to the authorities," he said.

"I guess it's possible. Nana's friends always did stick their noses where they didn't belong."

"I wouldn't be surprised if Brian stole the gas," Dax said. "Meth labs don't come cheap. I also wouldn't put it past him to have taken the pot shots at my truck, but I'd chalk that up to jealousy."

"Jealousy? Because we're working together?"

"Yes."

"If he really cared for me," Jessie said, "he wouldn't have shot me."

Amanda, who was perched outside the driver's side window, leaned in. "Maybe he wanted to sideline you for a while to stop you from asking questions so he could build his lab."

"I never thought of that."

Dax nodded. "I just saw Quentin wave. They're in place. Time to go."

As Amanda ducked back to her vehicle, Jessie checked that her weapon was secure in her holster. Nervous, she focused on the drive up the hill and not on what was about to happen. She prayed Brian would go quietly, but her gut told her that wasn't about to happen.

When Dax stopped at the house, she eased out of the cruiser, rubbed her sweaty hands on her pants, and hobbled around to Dax's side. Rock music blared through the walls, reminding her of the good old days. Brian always did like his sound loud.

Don't be a wimp, Jess. Take charge. "I'm going in."

"Jessie." Dax's voice came out strangled. "I know you want to do this your way, but you gotta trust me. Let me do the talking."

"Brian is *my* friend. He won't hurt me." She limped off before Dax could talk her into staying behind.

When she reached the front stoop, Jessie lifted one her crutches and knocked on Brian's door. The music shut off, and a moment later Brian answered. He smiled, and Jessie nearly turned around.

"What's up? You want—" He then noticed Dax. "What's he doing here?"

"Can you step outside for a minute, Brian?" she asked.

"Why?" His tone turned hostile.

Not wanting any violence, Jessie didn't want to pull her gun, but she had a duty to do. "Brian, I need to take you in."

"What the hell for?" He remained in the doorway.

"We suspect you're dealing drugs."

Quicker than she could draw her weapon, Brian stepped back and tried to shut the door, but Dax was faster. Gun drawn, he aimed his weapon and shouted. "Stop or I'll shoot." His voice came out so deadly even she froze.

Brian looked right then left, obviously trying to decide his odds. He turned to Jessie. "You and gimp going to take me in?"

"And the two Stanport deputies around back and Amanda parked in front."

Brian stared at them for a moment then raised his hands. "Well, shit."

***

Thank God the bust hadn't turned into the violent blood bath Dax predicted, and that they were able to lock Brian up in the Kerry jail without incident.

"I want a lawyer," Brian said to Jessie the moment she closed the jail door.

"Sure. You're allowed one phone call."

His bravado disappeared. "Can you suggest someone, Jess? I've been gone a long time and don't know anyone."

Brian seemed so distressed she wanted to cry, but he'd broken the law—maybe even more than one. "Try Stanley Cummings. We only have a handful of lawyers who stayed after the mine closed."

When she went to look up his number, Dax stepped up to the jail cell. "Tell me about Clinton DuPree's murder."

Brian's eyes widened. "You think I had something to do with that? You're crazy man. I'll admit to having a meth lab, but that's all."

"Did you shoot out the camera at Barton's gas station and steal the gas?"

"Hell no. I'm not saying anything else until I speak with my lawyer."

"Dax, leave Brian alone." Sheesh.

He came over to her. "He's not admitting anything."

"Can you blame him?"

"Nope, but I had to ask."

After Brian made his one call, Jessie phoned Hardy County and asked the deputy to meet them where his men had found Clinton's car.

Quentin LoRe had agreed to keep the prisoner company while she, Dax, and Amanda picked up the cruiser. Jessie said she'd stay behind, but Quentin insisted she go and fulfill her duty. He said he could use the peace and quiet for a few hours.

"I really appreciate you doing this, Quentin. We should be back in two hours tops."

"No problem. I know John's happy to spend a few hours here too. He and Loretta Stevens have been dating."

"No kidding. I had no idea."

He held up a hand. "I swear."

Jessie smiled. She liked the owner of the bookstore. She was a sweet girl.

"Amanda's waiting outside," Dax said. "The sooner we get going, the sooner you'll be back."

"Now you sound like Nana."

"Wise woman." He grinned, his cheeks dimpling, and her traitorous body melted. God, what she wouldn't give to delve into his luscious body. *Stop it. I have a job to do, but when this is all over, I might ask for one taste.*

"Let's go," she said, trying to use her most authoritative tone.

The morning sun had warmed the air and energized her. Once she was rid of these damned crutches, she'd be a lot happier.

"You guys took long enough," Amanda said, as she ran her fingers through her short spiked hair.

"Had to make sure Quentin was settled in."

"I get shotgun," Amanda called. Jessie was about to protest, when Amanda added, "With your bum leg, I figured you'd be happier stretching out in back."

"You're right." She appreciated Amanda's concern.

Jessie crawled in back. "You know with Brian in jail, Kerry

just might get back to normal." Jessie tossed her crutches on the floor.

Dax glanced in the rear view mirror. "That's assuming he's guilty of all the unsolved crimes."

"I know, but we have no other suspects." They drove in relative silence to Hardy County.

"Over there," Amanda shouted as she pointed to Clinton's cruiser off to the side of the road.

Jessie's stomach roiled. Poor Clinton. Whatever he'd done, it wasn't worth dying for—assuming he was dead.

Dax pulled to a stop on the berm near the cruiser where a Hardy County deputy was leaning against the hood waiting for them. He pushed off and strode over.

Perhaps now they'd finally find out what happened to her boss. Thank goodness, the deputy hadn't indicated there was a body anywhere nearby, giving her slim hope that he might be alive.

Dax helped Jessie out and handed her the crutches. She hobbled over to the officer and introduced herself. "Jessie Nash. This is my deputy Amanda Simmons and a private investigator friend, Dax Mitchell, who's helping me."

"Deputy Milton Kriebel, ma'am."

Amanda stepped in front of her, acting as if she were in charge, but Jessie refused to let Amanda take center stage. "So what do we know, Deputy?" Jessie asked.

"Hard to say. There were no skid marks, just a broken right headlamp and a crumpled left front fender from when he ran into the pine tree."

The implication was that he ran off the road. Jessie, Dax, and Amanda circled the car. When Amanda pulled open the driver's side door, Jessie yelled at her. "Amanda, don't touch anything. What's wrong with you?"

Her deputy smiled and shrugged it off. "I wanted to see if there was any blood inside."

"Ever heard of gloves?"

"Jessie, come on. I'm sure the Hardy County boys have had their paws all over this vehicle. One more set won't make a difference. Besides, we can separate our prints from the others later."

"You're mistaken, ma'am," deputy Kriebel said. "The moment we spotted the cruiser, I called your sheriff. We haven't touched a thing—and that includes not opening the trunk."

Jessie's heart sank, and she sniffed the air to see if she could detect an odor of decaying flesh, but nothing but the sweet smell of grass filled her nostrils.

"Well," Amanda said with her hands on her hips, "it's obvious you don't think I can do this job. I better just wait in your cruiser while you *experts* figure out what happened to the sheriff."

What got stuck up her butt? Amanda's days at the Kerry Sheriff's Department wouldn't last very long if she kept up her crappy attitude. When Jessie had called her former place of employment, the sheriff there gave her high marks. She wondered what had changed.

Jessie turned back to Milton, embarrassed by her deputy's outburst. "How do you know someone didn't come by at night and mess with the scene?"

Milton looked confused. "I guess I don't know for sure, but people around here respect the law."

Jessie let his explanation slide as she moved to the rear to see if there was any evidence that the car had been run off the road. Dax donned his rubber gloves. He leaned inside while she studied the bumper. Unfortunately, she detected no cracks, dents, or damage of any kind. An animal could have darted in front of the sheriff, but if that had been the case, how did Clinton end up in town? Had he been given a lift and then was killed? Or was this car staged to make it look as if Clinton had driven into a tree? Damn. She had too many questions and not enough answers.

When Dax stood up and surveyed the area, she spotted a glowing red light aimed directly at his head. Oh, shit. She whipped around to find the source of the laser light, but saw no one.

The meaning of the dot finally registered. Someone wanted Dax dead.

Her muscles bunched and her heart jetted into overdrive. Needing to push him out of the way, she sprang up and threw herself at him. When she collided with his hip, her shoulder buckled, her leg screamed, and glass exploded right where his head had been. The air rushed out of her lungs as she landed on the ground with a thump. When her knee smashed into a rock, pain raced up her thigh. All she could think of was that Dax had almost been killed.

CHAPTER EIGHTEEN

When Jessie finally managed to raise her head, she was sprawled on top of Dax, his arms wrapped tightly around her. She tried to wiggle free, to get away from the shooter, but Dax held on.

"Get out of there," Milton shouted before she had a chance to ask if Dax was okay. The deputy ducked behind his cruiser and motioned they join him.

Dax scooted out from under her and half-carried, half-dragged her around to the other side of Clinton's cruiser. Her legs ached and her heart raced. His hold on her loosened, and she slid to the ground, her rear end landing on a sharp rock. "Ouch."

She hadn't been shot, and she believed Dax hadn't been either. After quickly checking him out to make sure, she was relieved to see there wasn't any blood on him. Her leg was a different story. Red splotches covered the knee of her new sweat suit.

"Are you okay?" he asked. The look of horror on his face made her believe he really cared, and her pulse fluttered.

No need to tell him about the slight injury. "Yes."

He drew his weapon and motioned for the deputy to stay

down. The young man looked scared shitless and did as he was told. He'd probably never been this close to a shooting before.

A vehicle slowed down in front of them before driving past, and then a car door opened then closed. Amanda dashed the ten feet from the passenger's side to behind DuPree's cruiser. "You guys okay?" she asked, her voice cracking.

"Yes," Jessie and Dax said in unison.

"Thank God."

"Did you see who took the shot?" Dax asked Amanda.

"Hell no. The second I heard the glass explode, I ducked down. I figured when no more gunfire erupted, I'd chance coming out."

"Damn," Dax said with more animation than usual.

Jessie leaned back against the car door and hiccupped. "I saw a r-red light on your head, Dax. It took a second for me to realize someone had you in their sc-scope."

"Then I guess you saved my life." He winked and her stomach flip-flopped. Stupid hormones.

He had no right to be even remotely cheerful at a time like this. "Aren't you upset?"

"Sure, but I'm used to it. Tell you one thing, this proves we're getting close. Real close."

"Well, we know it wasn't Brian," she said.

"True, and that means we're back to square one."

***

A soft knock sounded on Jessie's bedroom door, and she figured it was Nana wanting to find out why she was still in bed. "Come in."

To her surprise it was Doc with his little black bag. "Hi, Jess. How are you feeling?"

"My stomach's still in knots from Sadie's death, my life's in a spiral, and my heart has more ups and downs than a yoyo. I guess that means I'm doing great."

Doc shook his head. "It's time to change the bandage on that leg of yours. I want to make sure it's not infected."

"It's getting better but have a look."

Doc did his usual fussing at her, then cleaned and changed the bandage, which was not fun from a pain perspective.

He pointed to Jessie's other knee. "Now how did you get that cut? I don't remember the wound from the shooting."

"I was playing touch football."

"Not funny, Jess. You need to take it easy. Doctor's orders."

"Yes sir." Jessie saluted.

He cleared his throat. "You know Roberta Barton and I have been seeing each other for the last couple of months, right?"

She nodded. "Nana mentioned it."

"Well, Roberta and I were supposed to go to the movies last night, but when I arrived at her house, she wasn't there. The lights were off, her car was gone, and she didn't answer her landline."

A slow dread came over Jessie. She didn't want to consider that Roberta had disappeared too. "What are you saying? Do you think she was killed, like Sadie?"

He shook his head. "I don't know. Roberta would never stand me up. She's not like that. In fact, we'd made plans to have a fall picnic this Sunday."

"I wish I had an answer." All she could do was clasp his gnarled hand and hold on tight. "I'll check into it today, I promise."

"Thank you, but you shouldn't be running around on that leg of yours."

"I'll be fine. When can I get off these crutches?"

"As a matter of fact, I left a cane downstairs for you."

Not exactly sexy, but anything was better than hobbling around. "Don't worry about a thing, Doc. I'm sure Roberta had some emergency and either didn't think to call or couldn't call. I'll let you know what I find out, okay?" Jessie smiled, hoping to fool him into believing she was almost good as new.

"Thanks, Jess."

After Doc left, she dressed. It was too cold to wear the A-line skirt Amanda had bought her, so instead, she pulled on a pair of stretch pants Nana had given her many Christmases ago. The soft fabric would be kinder to her leg than scratchy jeans. She then threw on a sweatshirt, along with a pair of sneakers, and headed out her door, this time without crutches. Yay!

The smell of bacon and eggs floated up the stairs and her stomach grumbled. As she turned to go downstairs, the bathroom door opened. Whoa. No, make that a double whoa. Dax had on a pair of jeans. That was it—no shoes and no shirt. He was freshly shaven and his hair was slightly damp as if he'd taken a shower. His chest had just the right amount of hair and his abs were to die for, just as she'd suspected.

Their gazes met. "Good morning," Dax said with a smile.

She could have sworn he stuck out his chest a little and sucked in his belly. Hopefully, he couldn't tell her mouth watered at the sight of him. Jessie blinked to stop from staring then wondered why he hadn't put on a shirt. He must realize what a distraction he was to her.

You want him. I do, but he'll be leaving soon. Then I'll need to convince him to stay.

"Good m-m-orning." When would she stop stuttering? Easy. When she stopped being nervous.

"Where are your crutches?"

"Doc stopped by and gave me the all clear."

"Fantastic."

When he didn't move, Jessie edged closer. The longer his gaze remained on her face, the hotter she became. "You know you shouldn't be walking around without a shirt on."

Oh, God, that was so lame.

He looked down at his chest, acting as if he hadn't realized he didn't have one on. "Why not?"

"If Nana sees you, she might..." Jessie couldn't even come up with something to finish her sentence.

"Want me?" he asked with a chuckle. "Or do *you* want me?" *Tell him yes. Ask him to stay!* "I, ah…"

Before she could finish her sentence, Dax drew her close, leaned over, and kissed her. Yes! Stars swam in her head, bathing her brain in intense colors, stimulating every part of her body.

Without thinking, she begged for entry. When he opened his mouth and their tongues touched, her legs weakened. Never had a kiss made her this hot. She wrapped her arms around his neck and held on tight, thrilling to the way he tasted. His languorous movements had her panting for more. She hadn't meant to moan but being pressed against him felt so damned good.

His hands roamed down her back and then pressed firmly on her butt. His erection against her stomach hardened. Oh, my. The rational part of her brain said to stop, but the emotional side told her to drag him into her bedroom and make love with him. She deserved to experience Dax one time before he left.

Jessie dragged her hands down his shoulders, ready to take his hand, when someone behind her cleared her throat.

"Jessie?" Nana said.

They broke apart so fast, she nearly fell backward, but Dax steadied her.

"Sorry, Margaret," Dax said. "It was my fault."

"Oh, I'm the one who's sorry. I certainly didn't mean to interrupt. By all means continue." She grinned.

Heat raced up Jessie's face. "Is breakfast ready, Nana?"

"Yes. I came up to see what was taking you so long. I thought I heard voices."

"We'll be right down."

With her grin firmly in place, Nana nodded, turned around, and headed back down.

Could Jessie be any more embarrassed? Thank goodness, the man couldn't read minds. He'd either decide to leave earlier than planned, or suggest they have a quickie before breakfast. She inwardly groaned at that decadent thought.

Jessie faced Dax. "I didn't mean to…."

He held up a hand. "If you apologize, I'll never forgive you."
He grinned. "Come on. Let's eat."

They went downstairs. When they rounded the corner, Nana
was setting the table and looked up, acting as if nothing had
happened. Dax pulled out Jessie's chair and then sat down across
from her.

"So what did Doc say?" Nana asked, as casually as could be.

Jessie wasn't sure if Nana was referring to Roberta's disappearance or her leg. "He said I could go without crutches. If I
need to walk a lot, I can use a cane."

"Oh, my, I didn't notice you were walking by yourself. How
does your leg feel?"

"Improved, but still sore."

"Good. Sit down and I'll bring breakfast out."

Nana disappeared into the kitchen, and Jessie didn't know
how she was going to tell her grandmother that another one of
her friends might be missing. *Don't think so negatively.* If Nana
didn't have any information about what had happened to
Roberta, Jessie and Dax would have to look around today.

Nana came out with a bowl of scrambled eggs and a plate of
bacon. "Toast is almost ready, and coffee's perking."

"Nana, do you know where Roberta is?"

Nana's lips pressed together. "No. Why would I?"

"Because you know everything that goes on in this town."

"I do not." She waved a hand without making eye contact.
"Why do you ask?"

Ah, she did know something. "Because she stood up Doc last
night. They had a date."

Nana looked like she'd swallow a pickle. "They don't date,
not in the real sense. The man isn't capable of getting it up."

"Nana!" Jessie purposefully didn't glance over at Dax. "I
wonder why I ask you any questions. You have no internal filter."

"Honesty is the best policy," she said smugly.

As soon as Nana went back into the kitchen, Jessie whispered. "Doc told me Roberta has disappeared."

He scrubbed a hand down his jaw. "Are you sure she didn't just wander off?"

Nana came out again with a carafe of steaming coffee. "Don't wait for me; you two, dig in."

Jessie hadn't told Nana about the shooting yesterday over in Hardy County, although she did mention Brian's arrest. Hiding that from her would have been impossible.

"Dax, did you hear that Jess and I are going to get beautified today?"

"Oh, Nana. I can't go today." Roberta came first. "But you go."

Her grandmother's face sagged. "I wanted us to go together."

Jessie looked over at Dax then back at Nana. "Can we make it tomorrow?"

Nana leaned over and patted her hand. "Sure we can. In fact, Mary Alice called this morning all excited about something. I'll call her back and tell her I can meet with her today. Tomorrow will be our day."

Glad they'd reached a win-win resolution, Jessie dug into her meal.

***

Lunch at The Sugar Shack seemed rather noisy for a Thursday, but then again, it was Halloween. Dax said he hoped Roberta's disappearance was merely a case of a woman wanting some adventure, but given everything that had happened, they had to check it out. Jessie sat in the booth sipping her tea. She sat across from Dax who was seemingly lost in thought.

Now that Brian was being held at the station, someone needed to stay there. It couldn't be Amanda, as she was needed to take care of other issues that had cropped up. That meant Jessie had to hire someone, at least temporarily.

"So what do you know about this Frank Matthews guy?" Dax

asked plucking his napkin from his lap and tossing it on the table.

"He was Clinton's deputy before he retired, and he likes to help out when he can."

"How long do you plan to keep Brian locked up?"

"Until the judge releases him on bail. That assumes Brian has enough money to pay it."

Dax leaned forward on his elbows and steepled his fingers. "Isn't Amanda's dad the judge?"

"Good memory, but he's doing a trial in another town and won't be back until tomorrow."

Lena waltzed over. "Can I refresh your drink?"

Jessie shook her head. "No, thanks. Lena, when was the last time you saw Roberta Barton?"

Lena looked off to the side. "It's been days, why?"

"Nothing. I just needed to chat with her, that's all."

As soon as Lena was out of earshot, Dax checked his watch. "Given Roberta's not home, not with Doc, and not with your grandmother, about the only place we haven't checked is the mine."

She cocked a brow. "The mine? What reason would she have for going there?"

"Remember when my truck tire was shot out, your grand-mother, Mary Alice, Eleanor, and Roberta were on the way there, but they never got out of the car because they had to drive me back to town. Roberta might have decided to return."

"Why? She knows Sadie's dead."

"Perhaps she's looking for alien love."

Jessie almost spit out her ice tea. "I can't believe you're buying Nana's theory about aliens."

"Not me, but Roberta sure has."

She shrugged. "Well, it's worth a try. No one seems to know anything about her whereabouts in the last forty-eight hours, so perhaps she did take off on her own. With my grandmother's friends, nothing would surprise me."

Amen. "Let's go."

***

Dax tossed down enough money to cover their food and a tip. He took it slow so as not to make Jessie self-conscious about her walking. Doc shouldn't have told her she didn't have to use the crutches. She'd refused to use the cane, saying it made her look like an old lady. Old indeed. She was young, vibrant, soft, and sexy.

Outside, the sun had turned the day balmy. "Seems like Indian summer snuck up on us this year," he said, wanting to keep the conversation light.

She smiled, closed her eyes, and raised her face to the sun. "Yes, isn't it wonderful?"

My, she was pretty. Even though she wasn't wearing the sexy red dress, the tight leggings enhanced her figure. If only he could get her out of that baggy sweatshirt he'd be a happy man.

Dax had been able to park in front of The Sugar Shack, which made the hike to the cruiser a short one. He was about to open her door, but she beat him to it. Chivalry must not have materialized in this town.

By now, Dax knew the way to the mine as well as he knew Baltimore's roads. He rolled down the windows to enjoy the fresh air. Between the clear skies, bright sunshine, and the scent of pine, he couldn't ask for a better day.

They reached their destination fifteen minutes later. "Except that my truck has been towed away, it doesn't look any different from when we were here the other day," he said, a bit disappointed they didn't find Roberta.

"True." Jessie slid out, shielded her eyes from the sun, and looked around. "Dax?"

"What?"

"Look over at the ridge to the east of the mine at Cyril Harper's farm. He's been dead quite some time, but doesn't it look like there's a car by the barn? It could be Roberta's."

"Dammit. My binoculars are in the truck." He squinted. "How do we get over there?"

"There's a turn off about a mile back up the road."

"I say we check it out."

They arrived a few minutes later. "Given the roof on the house has collapsed, I'd say the place is abandoned." That made the car being there more suspicious.

"It has been empty for more than five years, but it still gives me the creeps every time I come here. I know Cyril is dead, but I swear his ghost is still roaming about."

"That bad, huh?"

"Worse. As a kid I used to sneak over here hoping for a taste of one of Evie Harper's apple pies. She was the nice one—the total opposite of her husband. He always yelled at me, but then, he yelled at Evie too. After she died, I was afraid to go near the place."

"Did he ever get violent?"

"Let's just say, the man used to carry a big scythe around, and one time he told me he liked to cut off little girls' heads."

Dax loved hearing stories of her youth. It gave him a better picture of what her life must have been like. "I guess that would have kept you away."

"It did for a long time. I only returned about three years ago. His son, Wesley, who lives in Charleston, keeps saying he wants to move to Kerry and fix up the place, but he's never followed through. Good thing too, since he took after his dad in the mean department."

"Why did you go back there?" Dax gripped the wheel.

"One summer Clinton decided it was my duty to make sure no one messed with the property. I'd gotten wind that some vagrants had taken up residence in the house, so I sucked up my courage to investigate. Sure enough, three men were living there. I kicked them out, but in the last year, the world thankfully seemed to have forgotten about the place."

The long dirt road to his farmhouse had become pitted from disuse, and the cruiser was taking a beating as they inched their way up the property. The grass was overgrown to about two feet tall and vines had snaked their way up the trees.

They rounded a bend, and she sucked in an audible breath, and pointed. "Dax, that's Roberta's car. I've not seen any other VWs like hers."

He sped up, and the rocks hitting the undercarriage sounded like gunshots. He slowed then pulled to a stop about fifty feet away. "Can you walk the rest of the way? The ruts are so deep, I'm afraid the cruiser might rebel."

She straightened in her seat. "I sure can."

Unfortunately, once she stepped out of the car and began to climb the hill, her limp became more pronounced. Jessie should have used the cane or else asked that he drive slower.

Dax wrapped an arm around her. "It's a little rough. Let me help."

"Thank you. My balance hasn't been the same since my calf muscle was cut."

When they reached Roberta's car, Dax pulled open the passenger side door. "I'm glad she saw fit not to lock it."

"Maybe she wasn't driving. Someone could have used her car to bring her up here against her will."

Dax looked at her in surprise. "Since when did *you* become the cynic?"

"Oh, I don't know. When people I cared about started disappearing. I used to think the best of everyone. It's that old silver lining thing, but now I suspect everyone and everything."

"It didn't help that Brian wasn't who you thought he was, I suppose." Dax yanked something out of the glove compartment and unfolded a piece of paper. "It's Roberta's registration."

Dax took her hand again, and even though they were on flat ground, Jessie thankfully didn't pull away. They hiked to the barn where he drew open the door. Instantly, the smell of old straw and mold assaulted him.

Jessie held a hand over her nose. "I don't think anything could stay in there for long. It's foul."

Dax stepped a few feet inside. "Hello?"

"I've got a flashlight in the cruiser if you want to check it out," she said.

"Nah. Let's look elsewhere first."

They walked to the backside of the barn but only found a rusted out tractor, a pile of decayed wood, and some plowing blades.

Jessie nodded toward the house. "As long as we're here, we might as well check out the old homestead."

"It doesn't look safe."

Her shoulders slumped. "At one time, the Harper place was something to be proud of but not anymore."

As they picked their way down the hill, sweat formed on Jessie's forehead from the exertion. The cloudless day had heated up the air, but shouldn't have been enough to cause her to perspire. Dax didn't like it. He'd suggest she sit in the cruiser if he didn't think she'd balk.

She fanned her face. "It must be at least seventy out here."

Dax looked down at her and smiled. "It's nice, isn't it?" He stopped then faced her. "I just thought of something," Dax said. "Roberta's last name is Barton. Harold Barton owns the gas station. Are they related?"

"He's her son."

"That might not be a coincidence."

"You're not thinking Harold had anything to do with his mom's disappearance, are you?"

"Who said she disappeared? I was wondering why we didn't ask Harold where she might be."

"Ah, Kerry's dirty laundry is about to come out. They don't get along, shall we say." She stopped in her tracks and grabbed his forearm. "It can't be." She pointed to the Cadillac.

Off to the side of the house sat her grandmother's car. "What the hell is Margaret doing here?"

"That's what I'd like to know," Jessie said.

They were half way to the car when he heard laughter out back. "Maybe she and Roberta are having a picnic," he said.

"With those two, I wouldn't be surprised."

They snuck around to the other side of the house, keeping clear of the broken crates and assorted car parts.

Behind the house was a large mound of dirt, and on top of the dirt was a sight Dax couldn't believe.

CHAPTER NINETEEN

"What the hell?" Dax said.

Jessie broke away from him and hopped toward the group of ladies—or rather the group of hussies. Her calf screamed, but the view before her demanded she take action. Now she wished she'd brought the cane, mostly to beat some sense into Nana and her friends.

Nana, Mary Alice, and Eleanor were lying on their backs on some kind of shiny, aluminum foil type blanket holding hands, clad only in their underpants and bras. Each had what looked like foil antennae on their heads, implying they weren't there to sunbathe.

Jessie loomed over her grandmother. "What the hell is going on here?"

Her grandmother sat up and crossed her arms over her chest. "Jessie? I need to ask you the same thing." When her grandmother caught sight of Dax, she lowered her arms. "Oh, hi, Dax."

Gross. Jessie had enough. "Answer me, please. Have you all lost your marbles?"

It was Mary Alice's turn to sit up. "Shh. We're trying to contact Roberta."

"Roberta?"

"Yes. Roberta."

"I don't understand."

Mary Alice sighed. "You young people. Sheesh. Roberta wants a real man, not some over the hill, limp dick guy, like Doc. Since this is one of the highest elevations in Kerry, we thought we could contact her from here. She said she was going to find the mother ship, and everyone knows the reception is best this high up."

Jessie couldn't put into words what was going through her mind. Her grandmother and her friends were plum crazy. "I can't believe this. You'll catch cold." Stupid comment, but she was in too much shock to say anything intelligent. It didn't matter she was sweating. "Nana, get dressed. You're coming home now."

Her grandmother's lips pinched together. "I will do no such thing." She turned to Dax and her face softened. "Dax, dear, why don't you take Jessie to the movies or better yet, go to the house. It's empty." She winked. "Surely a young, virile man such as your-self can find something to keep her occupied while we old ladies contact our friend."

"Nana!" Though snuggling in bed with Dax held a lot of appeal, she wouldn't admit it to them. Knowing her grand-mother, Nana had already told them about catching her and Dax in a hot kiss.

Jessie was about to stomp off when she decided these women might know something about Roberta's disappearance. "Do any of you know for certain what happened to her?"

Eleanor sat up. "Roberta called me last night and said she didn't want to settle for Doc. She wanted a...what did she call him, Margaret?"

"A stud."

"That's right. Roberta wanted an alien stud. Mary Alice here convinced her that the mother ship had landed at this house at one time."

Jessie shook her head in disbelief.

Dax tugged on her arm and leaned over. "We need to search the place. If Roberta drove herself up here, she's got to be somewhere."

"Right."

Jessie looked at the three women. "We'll be back."

She waited until they'd traveled out of earshot before looking over at Dax who was actually smiling.

"What's so funny?" she asked.

"Your grandmother and her friends. They're hoots."

"They're crazy and horny."

"That may be, but I hope I'm that feisty when I'm their age."

Jessie turned wrong and her knee gave way. As she reached out to catch herself, Dax grabbed her around the waist. "Easy." He made certain she was steady before letting go. "Take hold of my arm. The path is too uneven."

"Stupid leg." She inhaled to calm her racing heart. Thankfully, Dax took his time going back to the cruiser. "Where could she be?" Jessie asked.

"I don't know."

She leaned back against the cruiser door and then he stepped in front of her. The moment he placed his palms on each side of her head and gazed down at her, all thoughts of finding Roberta flew away. Dear Lord, the man had warm, rich eyes that actually sparkled in the sunlight.

"You're grandmother's a smart woman. Even she can tell that I want you, Jess." His voice came out husky, hunky, and sexy.

She swallowed and opened her mouth to respond, but her gaze couldn't leave his lips. Make those incredibly kissable lips.

Go for it. Sadie's voice came in loud and clear as if the woman were standing next to her.

Aw, what the hell. She didn't get her fill before. There was no time like the present. As Jessie touched Dax's cheek, her lips parted and Dax leaned closer. He rubbed his thumbs along her jaw, and she couldn't breathe, couldn't think, couldn't move. Every fiber of her being wanted him.

Jessie closed her eyes and when she tilted up her head, his mouth and hips met hers. She wanted to enjoy the sensation of his soft, pliable mouth, but his hard erection stole all thoughts. She let go of her pent up inhibitions and blocked out every objection her inner voice shouted at her. Her body flooded with hormones, as she entwined her fingers in his soft hair. Dax groaned then palmed her breasts. She couldn't help but melt against him.

"God, you feel so good," Dax whispered in the sexiest voice she'd ever heard.

The wind whipped through her hair and her body caught fire. Jessie lowered her arms to around his neck and opened her mouth to receive him more fully. He tasted like mint and honey, all wrapped together, and as their tongues tangled, probed, and explored, she couldn't get enough of him. Wetness raced between her thighs with every breath. She'd never experienced anything like this in her life. Being in his arms seemed right— too right. Forever right.

Jessie tried to memorize the feel of his cheek, the softness of his lips, the hardness of his chest, and the size of his—

Dax pulled away.

Devastation slammed into her. "What's wrong?"

"I don't want to hurt you."

Physically or emotionally? "You weren't."

"But I might." He stepped back and grabbed her hand. "Come on. We need to find Roberta."

Was he kidding? It didn't matter if he was right, she wanted to forget all her obligations and kiss him forever. Sometimes, life wasn't fair. He certainly had seemed willing this morning. So what had changed?

Jessie wanted to believe that if they'd continued, he'd end up needing to make love in the backseat of the cruiser. With her leg, it might not have been pleasant.

He retrieved her cane from the back. "Use this. I don't want you to fall."

"Spoilsport." And to think she had him right where she wanted him. Hell, she was almost willing to drag him into the barn and have sex with him, not caring how bad it smelled. "Where do you think we should look?" She tried not to pout, but even she could hear the disappointment in her voice.

"Inside the house, if we can get in," Dax said.

"The last time I checked, the place was unlocked. Vagrants had broken a few windows, and the owner's son never fixed anything, so we figured why bother putting security on the door if he didn't care."

"Works for me."

The sun continued to beat down on her face, and a few crows squawked loudly as they walked to the abandoned building. Dax held her hand as she hobbled up the three steps to the front porch. As she moved close, the smell of mildew almost took her breath away. "I can't imagine anyone willingly going inside this place. The stench is worse than in the barn." She didn't want to consider a decomposing body could be inside.

He smiled. "Be thankful you're a cop in a small town. In Baltimore, we've experienced a lot worse than this."

"I'll let you handle that duty." Though, if he ever asked her to go with him, after that kiss, she might consider the move.

Dax had to use his shoulder to push open the front door. "Sticky little bugger."

White sheets covered the furniture, though she doubted it did much good. She bet vermin had already eaten through the fabric by now. "How about you take the upstairs and I'll look downstairs," she said.

"Fine, but be careful."

"Me? You're the one who has to pay attention to the collapsed roof."

Dax eased his way up the creaky steps while she headed back to the kitchen where Jessie could almost see Evie baking her pies. Poor dear. She'd had such a hard life being married to that tyrant.

Jessie's foot slipped, and she almost went down on one knee but caught herself on the counter. Eww. A puddle of gray slime had slickened the floor. She bent down to examine the gooey substance, but it didn't look like anything she'd ever seen before. It had the consistency of paint but wasn't animal feces or blood. Plant material, perhaps?

"You find anything?" Dax said behind her.

Her heart pounded. "Don't sneak up on me like that."

"Sorry. What did you find?"

"Nothing. Just some goo."

He studied the puddle. "Looks like alien juice."

She looked up at his smiling face. "Funny."

"Hey, don't believe me? Get a sample. Maybe it's some cosmetic lotion Roberta used to attract her alien. She could have dropped the bottle."

"Then where's the glass?"

He threw her an appreciative look. "Good point, unless it didn't break."

Speculation wouldn't get them anywhere. "You find anything?"

"Nope. I say we look in the barn."

"We already did."

"I only said *hello*."

Not having anything to hold the sample, she let the mystery material remain untouched. If need be, she could come back later. As they left the house, she glanced up at the hill. "How can my grandmother who is so sharp lose it so fast?" She knew Dax couldn't answer her, but she needed to vent her frustration at her grandmother's decline.

"Oh, I don't think she's losing it. She's having the time of her life."

"I hope you're right." Jessie's mood lightened. She nodded to the barn. "I'm sure Roberta wouldn't go in there. It's too nasty."

"I'll be back in a sec. Let me get a light."

Jessie waited at the barn door while Dax retrieved his

precious beacon. She thought about suggesting he wear the damned thing around his neck but that would be cruel. The man had issues, ones she figured stemmed from his time in the service.

He turned on the light. "Let's go."

"What do you hope to find?"

"Something she might have dropped that could give us a clue as to her whereabouts."

If Dax thought it possible that Roberta had gone in there, it was her duty to check it out. Once inside, Jessie tried holding her breath, but it didn't work, so she placed a hand over her nose to prevent the gag reflex from kicking in. Jessie was rather disgusted with herself. Her father had brought up stronger stock. Lowering her hand, she inhaled and coughed. Her sense of smell was too acute. Nana always claimed Jessie must have been a bloodhound in a former life. How true.

They shuffled around the floor, kicking up the straw as they went. Her toe hit something hard, prompting her to bend down and fish around until she found a triangular object one inch thick and about five inches on each side. "I found something."

"What is it?" Dax flashed the light on it.

"I don't know. Could be a GPS, though if I remember my Star Trek episodes, it looks like a tricorder."

"A what?"

"A tricorder. Bones used it to heal people."

"Bones? Whatever." Dax held out his hand and Jessie placed the weird object with the shining circles in his palm.

"It's a bomb detection device. We didn't use one like this, but I've seen something like it."

"I wonder what it's doing here?"

"Excellent question," Dax said.

"It looks like one of those things restaurants give out when you're waiting for a table."

"It does at that." He stuffed it in his pocket for safe keeping.

Five minutes later, after taking too many bad breaths, Jessie moved toward the exit. "I need some fresh air."

"Me too."

As she stepped outside, Jessie shielded her eyes against the bright sun. "Now what?"

"The only place left is the field."

Her shoulders drooped. The field was a good twenty acres of high grass. Good thing she had on leggings or else the bugs would eat her alive. "Let's do this."

He turned toward her and when he cupped her cheek, heat flushed her face. Her pulse raced with the hope he'd kiss her again.

"Why don't you sit in the car while I have a look. It'll be faster and a lot less painful."

She didn't want to give in, but with her bad leg, she'd only slow him down. "Thanks."

She waited in the front seat, but after forty minutes, she began to wonder if he was moving each individual blade of grass looking for alien artifacts or something. As much as she loved Indian summer, it had its drawbacks when sitting in a car.

Just as she was about to get out and look for him, Dax came down over a crest in the field, and Jessie jumped out of the car. "You find something?"

"Yes, but you won't like it."

CHAPTER TWENTY

With Doc standing over the gravesite while Dax dug, it was déjà vu all over again. Jessie's heart broke watching the old man. Even in the bright sunshine, his skin was sallow. He'd already lost his wife five years ago to cancer, and if Roberta was the one in the grave, Doc might lose it, and she wasn't sure she could handle his tears without sobbing herself.

"Someone went to a lot of trouble trying to hide the smell," Dax said. "There's a ton of lime on the body. From the amount of scattered dirt, along with the matted grass near the site, the grave's fresh." Dax picked up the digging pace, tossing the lime away from them.

Jessie stepped back. "Careful, Dax. The wind is pushing the dust back on us." She waved away a plume of lime and coughed. "You need a mask. Lime can do some lung damage if you're not careful."

"Hold on a sec." Doc bent down and pulled out three face shields from his black bag. As a kid, she used to wonder if he had a rabbit in there since the man seemed to carry everything.

Doc put on his mask then handed the others to them. Dax slapped the white cover over his face then continued to dig faster and faster, as though removing the victim from the ground sooner rather than later would save the person somehow.

"Be careful, son. We don't want to harm the body."

Dax stopped. "Sorry." He looked up at Jessie and wiped the sweat from his brow with his sleeve. "Jess, if you want to go back and be with Margaret, I'm sure I can get Doc to give me a lift home."

Doc nodded. "Sure."

"No. I want to see who it is before I break the news to her."

"I understand." Brown streaks stained his face and fatigue marred his forehead. Dax had come here to find Sadie, not baby-sit his employer, or help Jess keep her job. He was a truly good man.

A single cloud covered the sun for a moment, giving them respite against the heat. She never remembered October being this warm.

Dax dropped to his knees and began digging out around the body with his hands like he had with Sadie. His back muscles bulged and her fingers itched to touch him, to comfort him, to know him deeply.

Move on, Jess.

She studied the grave, the shape of the body seemingly too large to be Roberta, but maybe the excess dirt threw off the actual size, or else gases had filled the body. Jessie shook her head not wanting to think about what really happened when someone died.

Dax brushed dirt away from the face and Jessie sucked in a breath. "Ohmigod. It's Clinton."

While still horrible, she was relieved it wasn't Roberta. Jessie had suspected...no, known in her heart, that Clinton was dead, but there had always been that seed of hope he'd merely run away.

She looked up at Doc. "Can you tell how he died?" She didn't see any bullet hole to the head, but the dried blood on his temple indicated there'd probably been a fight.

"Finish cleaning away all of the dirt and lime from his face, will ya, Dax? I can't tell a thing yet." Doc stepped closer and squatted next to Clinton's head.

Dax moved to his right and hovered over the body, blocking her view. He looked over his shoulder. "Jess, you really don't need to see this. Why don't you go home or back to town?"

"Go home? Like a good little girl? Have you forgotten I'm the sheriff and you're... you're..." She threw up her hands. She didn't know what he was. Her hero? Dax had practically led every investigation since he'd arrived, but that didn't mean she was a nobody or that she hadn't contributed.

Forget it. It wasn't worth fighting over. The real question was did she *want* or *need* to stay? She couldn't help lift the body or aid them in any way. "Fine." She held out her hand. "Keys. Of course that means I have to drive. Me, the person who wasn't capable of driving a few hours ago." Dax had been adamant that her injury prevented her from being able to brake effectively.

He looked rather sheepish. "Here," he said dropping them into her palm. "If you drive slowly you should be fine."

"I'm leaving, not because you told me to, but because I don't want Nana looking for me and finding Clinton's grave instead. I need to head back to the office to relieve Frank. He's probably wondering where I am. I also need to make sure Brian gets fed, and then I have to fill out the necessary paperwork for Clinton." She turned to Doc. "How long before you get the results of the autopsy?" She sounded professional, calm, and in control.

"On Clinton or Sadie?"

She nearly sucked in an audible breath. How could she have forgotten Sadie? Though the bullet to the head confirmed the cause of death in her humble opinion. "Clinton."

"You've got to give me at least three days."

"No problem."

Jessie glanced back at the Harper's dilapidated house. Nana's car was still parked next to it. Jessie would have to tell her about finding DuPree—later, and then she'd contact Clinton's family.

Jessie hobbled back down the hill to the cruiser. Her curiosity about dead bodies had been totally satisfied after seeing Sadie, so she didn't need another full view of Clinton. Jessie wanted to remember what the kindly man was like when he was alive.

Once in the car, she stabbed the key in the ignition, rolled down the windows, and took off. Only after she hit the pavement, did she stick her head partly out the window to catch the breeze.

Despite taking Dax's advice about driving slowly, her right leg throbbed every time she lifted her foot off the pedal and onto the brake, convincing her she might have to wait a wee bit longer before she resumed her normal driving duties. She hated when Mr. Know-It-All was right.

Needing to take her mind off the horror, she flipped on the radio to the only station that came in clear—Country Western. She hadn't heard music in forever and missed the comfort it brought. She'd been with Dax so much she hadn't realized how long it had been since she'd heard her favorite songs.

Just her luck—the song playing was about unrequited love, a topic she didn't need to hear, so she changed the station. The jazz song came in weak, but at least it had no words to remind her of anyone—like Dax.

To be sure, the man was an enigma. He seemed to care so much for the town, yet he kept telling her he would be heading back to Baltimore soon. Hell, perhaps she should jump his bones, as Nana would say, if only to have memories of the incredible experience after he left. A tear trickled down her cheek and she wiped it away. She couldn't decide if she was crying for Clinton or for Dax's imminent departure.

Without any traffic, Jessie pulled in front of the office in less than sixteen minutes. As she climbed the steps, the normally pretty flowers by the door appeared to be wilting before her eyes. Clinton always remarked how much they brightened the entrance, but they must have sensed his passing and were in mourning. A lump formed in her throat. He'd been like a dad to her and now he was gone.

Jessie took a deep breath and pulled open the office door, working hard to compose herself. Frank was sitting in a chair next to the jail cell chatting with Brian. The second he saw her, he stood up.

"Howdy, Jess. You took longer than you said." His tone wasn't accusatory, just factual.

"I know. I'm afraid we ran into a little trouble."

Worry creased his brows. "What kind of trouble?"

She stepped to the desk area, sat down, and motioned him over. Frank dragged the chair back to Clinton's desk and did the same.

She glanced over at Brian whose gaze was locked onto hers. "We found Clinton's body," she said loudly enough for both to hear.

Brian's expression didn't change—no shock, no sadness, no reaction. She prayed he didn't have anything to do with her boss's demise.

Frank let out a deep sigh. "Jess, I'm so sorry. Clinton was a fine man."

"Yes, he was. I'm staying, so you can go home now. I'll call you when I need you to come back."

His face seemed to brighten. "You sure?" He checked his watch. "It's my weekly poker night tonight, though I'm not sure if I feel like playing with Clinton dead and all."

"Get going," she said in a pretend stern voice. "You know as well as I do that Clinton wouldn't want you to stop enjoying life just because he's not here." Especially since Frank had to be pushing eighty.

"You're right."

Frank used the chair arms to help him stand. For a moment, she thought he might lose his balance, but he didn't. Shoulders hunched, Frank ambled off. From his back pocket, he pulled out a handkerchief and blew his nose, and then quietly closed the door.

Boy, was this town going to need a long time to heal.

When Jessie turned around, Brian had moved back to the cot. "You hungry?" she called out.

"Could eat a horse," came back the reply.

"I'll order something from The Sugar Shack. What do you want?"

"Whatever you're having."

Easy enough. She dialed the restaurant, and Cherise answered. Jessie ordered two hamburgers, fries, an iced tea for herself and a lemonade for Brian, just like old times. She waited for the melancholy to grab hold about the past, but it never came. Only Dax's face appeared in her mind's eye.

Did she have it bad or what?

"I'll bring it right over when it's done," Cherise said, sounding way too excited.

"You don't have to. I can pick up the food." Even though the pain might take her appetite away. In the five minutes she'd be gone, she didn't think anyone would try to break Brian out of jail.

"With your bad leg? Honey, I can walk a block or two. Besides, it's a way for me to get out of here for a few minutes, if you know what I mean."

"All right. Thank you."

Jessie knew the real reason for the visit. Cherise had the hots for Brian—or least she used to. From what she'd heard, all the eligible women had their sights on him at one time. Too bad, they'd have a real long wait until he was released from prison this time.

Ten minutes later, a light knock sounded on the door. "That was fast."

Figuring Cherise's hands were full, Jessie opened the door, only to find it wasn't Cherise at all, but rather Lena.

Lip split and bloodied, along with an eye swollen shut, she looked like she'd gone five rounds with a prizefighter.

"Dear God. Wh-what happened?"

CHAPTER TWENTY-ONE

As Jessie guided Lena over to an office chair, her friend covered her bloody lip with her hand.

"Sit down and tell me everything," Jessie said grabbing a tissue box from her desk. "Here."

"Lena?" Brian called through the cell bars. Concern and anger laced his tone, surprising Jessie at the hidden passion, until she remembered the abuse his brother suffered at his dad's hand.

Lena looked up. "Brian? What are you doing here?" She dabbed her lip with the tissue, blew her nose, and then threw Jessie a questioning look.

Jessie would have thought Brian's arrest would have reached her by now, but apparently Deputy Frank must not have spilled the beans.

Jessie pulled up a chair and sat down next to her. "He ran into a bit of trouble." She didn't need to go into the reason for Brian's arrest and have Lena off track. "Now tell me what happened to you."

She swallowed hard. "It was... ah, ah Seth," she choked out.

Jessie wasn't sure she'd heard correctly. "Seth? The dream man you were with in the bar on Saturday night?"

She nodded. "He thought I'd tell, but I swore I wouldn't; only he didn't believe me." She looked up at Jessie with tears streaming down her face. "Why do men have to beat me?"

First her ex-husband, now Seth. Jessie didn't want to say that some women attracted abusers like knick-knacks to dust. Thank God, the men she'd dated had all treated her with respect, though toting a gun might rein in the worst trait in a man.

In her most gentle tone, Jessie tried to coax Lena to tell her story. "Start at the beginning and leave out no details."

"He, um, spent the night at my place last night, and it was wonderful." Lena broke down again and Jessie wrapped an arm around her shoulders.

"Go on."

"This afternoon we just hung out in the living room watching movies. I don't think I'd ever been happier. Thursday's my day off, and Seth didn't have to be at work until five." She hiccupped and wiped a strand of hair from her face.

Jessie worried Lena's injuries might worsen without some medical help. "Hold that thought while I get an ice bag for that eye, okay?"

Lena nodded. Glad to have something to do with her hands, Jessie snatched a baggie from her drawer and filled it with ice from the small refrigerator. She wrapped it in a thin towel to make it less painful for Lena. "Put this on your eye. Do you know what set Seth off?"

She covered part of her face and winced. "Someone called him about an hour ago, so he went into the bedroom to talk because I thought he didn't want to disturb me. Now I realize, he didn't want me to hear what he had to say. I even turned down the sound on the TV so as not to bother him. When I didn't hear his voice for a minute, I figured he was finished, so I went to the bedroom thinking I could entice him into an afternoon delight."

Dax's image flashed in Jessie's mind, but she cut off the thought. She needed to concentrate on Lena—not on her own fantasy. "And then what happened?"

"As I reached the bedroom door, I realized he was still on the phone." She glanced up, as though looking for some kind of affirmation, but Jessie couldn't help but raise a brow. "Okay, so I listened. It's not a crime since it's my house."

Jessie patted her hand. "You're right." Though the moment Seth closed the door, he was telling her he wanted privacy.

"I couldn't hear real good through the closed door, but I thought he said something about a kidnapping and then something about hiding in the mine."

Jessie's mind went on high alert. "A kidnapping? Was he more specific? Did he say a name?"

She shook her head. "Like I told Seth, I really didn't hear anything, but he didn't believe me. That's when he wailed on me."

"Oh, Lena, I'm so sorry." Jessie needed more information. "Could it have been Roberta he was talking about?"

"Roberta? I don't know. He never said a name. That's all I know, I swear." Lena seemed to shrink back against the seat.

"That's fine. You did good. Real good." Jessie went over to her desk and pulled out a ring with a key attached for the second cell. "Why don't you lie down on the cot?" She motioned toward the cell next to Brian's. "I just changed the sheets."

"You want to lock me up?"

A small smile lifted her lips. "No, silly." She handed Lena the key to her cell. "You'll be safe in there. I need to check something out." She had to see if anyone was being held hostage in the mine. Then she'd bring in Seth. "You can get out anytime you want, but if Seth comes looking for you, he won't be able to get you."

Lena grabbed Jessie's hands. "I can't thank you enough."

"There's aspirin in the bathroom above the sink if you want something for the pain. Cherise will be here in a minute with two hamburgers, so eat." Jessie dug out a twenty-dollar bill from her purse and handed it to Lena. "This is for the food."

"What about you? You need to eat too." Lena took the money and stuffed the bill in her jeans.

"Don't worry about me. I'll eat a power bar. I live off them."

Lena tried to smile, but the moment she did, her hand flew to her mouth. "Ouch."

Jessie's heart ached. "I won't be gone too long. If there's an emergency, call Bruno at the bar. I'm sure he can round up someone."

"Thank you."

If Seth had kidnapped anybody and took that person to the mine, he must have turned on the electricity since a mine elevator couldn't move on its own. She doubted cheapskate, Catchman, would have paid for power after the mine closed. If Seth had trespassed on the man's property to do harm, she had probable cause to cut off the lock and see for herself what was going on.

Jessie stepped to the back closet and pulled out a pair of lock clippers. Good ole Clinton. She remembered laughing the day he bought them. "We'll never use these," she'd said, and he'd wagged a finger at her. "Just you wait and see."

Her throat clogged with tears. He was a wise man, and Jessie missed him already.

She didn't like leaving her friend at the office, but Lena would be safe there. If Frank hadn't said he had his card game tonight, she'd have asked him to come back and watch these two.

Time was of the essence, so she couldn't ask around for someone else to keep an eye on them. Jessie would take a few minutes, however, to look for Dax before she went to the mine. Clinton always preached to take backup whenever possible.

She drove past Doc's place, hoping his van and Dax would be there, but they weren't. Not only did Jessie want him with her because of the added protection, she could use his extensive police experience.

Be honest. Dax was smart and she enjoyed being around him.

She liked when they flirted and even enjoyed arguing about the best way to investigate.

Bottom line, he wasn't around, and unless he was still at the farm digging up Clinton, she'd have to go solo. Jessie would have to accept that she would be on her own once Dax was gone anyway. At least for the next few weeks, she was sheriff, and relying on Dax wouldn't do her career any good.

Once in the car, she radioed Amanda's cruiser to see where she was, but her deputy didn't respond. Jessie had little choice but to go it alone. A few minutes later, she turned down Orchard Avenue, refusing to count the number of times she'd been on this road in the last week.

When she spotted the turn off to Cyril Harper's farm, she headed on up there, hoping to find Dax. She entered the property, and the car jostled and bounced on the uneven terrain, almost worse than the first time. If the son didn't want the place, he should put it up for sale since the land was prime real estate. If he sold the property, maybe the new owner would pave the entrance.

When she reached the barn, it was apparent everyone had left. Only Roberta's car remained. Maybe it was better that her grandmother wouldn't learn about Clinton's death until tomorrow.

Frustration filled her, yet if she hadn't checked and Dax had been there, she'd have been angry with herself for not covering all her bases.

As Jessie made a U-turn to head back to the mine, a gust of wind threw open the barn door, and out of the corner of her eye, she spotted Amanda's cruiser.

The only reason she would have to be up here was to look for evidence of Clinton's murder or Roberta's disappearance, though Jessie hadn't mentioned either event to her. Then again, Amanda could have passed Doc and Dax in town, and they could have told her. Jessie relaxed at that logical conclusion. Amanda was probably being her usual proactive self, trying to solve the crime, though how she'd do that, Jessie couldn't guess.

She turned off her engine and got out. "Amanda?" she shouted.

She was surprised Amanda would step foot on the place since her friend never liked this farm any more than Jessie did. She remembered hearing that when Amanda was twelve, her dad had given her a good spanking when he learned she'd come to old man Harper's property. As far as Jessie knew, Amanda had never returned.

Jessie called again, and when she heard nothing, she took a deep breath and walked inside the dark, dank barn. Holding a hand over her nose, she did a quick check in the tack room before looking inside the cruiser for a clue as to where Amanda might have gone. Wanting to be thorough, Jessie popped the trunk and found a pink and gray suitcase. This didn't look good.

Jessie's armpits dampened as a small ache began to grow in her belly. She clicked the case open and found women's clothes and toiletries, which surprised her since Amanda hadn't mentioned anything about needing to go somewhere. Jessie didn't think her friend would consider leaving her seriously ill mother.

Trying to gather her thoughts, Jessie placed a hand on the hood and found it warm but not overly hot. She estimated Amanda had parked about a half an hour ago, and assuming the aliens hadn't sucked her off the earth, the only place left for her to be was at the house.

As she headed out, the fact the cruiser was hidden in the barn still bugged her. Nothing was making sense, and she concluded the smell must have corrupted her brain cells. Then a new, more sinister scenario flitted through her mind. It was possible that Amanda had come here, and someone who didn't want her snooping around had killed her. Shivers raced down her body at the possibility.

Clinton would tell her not to jump to conclusions, but two

people were already dead and one was missing—no make that two people missing. Jessie whipped around to make sure she wasn't the next target and hurried the best she could to the house. Inside, she performed another quick search. No matter how often she called Amanda's name, her deputy didn't answer, causing dread to pool in her belly.

Needles of fear stabbed her gut, urging her to get the hell out of there and find help.

Jessie would have driven straight to town to locate Dax, but someone could be trapped in the mine—someone who needed her help more. What she wouldn't give for a clone.

Jessie slid into her cruiser and locked the doors, something she rarely did, but the world was off kilter, and she needed to take extra precautions.

At the turn off, she zipped through the forested lane until she hit the road to the mine, constantly checking her rear view mirror. The sun was setting, and the air had finally turned chilly, so she rolled up the windows to keep the warmth inside.

Several times, she'd questioned if she was doing the right thing, but each time, she came to the same conclusion. She'd check the mine to make sure no one was trapped below and then head straight back to the station to find Dax. Together, they'd figure out what happened to Amanda.

Jessie parked close to the entrance, grabbed the metal cutters from the trunk, and headed to the mine's door.

As she raised her arms to cut off the lock, the click of a revolver sounded in her ear.

"Put down the clippers and raise your hands."

Oh shit. No, make that double shit.

CHAPTER TWENTY-TWO

"Amanda? What's g-going on?" Jessie tried hard not to show any fear, but she failed. To think Jessie had been worried about her deputy. She'd never make that mistake again.

When Jessie started to turn around to ask for an explanation, Amanda jammed the gun harder against her head. "Don't move."

"Ouch. W-Watch it." Wait a minute. It was October 31th. This must be a Halloween prank. "Oh, I get it. Trick or Treat." Her body sagged in relief, but when she tried to step away from the pressure, Amanda clamped a hand on her shoulder, preventing her from getting out of the gun's range.

"What are you doing here?" her deputy asked with more bitterness than had ever come from her mouth.

Jessie's heart stammered in her chest. Oh, shit. Anger overtook the fear that had soured her stomach. "What am *I* doing here? The real question is what are *you* doing here? And with a gun to my head for God's sake?" Jessie struggled to get out of her grasp, but Amanda held tight.

Holding her hostage, Amanda ripped the cutters from her hands and tossed them on the ground before Jessie had the chance to use them as a weapon.

Amanda then grabbed Jessie's right wrist. "You've gotten in my way one too many times, bitch."

Bitch? Who was this woman? Amanda shoved a palm against Jessie's back, smashing her face against the rusty steel door, forcing her to gasp for air.

Don't panic. Think.

The pressure against her head temporarily disappeared, and Jessie took the opportunity to rotate toward her assailant. In her brief moment of freedom, she reached across her body to grab her gun from her holster, but before she could, Amanda latched onto Jessie's wrist again. The click of the steel cuffs made Jessie's heart almost stop.

Jessie whipped her other arm out of the way, hoping to avoid capture, but Amanda wrestled it back down, flipped her back around again, and clipped on the other cuff so that her hands were behind her back. Man she was strong. Being in the Navy must have whipped her into shape.

Now Jessie was really pissed. "How dare you cuff me, and what do you mean I was in your way?"

Amanda spun Jessie around, grabbed her gun out of the holster then lobbed the weapon a good twenty feet away into a pile of rubble. When she pushed Jessie back again, the door handle bit into her spine, radiating an intense ache in every direction. The metal cuff caught the skin on her wrist and gouged a hole that caused a slow burn to crawl up her arm. Then blood dripped down her hand.

"We're going below," Amanda said, her face contorted.

Sheer panic gnawed at her gut. No way she was going into a mine with a mad woman. It was one thing to go on her own, and yet another to be forced down. "Don't do this, Amanda. We can work something out," Jessie said in as calm a voice as she could manage given the adrenaline was running rampant through her system.

"No, we can't."

She couldn't let Amanda ruin her own life—or Jessie's. *Think fast.* "You don't need to keep me cuffed. I won't try to run, I promise. I can barely walk." She softened her voice. "Amanda, tell me what's wrong. I can help, I swear."

Amanda laughed. "You are a piece of work. You don't get it, do you?"

"Get what?"

Amanda stepped away to unlock the mine entrance but kept the revolver pointed at Jessie's chest. "Get inside and don't make me ask again." She cocked the gun and firmed her lips. Her blue eyes turned steel gray.

Once Jessie stepped into that elevator, she'd never come out alive, which meant she had to disarm Amanda. With her hands behind her back, she didn't know how she was going to do that. If Dax had been with her, Amanda never would have gotten the drop on her.

Jessie glanced at her cruiser. Even if she made it to the car before Amanda reached her, opening the door would take time and driving away would be impossible. What was she thinking? Amanda would shoot her dead if she tried to escape.

What Jessie needed was a diversion. She sorted through her few options and decided her best tactic was surprise.

Amanda shoved her. "Move."

Now! Standing on her good leg, she rocked back on her heel to deliver a sidekick to Amanda's midsection. As her foot was about to connect to Amanda's body, her deputy feigned to the right, lifted her arm, and smashed the butt of her gun into Jessie's temple.

The blow staggered her. A second later Jessie's butt hit the ground and then her face smashed against rough cement. An ache worse than a hundred migraines nearly took off her head.

"Why?" Jessie managed to spit out.

"Get up and do as I say."

She couldn't get up. She couldn't even move. Pain had paralyzed her. Amanda delivered a swift kick to her belly. *Ooof.* Bile raced up her mouth, and a trickle of blood dribbled out.

She couldn't die now. She had to fight, had to stay alive.

Amanda yanked on her arm, nearly ripping her shoulder out of its socket, and jerked her to her feet. "Obey or pay," Amanda said. "Get it? Obey or pay? It rhymes. Like it?"

"You're a real laugh a minute." Jessie spit blood out of her mouth from where a tooth had come loose.

In high school, Jessie used to enjoy Amanda's clever use of puns and rhymes, but no longer. The girl, or rather the woman, had lost her mind. Jessie couldn't believe she'd suspected nothing. To think Amanda had bought Jessie clothes, found confiscated photos, and helped her investigate. Their friendship was clearly a ploy to mislead, and that hurt.

She needed answers. "My shooting wasn't an accident either, was it?"

"Not by a long shot. Ha, ha. Get it? Long shot." She waved her gun when Jessie refused to laugh. "Actually, I was trying to save you."

Her arrogance amazed Jessie. "Like I'm supposed to believe you?"

"It's the truth. I thought if you were bedridden, you wouldn't come snooping around the mine." Her demeanor changed—evil-eyed, bitter, disgusted. "But not the great Jess Nash. Oh, no. You wouldn't lie still." She shook her head. "You always were an overachiever, and I had work to do, which meant I couldn't let you interfere."

Without warning, Amanda opened the elevator door and shoved Jessie inside. Her heart pounded so hard she thought it would leap from her chest. She twisted her wrists, hoping her sweat and blood would provide enough lubrication to get them off, but nothing worked. Her skin burned, but she kept trying. Amanda stepped into the cage with her, keeping the gun at Jessie's chest. As they descended, cold air, along with the musty smell of dust and dirt, shot up the shaft.

Amanda smiled. "I bet you never thought I would do something like this, did you?"

"You mean kill me? No, I didn't, but then, ten years is a long time, and people change." Jessie softened her voice, trying to win her over. "What happened?"

Amanda's face contorted. "The stupid President kept sending more and more troops to Iraq instead of where they were needed —to Darfur, where women are abused and treated like slaves. Congress claims the United States is a humanitarian nation, but that's a crock of shit. Women and children are starving in Africa, and we stand around doing nothing."

The bitterness seemed to run deep. Whatever happened to Amanda in the service must have messed her up. "How does killing me help your cause? You're no better than those who imprison and enslave women in Darfur." Jessie's voice cracked. The slap across her face came so fast and hard, her vision blurred.

"Don't be so naïve."

Okay, Amanda was seriously unbalanced. She'd served off the coast of Somalia, so Jessie could understand her wanting more aid to the women in Africa, but why Darfur specifically? She'd never mentioned it before, or had she befriended someone from there? The cage stopped, seemingly caught on a cog, but then rattled for a shaky moment before jerking downward again. The air turned chillier and Jessie shivered. If Amanda was insane, what other things had she done? "Did you kill Cl-Clinton?"

Maybe that was why Amanda's car was at the farm, but then she realized he'd been killed a week or so ago. Or was she there to check up on the body?

"Yeah, I killed him. Showed you those photos of the mayor and his lover to keep you and that P.I. from looking in my direction." She almost sounded proud.

"It didn't work, did it?"

Amanda jammed a fist into Jessie's stomach and white pinpricks of pain stole her breath. She'd never been more pissed off or scared in her life.

"You are so stupid. You and your questions. Now that I've confessed to murder, I gotta kill you. Good going, *Sheriff*."

While Jessie couldn't decide if Amanda was bluffing about murdering Clinton, she was certain Amanda was serious about doing her in. "How did you kill him?"

"Ah, I see you're testing me. A blow to the temple, just like the one I delivered to you, only he died."

Jessie swallowed hard, trying to keep the tears at bay. "Did he suffer?"

"How the fuck would I know? I came at him from behind, smashed him on the temple, and he went down. End of story." Amanda leaned back against the cage with a smug look. "Your own grandmother sealed his fate, you know. She found a pair of night vision goggles, or rather Sadie found the NVG's, and your Nana turned them in to Clinton. The good sheriff was suspicious and came snooping at the mine just as I was coming out of the shaft. When I ran into him, what was a girl to do?"

If life meant nothing to Amanda, why care about the women in Africa? "Did you kill Sadie too?" Jessie's mind reeled with horror.

"I had to. She was a bigger snoop than the sheriff."

As long as Amanda was in the confessing mode, she might as well learn all she could before she died. "And the attempt on Dax's life?"

"All me. Well, not actually me, since I was with you both, but one of my men tried to take him down. The same one who shot you—on my command of course." Her face looked disgusted but only for a moment. "Brilliant plan if I do say so myself. Too bad you pushed your man out of the way." Amanda spread her feet and stepped closer to Jessie. "I'm disappointed in you. You didn't ask about the gas theft or the grocery store heist. Can't connect the dots yet?" Amanda got in her face.

"I suppose you're going to tell me you pulled those off too?" The woman seemed ready to take credit for everything.

"Of course I did. After the nuclear waste begins to spread, I have to have food, fuel, and supplies. Didn't see any need to spend my hard earned cash." Amanda sighed. "The good folks of Kerry are going to feel the effects of the radiation and will die a long, painful death, but not me and my crew. We'll be safe and sound down here. When the waste blows over, we'll surface."

Jessie couldn't wrap her head around anything Amanda was saying. "Nuclear waste? Are you crazy?" Jessie couldn't fathom her hate. "What are you going to do? Drop an atom bomb?" There was no way she could pull that off.

Amanda shook her head. "Jessie, Jessie, you live such a sheltered life."

"If not an attack from the air then what? You going to blow up a nuclear power plant or something?" She wracked her brain to come up with one that was nearby but failed.

Amanda laughed. "No, no." She turned serious. "I can't blow up a plant. Don't you know anything? For your information, a nuclear sub is about to arrive in Annapolis for repairs. A little C-4 on the cooling pipe and voila, a nice, little unstoppable leak."

"A sub?" Annapolis was near Washington, D.C. Oh, my God.

"Don't you worry your last few hours of life about something you can't stop."

"What about your father? You want him to suffer too?" He lived in town.

"Of course I do. God only knows my father deserves to get cancer. Why do you think I left town right after high school?"

Jessie had always wondered. "Why?" She needed to keep Amanda talking. Perhaps she'd lose focus and give her an opening to escape.

Amanda's features hardened. "My father decided I was a better lay than my mother."

The revulsion nearly strangled her. "Your dad's a judge." While she'd never liked him, she never imagined he'd abuse his own daughter. Perhaps that was why Amanda wanted the women of Darfur to be saved.

"He might be, but he still has a dick and likes to use it. Doesn't seem to matter where or when."

No wonder Amanda was so screwed up. If only Jessie had known, she might have been able to help.

The car reached the bottom of the shaft with a thunk and a loud groan. With the gun still trained on Jessie's chest, Amanda opened the squeaky cage door and motioned her out. Even though lights lined the walls every fifty feet, they barely lit the gloomy mine. Apparently, Amanda had found a way to turn on the electricity or else she had a generator.

"I hadn't planned on you being the one to use my special tunnel," Amanda said, "but it's all yours now."

Jessie's stomach revolted, and vomit rolled into her mouth. Amanda really was going to leave her in the mine to die— without saying goodbye to Dax or Nana. "You c-can't d-do this!"

"I already have."

Amanda shoved her backward, and Jessie's feet tangled up. She landed on her butt and the air rushed out of her lungs.

Amanda hovered over her. "You are so clumsy. Get up."

Jessie rolled onto her knees. Without the use of her hands, she fell again. Her head ached and her stomach threatened to erupt.

"I can't."

"I can't," Amanda ridiculed, then kicked her again, this time in the leg.

Jessie cried out.

"Wimp." Amanda grabbed her by the shoulders and dragged her another twenty feet into a short tunnel, one that went nowhere. Rocks scraped her legs through her tights. Amanda dropped her and Jessie's mouth slammed into the ground.

"Oh, God." Jessie didn't have the strength to fight back as tears stung her eyes.

"God ain't going to help you now," Amanda said.

Jessie managed to roll onto her side and look up at her captor. "Why? Why are you doing this?"

"I already told you. I want to get Congress's attention. If they don't send troops to Darfur, my friends and I will set the charges. Now, if you get any ideas about getting out of here, I need to tell you I've set a few charges in some of the shafts. If you cross one of them—kaboom! It'll be bye-bye, Jessie. If, by some miracle, you do reach the surface, the door will be locked from the outside." She laughed.

Jessie was tempted to ask her to kill her now and put her out of her misery, but she had to believe there was something she could do to save herself.

Amanda strode off, kicking up dirt in her wake. Jessie sank back to the ground to gather her strength, to plan, to plot. The gate grated closed. She was now all alone and scared to death.

CHAPTER TWENTY-THREE

"You keep up that pacing, son, and you'll wear a hole in the floor." Margaret took a swig of her gin and tonic and leaned back against the living room sofa, appearing calm.

"Jessie should have been back by now," Dax said.

Margaret checked her watch for the tenth time in as many minutes. Perhaps she was more worried than he'd first thought. "She doesn't usually miss dinner, and she's good about calling. Did you check the office?"

That was the first placed he'd called. "Yes, but nobody's answering. I thought she said someone would be staying with Brian."

Worry churned his gut. "Maybe Frank took ill, and she had to drive him home. He's getting on in years."

"Even if that were the case, she would have called. Something's wrong. I'm going to town to find her."

Jessie's grandmother polished off her drink. "Maybe she's at the bar trying to calm down some drunk or helping someone in need."

Dax didn't buy her reasoning. "The night we found Sadie, we stopped at the bar. Even when her mind was elsewhere, she called you so you wouldn't be upset."

Margaret pressed a finger to her lips. "She is good about that."

Dax headed for the door. "Keep your gun handy."

Her jaw dropped. "Whatever for?"

He whipped around. "Do as I say." Margaret flinched at his harsh tone and guilt attacked. "Please?" he said as gently as he could.

"If you think there might be trouble, I will." Margaret stood up. "Wait a minute. I have something for you."

A moment later Margaret returned with a large flashlight, one that used a heavy-duty battery. "Bless you," he said.

"Oh, and you'll need these too." She dropped the keys to her car in his palm.

He'd forgotten Jessie had the cruiser and his truck was safely tucked away at Walt's. Doc had dropped him off at the house after they finished with Clinton's body. "You are a lifesaver." Dax leaned over and kissed Margaret on the cheek, and she actually blushed.

She made a shooing motion. "Now go and bring back my granddaughter." For a split second, he heard Jessie's voice in Margaret's, and his heart kicked up a notch.

"You got it."

Dax rushed down the steps and jumped in Margaret's Cadillac, ignoring the throbbing in his leg. It then took a moment for him to figure out how to turn on the headlights, but once he did, he couldn't leave fast enough. His first stop would be the office. Brian should still be in jail, and Jessie might have told her ex where she was headed.

Even though the town was four miles away, it was the longest four miles in his life. He prayed like he'd never prayed before that Jessie was all right.

Just as he turned down the main street, a car pulled in front of him and slowed to ten miles an hour. Dax honked. The person must have recognized Margaret's car and waved. Since Margaret's car was bigger than a boat, he wasn't able to pass her and not hit the cars parked along the side of the road.

Dax tried to relax, but the tension in his body made his pulse speed. *Come on, move.*

Margaret's friend pulled into a parking spot on the main drag and Dax sped by. A half mile later, he stopped in front of the station, the brakes squealing in protest. As soon as he ripped the keys from the ignition, he jumped out, and then took the stairs two at a time. Dax burst through the door, hoping to see Jessie at her desk.

Brian jumped off the cot in his cell. "What's wrong?"

"Where's Jessie?" Dax asked.

Brian pointed to a curled up ball in the next cell. "Ask Lena."

Lena? What was she doing in jail, and where the hell was Jessie?

***

Even with his headlights on high, the road to the mine was darker than sin. Dax's hands trembled and his pulse raced. He despised how his phobias controlled his life, and anxiety only made them worse.

He forced back the horror the best he could and tried to make sense of the concept that Lena's boyfriend might have kidnapped someone. Seth had only been in town two weeks, which meant he might have come to Kerry to do harm. Lena also mentioned that Jessie believed Roberta might have been the victim.

He slapped the wheel, fearing Jessie might have decided to track Seth down and then confront him. He should have found out from Lena where her beau was staying. If Dax weren't so close to the mine, he'd have considered turning around.

After making the last curve, his lights spotted her cruiser, and relief blanketed him. He floored the car to reach her.

Seconds later, Dax parked behind her cruiser and jumped out. "Jessie?"

The only response came from the howling wind buffeting the leaves, and the blood rushing in his ears blocked out all other sounds. He placed his palm on the hood of her car. It was cool, implying she'd been here a while. His gut soured, not liking where his mind was headed.

A chilly blast of air snuck through his shirt, confirming the predicted cold front had followed closely on the heels of the short-lived Indian summer. Keeping vigilant, he shone his flashlight at the mine entrance hoping to see some evidence of Jessie's arrival. *There*. A red object was on the ground. As he moved closer, he identified it as a pair of lock cutters. Brian told him she'd brought a pair with her, so she had to be here.

"Jessie?"

He held his breath awaiting her answer. His gaze shot to the lock, and the metal loop was hanging open. Uncut. Guess she didn't need them after all.

"Jessie?" He yelled louder this time.

She would have heard him if she'd been outside, which meant she'd gone into the mine to search for the kidnapped victim where it was dark, dangerous, deadly.

As he reached for the handle to open the cage, he stilled, wondering why it was at the top of the mine instead of at the bottom. An ugly sludge filled his veins. Something was seriously wrong. She wouldn't have sent the cage up if she were still below.

Dax inhaled deeply and fought his demons as he stepped inside. Once more he called her name even though he doubted she could hear him hundreds of feet below.

Press the button.

He had to go down and find her, but all of his usual excuses surfaced—the elevator could break, the mine could catch fire, or he could die just like his dad.

Stop doing this; Jessie needs you.

As he tried to clear his head, his father's screams echoed in this mind. Dax slapped his palms over his ears to stop the death shouts from scrambling his thoughts. His knees buckled, and he lowered his hands to catch himself.

Oh, God. He wasn't sure he was even capable of saving her. His throat partially closed from the lack of air and sweat beaded his forehead, as the sense of doom nearly paralyzed him.

Jessie was down there, perhaps injured, alone, and scared. Or worse, Seth was holding her captive.

The best-case scenario was that she had tried to help the kidnapped person and had been injured in the process. Given she'd arrived a while ago, Jessie should have come back up by now. He inhaled, but couldn't detect any smoke, implying there hadn't been an explosion. Panic gripped his lungs and squeezed his chest, and the urge to jump in Margaret's car and drive back to town was strong, but he couldn't leave Jessie. He'd rather die from his fears than have any harm come to her.

With more courage than he believed he possessed, Dax closed his eyes and pressed the down button. *Clang, wheeze, grind.* The cage rattled and swayed as it made its way to the bowels of the earth. He gripped the iron bars tight, half expecting the elevator to stop in mid-descent, stranding him. Only this time, it would be forever.

Then the horror began anew. The walls started to close in, and as much as he willed his mind to ignore the imaginary threat, the panic gripped him harder. He reminded himself for the zillionth time that his dad's death had been an accident, and the explosion had been the result of a cave-in, but the tightness in his chest didn't ease.

A hint of reason intruded. With the mine closed down, there wouldn't be any working equipment to explode. There was no real danger going down there, or so he tried to convince himself.

Dax patted his side to make sure he had his gun, but a lot of good it would do him now. He couldn't shoot the dark. The cage descended at what seemed like ten feet a minute, instead of ten feet per second. *Come on, come on.*

The farther he dropped, the darker the cage became. The trouble light hanging above his head didn't help ease his fears, and the familiar smells made him sick. His breaths shortened. He was going to be sick.

Wimp.

Be a man.

Dax concentrated on sweet Jessie instead of on the claustrophobia that threatened to make him stop the death trap and return to the surface. When he imagined her beautiful, trusting face, his palms still slickened, but his quick breaths began to slow. Picturing her smile and how she always stood up to him brought the needed courage. Whatever it took, he was determined to keep her safe.

The elevator came to a clanging halt at the bottom, and he tried not to imagine what he might find. Anticipating the darkness to rush out and crush him, he waited a moment to calm down.

Go, go.

Gun in one hand and his light in the other, he stepped into the mine, and this time, his demons thankfully backed off, though they were bound to come rushing back with a vengeance at any moment.

He looked around at the serene tunnel. Railroad tracks narrowed to nothingness, and an old coal car sat abandoned. He almost expected to see his father's smiling face round the bend.

"Jessie?" he called.

Several shafts shot out at odd angles just like in his hometown mine. She could be in any one of them. He listened for voices—a command, perhaps, from Seth. Then someone moaned. It might be Jessie or the captive, and he rushed in the direction of the noise.

Sweeping his light in a wide arc, he spotted her sprawled face down on the ground, motionless. When no one else appeared to be there, he rushed to her, his heart ready to explode. "Jessie?" His voice cracked and his heart nearly stopped.

Dax dropped to his knees, set down the flashlight, and then gently placed his forefinger on her artery to feel for a pulse. The beat was faint but there, and relief washed through him.

"Jessie? Can you hear me?" The side of her face was covered in blood from her temple to her nose, and he wanted to kill the son of a bitch who had done this to her.

She moaned and her legs jerked, jacking up his pulse.

Her hands were cuffed behind her back. Shit. As gently as he could, he slid his hands underneath her, sat on the ground, and then cradled her in his arms, willing his strength into her and sharing his warmth. Christ, she was cold.

She cracked open one eye. "Dax?" Then she did something he never would have believed. She smiled, and his heart flooded with joy.

"How are you?" That was a stupid question given what she looked like, but he wasn't functioning on all cylinders right now.

"I hurt, but I'm okay now that you're here. I thought you were Amanda coming back, so I didn't move when I heard my name called."

He couldn't believe it. "Amanda is behind all this?"

"Yes."

He'd worry about her motives later. "Come on, I need to get you out of here."

"My wrists hurt. Amanda cuffed me. I have a key in my back pocket."

"Let me help you." He dug his fingers into her pocket and retrieved the key. "I'll have you free in a sec." He slipped the key in the lock and released the cuffs.

"Thank you." Her voice wobbled.

"Let's go."

She grabbed his arm. "We can't leave."

"Why?"

"Amanda said she set a charge around—"

"I don't care what that bitch said. We need to go—now. I

didn't trip any wires getting to you, so we'll return the same way."

Squatting, he lifted her up. Even with Jessie in his arms, he was able to hold the flashlight, but with each step, the light bounced around. Returning to the elevator wasn't as easy as he thought, as the darkness disoriented him. Even though he stepped carefully, he must have kicked something, because a second later, an ear-shattering blast knocked both of them backward. As he lost consciousness, he remembered he forgot to tell Jessie he was falling in love with her.

CHAPTER TWENTY-FOUR

Head pounding and vision blurry, Dax slowly roused. He spit out the dirt lining his mouth and tried to focus on what had happened. He'd been holding Jessie when an explosion ripped through the tunnel. Now dirt blocked their exit.

Oh, my God. "Jessie?"

The rays from the fallen flashlight shone low on the wall, illuminating a sea of particles. As he staggered forward to find her, dirt and rocks fell off his back, and he scoured the cave before him.

Not more than ten feet from him, her body stuck out of the rubble. He rushed over, knelt down next to her, and gently shook her shoulder. "Jessie? Can you hear me?" His heart nearly burst.

She moaned and joy spiked his pulse. He brushed away the dirt covering her lower half. Her skin looked scraped, but at least he didn't see any protruding bones.

"Jessie, talk to me."

Her eyelids fluttered. "Dax?"

"I'm here."

"What happened?"

"An explosion happened and caved in the entrance."

She coughed. "We're trapped?"

Considering that possibility would undermine all of his logical thought. He needed to stay calm and remain focused to get them out of there.

"Don't worry; it won't take me long to dig us out." He only half believed it, but he needed something to hold onto.

"If we ever made it back to the elevator, Amanda said she'd locked the door to the outside."

"I left it open."

"Oh, thank goodness." Jessie tried to sit up again but fell back.

Dax yearned to hold her, comfort her, and make sure nothing else bad happened to her. He slipped his hands under her legs and slid Jessie onto his lap. Shivering, she rested her head against his chest, and he wrapped his arms around her. "You're so cold."

"You feel good and warm." She sat up straighter and looked toward the entrance. "How are we ever going to get out of the tunnel to reach the elevator?"

"I'll dig our way out. It shouldn't take long." A thin shaft of light, coming from the direction of the elevator, peeked through the top of the rubble. The rest of the wall of dirt didn't seem to be more than a few feet thick.

"Do you think anyone will try to save us?"

"Lena knows I came out here to find you. She'll rally the troops when we don't return."

"She's sweet, but she doesn't move fast. Given her condition, I'm betting she's sound asleep on the cot. By morning we could be dead."

"Don't think negative thoughts."

He kissed the top of her head, not caring if she was coated in dirt. Jessie looked up at him, and even in the dim light, he caught desire in her eyes, causing his groin to shoot to attention.

Stop it. Jessie's injured. The last thing she needed was some horny bastard taking advantage of her. In her delicate condition, he couldn't make love to her, though as God was his witness, he wanted her worse than life.

Jessie squirmed on his lap, making his situation worse.

Her eyes widened. "How can you get an erection when I'm such a mess?"

Nothing ever embarrassed him, but her comment sent heat up his face. "You are not a mess to me. Your eyes are still this sexy blue-green color that reminds me of the Caribbean, and your hair is so brown and curly that I can't wait to dip my fingers in it."

"Dax Mitchell! I never would have thought you to be the romantic type."

As he ran his hands over her dusty mop, his good intentions evaporated. "That's not romance. I'll show you romance." He leaned her back against a pile of soft dirt and kissed her, brushing a smudge off her cheek with his thumb. "You taste good."

She laughed. "As good as dirt tastes, I bet."

"I want to kiss your lids, your forehead, your ears, and everything in between, but I'm afraid I'll hurt you. You have a pretty bad bruise next to your eye." He ran a thumb gently over her temple.

"What bruise?" she said in the sexiest voice he'd ever heard.

She reached up and tussled his hair. He wanted her in the worst way, but now wasn't the time or the place. Her lips parted, and she drew him to her. She might be willing, but Jessie deserved more than a rough tumble in a disgusting mine.

Dax cleared his throat. "We need to wait until we get out of here before doing anything."

"Here I am willing and mostly able, and you push me away?" Thank God there was humor in her tone.

He looked down at her. "When I make love to you, Jessie Nash, I want to have you naked on a bed of roses surrounded by candles."

"D-Dax."

He gave her a quick kiss and lifted her off his lap. He then shrugged out of his jacket. "Put this on."

"What about you?"

"I'll keep warm by digging."

He stood, grabbed the flashlight, and looked for a flat stone to help him with the excavation. After trying a few different sized rocks and discarding them, he found one that worked. Dax climbed to the top of the mound then turned around.

"You might want to stay at the back of the tunnel. I don't want the debris to get you, not to mention what the dust could do to your lungs."

Jessie eased her way to a stand, took two steps, and teetered. "I'm good." She straightened and turned back toward him. "I'm helping."

"Jessie, you need to rest."

"If we don't get out of here soon, I'll be resting until the archeologists unearth my bones."

She had a point. The woman never was one to back down from a challenge. "All right then. Find a rock and get to work."

To his surprise, the rubble was fairly easy to remove. After fifteen minutes of clearing, they finally dug a hole big enough to crawl through. He turned to her. "Let me go first and I'll then help you through."

"Okay."

On his belly, Dax slithered through the opening. Shades of war crashed down on him, and the image of Evan flashed in his mind. His best friend had finished removing all the charges in the field, but as he stepped out of the way, his foot landed on a missed mine—one Dax should have detected. His failure had caused Evan to die. He blamed it on the encroaching darkness. It had made him rush, which had made him careless.

"Dax?"

He jerked his attention back to her and then scrambled up the small mound and guided her down the pile of dirt. When they reached the main entrance, they dusted themselves off.

"Ready to get out of here?" he asked.

"What if Amanda returned and locked the door?"

"We come back down."

As much as he didn't relish riding up in the confining elevator again, it was their only way out. Dax pulled open the door, and the hinge groaned loud enough to make him lose confidence they'd even make it to the top in this rust bucket. Jessie stepped past him and leaned back against the bars. Between her wobbling chin and random intakes of breath, she seemed to be fighting to hold it together.

"Let's get out of here." Dax said. As he was about to press the button to ascend, all the lights in the mine extinguished, entombing them. Oh, shit.

***

"Dax? What happened?"

"Hell happened."

He flicked on his light, enough to light their cage. Jessie huddled close, and he wrapped his arms around her, his strength helping to soothe her fears. "We should push the button to make sure the power is off everywhere," she said.

His laugh sounded bitter. "Be my guest, but I'd bet you anything, there's no power anywhere in town. Amanda and that Seth character are probably in this together. It would have been too easy for someone to drive out here, cut off the lock and free you, like I tried to do." He squeezed her tighter and rested his chin on her head. "No, Amanda wanted you to die down here, and the only way to be sure that would happen was to cut the power."

Tears brimmed on her lids, and her stomach churned. "How can you be so calm?"

"Calm? Sweetheart, I'm anything but calm. I'm furious. I'm so disgusted with myself right now. I rushed to save you without gathering more facts."

His sweetness bolstered her courage, what little there was left. "So what do we do now?" A renewed ache stabbed her belly. "I shouldn't be asking you that question since I need to figure things out for myself."

"I say we look for another way out." His tone came out colder than before, acting as if the lack of electricity was somehow his fault. He opened the cage door and motioned they step out.

She faced him. "There isn't another way out. I'd know. This was my grandfather's mine, remember? He loved to show off this place to me." Another wave of depression walloped her. "Hey, wait a minute. I just thought of something. Come on." She slipped his light from his fingers.

"Where are we going?"

"Amanda confessed a few things to me. Some of it might have been bragging, and other parts could have been downright lies, but she said she was responsible for the grocery store theft and the gas heist. Apparently, her group of cohorts are planning to sabotage a nuclear sub to get Washington's attention to do something in Darfur, and they're going to hole up here until the nuclear waste dies down."

Dax stopped in his tracks, his hands clenched. "Nuclear waste? Is that her plan? What sub? Where?"

She flashed the light on his chest to read his expression, and his intensity almost scared her. "I don't know. She said the submarine is docked at the Annapolis Navy yard, or is about to be docked. I can't remember. What difference does it make now? We can't contact anyone to warn them."

"You're right." His fists loosened. "I say we look for this safe haven. I could use a hot shower and a good meal about now."

Jessie chuckled though there was little pleasure in her heart. "You're better off thinking a little more primitive."

He leaned down and kissed her, gently at first, before becoming more demanding. Most likely, he was trying to take her mind off the panic that had crept up her face. At this moment, she'd take pleasure any time over the pain.

Jessie leaned into him and gave into her urges, desperate for solace. She wrapped her arms around his neck and the flashlight she was holding clunked him on the head.

He jerked back. "Hey. You trying to kill me?" His eyes widened in an exaggerated fashion, and thankfully, his tone held some cheer.

She loved how he could make light—no pun intended—of the worst situations. "Hardly, I need you." In more ways than one, but she didn't want to explore those options right now. Not until they were free—assuming they would be. She grabbed his hand. "Come on, I think I might know where Amanda would hide the stuff." Jessie prayed she hadn't set more deadly charges.

As she guided him down the tunnel, Jessie worked to keep alert, pushing aside the throbbing at the back of her head from where Amanda had hit her.

"Did she ever run around the mine with you when you were kids?" he asked.

"Yes, and that fact might save us."

Dax slid alongside her and slipped the flashlight from her fingers. "Do you mind?"

She'd had enough of not understanding his phobia and stopped. "Okay. I'm not going one more step until you fess up to why you're afraid of the dark."

She wished she could see his face, but he kept the light pointed to the ground. Dax blew out an audible breath. "I'm claustrophobic, not *afraid* of the dark."

She grabbed his arm. "It's okay. It doesn't bother me. Actually, I think it's heroic."

"Heroic? You've got to be kidding."

"How many men afraid of the da...I mean who don't like enclosed spaces, would have come into a *dark* mine to save me?" He said nothing. "Well, I think that's heroic."

"Yeah, I'm a real hero. Too bad this hero didn't use any

common sense when he tried to save you." He shook his head and stabbed a hand through his hair. "I bought the whole Jessie's-saving-someone-in-the-mine scenario from Lena that I didn't even think to get backup. Stupid, stupid, stupid. I'm a trained police officer for God's sake. Or at least I was. There was no excuse for me coming alone."

The fact he rushed to get to her implied he cared a lot for her. "You came alone because you didn't know anyone in town. There wasn't much you could have done. I was the stupid one who came out here looking for some imaginary kidnapped victim. Alone, mind you." She stepped in front of him and trailed a finger down his chest. "I did try to find you, in case you were wondering."

"You did?" She heard the smile in his voice.

"Yes." She punched him in the arm. "Now don't distract me. Where were you by the way?"

"With Doc."

"I must have just missed you. So what happened to make you so panicky being in closed-in spaces—when it's dark."

He didn't answer for so long, she thought he wouldn't tell her. She hoped he didn't think she was making fun of him. As she was about to explain that she wasn't, he began.

"I was ten. It was my dad's birthday, but it also was a school day. I told my mom it was a teacher writing day for the third, fourth and fifth grade, but not for my brother's first grade class. He had to be in school."

"You lied to your mom?" Jessie could picture him standing with his hands behind his back, fingers crossed, being the most beautiful little boy in the world, convincing his mother with the straightest of faces. No mother would believe he'd lie.

"I had to. I wanted to surprise my dad with the present I'd made him."

Her heart tore. "What did you make?" She remembered the fishing lures she'd fashioned out of left over stuff in the garage for her dad one year. He never caught a fish with any of them, but he loved them all the same.

"I carved a whistle, though truth be told, I was the one who wanted it. Then again, ten-year-olds aren't known for their charity."

"That was so sweet."

"Once mom went off to work, I hightailed it to the mine where Dad worked. No one was around when I arrived, so I jumped in the shaft elevator. I was half way down when the mine below exploded. A cave-in had hit some electrical equipment and ignited methane gas. The place turned into what I pictured hell would be like—all flames and no way out." He squeezed his eyes shut for a moment. "With the power out, the elevator stopped half way down."

She could feel his chest rise and fall more rapidly as if he were reliving the terror. "Dax?" He opened his eyes. She wanted to grab his pain and carry it as her own. "How long before you were rescued?"

"Six hours. I blew that whistle a lot." She sucked in a breath. "The worst part wasn't how hungry I was or how cramped my legs became, but the fact my dad was probably dead and I couldn't do anything about it." There wasn't enough light to tell, but from the way his voice wavered, his eyes might be tearful.

"Oh, Dax. I'm so sorry." She rested her head against his chest, trying to give him some comfort.

He rubbed her back as if she were the one who needed the relief. "I've heard that when people are in car accidents, their short term memory disappears, that they don't remember the collision or anything, but I wasn't so lucky. I remember every damn minute of it—the screams, the smell, the heat, the hope-lessness. I prayed for God to take me and let my father live, but he didn't listen."

"I can't imagine losing your dad at such a young age. You must have been terrified. No ten-year old should have to shoulder the burden of having to be the man of the family."

He looked away. "I was scared. My mom never recovered. She began to drink heavily, and once her liver started to fail, I had to put her into an assisted living facility. She died three months ago." He sucked in a deep breath. "I miss her."

Oh my God. Could the man have had a more tragic life? Then she remembered the picture of his fiancée, but she didn't have the heart to bring up that horrifying topic.

"What ever happened to your brother?" She prayed nothing tragic had happened.

"David? He works in Simi Valley. Made millions in the dot com market, but we don't talk."

From his hardened tone, the subject was a sore one. "Nana mentioned you were reluctant to take the job of finding Sadie. Was it because this town reminded you of home?"

He looked down at her. "You could say that."

"Then why didn't you leave the moment we found her?"

The pad of his thumb caressed her cheek. "Because I found you instead."

Her heart exploded. Jessie never thought she'd ever find love, but here was a man, damaged but strong who seemed capable of loving her back.

Wasn't that just her luck? She finally found the man of her dreams, and she wasn't going to live long enough to have a life with him. At least they could be comfortable in their final days. "Come on. Knowing Amanda, she'll have the place stocked well. I could really use a drink. There are miles of tunnels that jetted off in different directions, but Amanda wouldn't want to lug equipment far from the entrance. If nothing else, the girl had always been practical." She shook her head. "You know what pisses me off the most?" She didn't wait for him to answer. "I actually bought Amanda's girlie-girl role. In high school, she was tough, and acted as if she didn't care what anyone else thought. She dressed anyway she chose and wore too much makeup, but deep inside, she believed in causes. Fu—" She almost swore. "Sorry."

"Don't worry about it. There are times like these, where decorum isn't necessary. Tell me more about Amanda while we scour the bowels of the earth for her hiding place." His tone came out lighter than she expected.

Jessie's respect for him grew. "Why?"

"The more we know, the easier it will be to find her and take her down."

Now she had to laugh. "You expect to get out of here?" He was crazier than Amanda.

"Once you've been to war, you've seen it all. I've been in foxholes with mortar fire shooting overhead, the enemy coming at me, and at the last minute some brave ass rescue team drops some bombs on the approaching enemy and saves us. As they used to say, it ain't over until the fat lady sings."

She stopped and hugged him. "I like your attitude."

"Then let's find Shangri La."

For the first time in hours, Jessie had hope.

***

Jessie cracked open her eyes but couldn't see anything. The power must have gone out at home last night, and she'd been asleep when it happened. A chill had seeped into the air, and she pulled the blanket up to her chin. Her body ached so much she decided she might as well sleep in. As she fluffed the too-small pillow, a soft droning sound caught her attention, and she stilled, trying to figure out what was causing the noise. When she rolled on her side, her senses shot to high alert.

Oh, crap. She wasn't in her soft bed, but on a hard cot in a dank, musty mine with Dax next to her. Everything came flooding back from Amanda's betrayal to the explosion in the mine. Jessie rolled onto her back again, depression swamping her. She saw no reason to wake Dax as they had no place to go. She rose from the cot and pulled the scratchy blanket around her shoulders, but she still couldn't see a damn thing.

Dax had set the light next to the bed since he'd wanted to keep it on all night, but then decided it would be better to save the battery, even if there were tons of Sterno cans and a generator. He'd been convinced the fumes would do more harm than good in the confined space.

Jessie shuffled over to his bed, and when her toe ran into the flashlight, she stifled a groan. They'd set the porta-potty down the tunnel and around a bend for privacy, and she had to pee really badly. Without waking Dax, she snatched the light and tiptoed away.

When she returned, he was sitting up on the bed. "I can't believe it's nine in the morning," he said. The glow from his watch face faded.

If she let the depression grab hold, she'd cry and that would be ugly. Keeping upbeat was the only way to handle the crisis. "So what's on our agenda today?"

"I figure we need to eat and wait to be rescued."

"You're convinced we will be?" Getting her hopes up would only bring her down harder when they weren't.

He rose from the bed and took back his light. "It's simple. Even if the whole town's power isn't out, when we don't come back, Margaret will round up someone. Just you wait. Half the town will be looking for us."

"So your plan is to eat and wait to be saved?"

Dax glanced at the ceiling. "I was trying to stay positive."

"I hope you're right."

As Jessie turned to find something to eat for breakfast, an ear-shattering blast knocked her to her knees. The floor shook, and dirt and rocks dropped down on her. She covered her head with her hands, and then Dax covered her body with his. Her pulse skyrocketed and Dax's grip on her tightened. Jessie held her breath and waited for the ceiling to fall and bury them alive.

CHAPTER TWENTY-FIVE

Stunned, Dax waited for another blast, but when none came, he sat back up. "Are you okay?"

"I think so," Jessie said dusting off the debris. "What was that?" Her voice shook.

She placed a hand over her heart, acting as if she didn't press on it, the damned thing might jump out of her chest. Her eyes widened, and then she coughed as another dust storm rained down on them. Dirt clung to every inch of their clothes, face, and hands.

Dax jumped up. "Stay here, and I'll check it out."

"Oh no, you don't, I'm coming with you."

Dax lowered the flashlight to her chest, away from her eyes. "No way, Jess. That blast might have made the mine unstable, and I won't chance you getting caught in another cave-in."

She swiped a hand over her face, and when she licked her lips, she scrunched up her face. "I don't care. It's my life and I decide when and where I do my danger. If the mine caves in, it will be collapsing on us both."

He held up a hand in surrender. "All right, you win." She'd never obey even if he insisted.

He grabbed her hand and led the way, not trusting she

wouldn't take off, though with only one light between them, she might behave. As they neared the explosion site, the more their cave looked like a big, dark monster who'd coughed up a lung—and they were walking right into its mouth.

"Pull your shirt over your nose and mouth. You won't want to be breathing this stuff," Dax said. His vision was even more limited with the particles floating in the air.

Thankfully, she did as he asked. When they reached the end of the shaft and turned into the main entranceway, he halted.

"Ohmigod," she cried.

Not only had the elevator crumpled on the ground, part of the rock wall had disintegrated, and an empty coal car lay on its side.

"Wait here, and I mean it," Dax said.

"Okay, okay."

He stepped over rocks, metal, and the broken trouble light that had been inside the cage. Part of a cable poked its head out from under the debris, and he peered up the long shaft. Helplessness clawed at his heart. "An explosion from above must have ripped apart the cables." He turned toward Jessie. "We are truly fucked, excuse my French."

He expected the evil talons of panic to take hold, but they mercifully kept at bay. Maybe having Jessie by his side helped. It would be ironic if she were his lucky talisman that warded off his demons when they only had a short time to live.

"How are we going to get out of here now?" She suddenly sounded young and fragile.

He maneuvered back and wrapped his arms around her. "I wish I knew. There's no way they can dig down five hundred feet and save us. When they see the damage from above, they'll assume we're dead." *Good going, Mitchell. Scare her more.*

Jessie squared her shoulders and stepped out of his embrace. "You think Amanda did this?" She sounded more angry than afraid, and that emotion was far easier to deal with than fear.

"That would be my guess. In doing so, though, she cut off her own escape plan. She probably figured with you here, her safe haven had already been compromised."

Jessie sniffled. "You're right. Needing to disappear for good, she'll probably go across country."

"Nothing more we can do here, so let's head back."

Jessie followed close behind him as he made his way to their living quarters, which, while dusty, almost seemed luxurious. Thank God they hadn't stayed near the elevator, waiting to be rescued, because they'd be dead for sure.

She coughed and coughed, clearly in respiratory distress. "I think it might be better to die from a blast than from starvation, dehydration, or some funky lung disease," she said.

"I thought you were a glass half full girl."

She cleared her throat. "I'm not in the mood today. In case you haven't noticed, things aren't going so well."

"It won't help to get down. We have enough gas to run the generator for quite a while and food to last a month or two. Amanda did leave us a ton of water bottles."

"What a way to die." Jessie picked up a gas lantern. "Can we at least turn on some of these? It's dark in here."

So it wasn't just his imagination. "No reason not to use up the supplies."

Once she lit the lamp, she began to pace. "Wasn't it enough that we're trapped down here? Why couldn't she have left us a way out in say, a week, after she'd done her deed?"

Jessie looked like she was going to explode. "Come here," he said in his softest voice.

She stopped and looked at him as though he were crazy. "Why?"

Obviously, she was upset if she had to ask. "I'd like to live my last few days in relative enjoyment. Come sit by me. Please." He eased onto the cot and patted the canvas bed.

Jessie stomped over and dropped down, arms crossed over her chest, gaze straight ahead. She was hurting, angry, and frustrated, and Dax couldn't blame her.

He leaned on one elbow and stretched out his legs behind her. "Jessie, lie down with me." The cot wasn't very wide, but she had room to snuggle up against him.

"Aw, hell. Why not?"

Jessie must have her own idea of lying down, because she crawled on top on him, and then winced as if in pain.

"What's wrong?"

She sat up, straddling him, and placed a hand on her ribs. "Wrong? Let me see," she said counting on her fingers. "One, I still have a hole in my leg, two, my face was smashed in by a gun butt, three, I was kicked in the stomach a few times, and four, Amanda slapped me across the face. Other than that Mrs. Lincoln, how did you enjoy the play?"

Dax burst out laughing. He lowered Jessie to his chest, making sure he didn't hurt her. "Enough talk of our dire situation. Let me show you what I want to do."

He leaned over, moved the beam of light so that it didn't shine in either of their eyes, and then kissed her. Jessie moaned, and when she returned the affection with more passion that he'd thought possible, his dick turned harder than any ore they'd ever mined down here. This time, he wasn't going to stop like he had many times before.

Good thing they'd found the stack of moist wipes last night and were able to get a decent sponge bath. He for one smelled better afterwards, and Jessie had been so happy to get clean, she'd twirled around. Except for the recent dousing of dirt from the last explosion, he was fairly confident they were as close to sanitary as possible.

Shutting off the internal sensors that told him not to take advantage of her, he let his passion and desire flow. If they were going to die in this cave, he wanted to enjoy his last moments in her arms.

Not wanting her to catch cold, Dax pulled the blanket over Jessie's back. Of course, once they got going, the last thing on their minds would be the dampness that could settle in their bones for days.

When she shifted her weight to get more comfortable, he could tell this cot wouldn't do. "Get up for a sec, okay?"

Her mouth dropped open. "So help me God, Dax Mitchell, if you pull away one more time, I'm going to chase you around the mine until I catch you."

He laughed. "I just want to spread the blankets on the ground. Not only will our experience be more comfortable, but it will give me better access to your delectable body."

She grinned. "Now you're talking."

He should give her a medal for bravery. He bet Jessie had never stared death in the face before, and she was doing a fine job of adjusting. His goal was to make her forget their troubles, if only temporarily.

Once he spread the blankets and pillows on the ground, he motioned she join him. Jessie slipped onto her knees and peeled off her jacket, or rather the jacket he'd lent her.

Dax reached up and molded a palm over her breast. "Firm, ripe, juicy. Just how I like 'em."

She swatted his hand away. "They are not melons."

"You aren't looking at them from my perspective." He winked.

Dax loved to banter with her, but there was a time for talking and a time for action. Right now, talking was highly overrated. For weeks, he'd put his own desires on hold, but that restraint was about to end.

Dax drew her to him and gently kissed her again, tying not to inflict any more pain, especially close to the small cut above her lip. She stretched out on top of him and kissed him harder. Her breaths increased as she nipped and tugged on his lower lip, causing his libido to shoot out of control.

"I could spend hours devouring you," she said.

"I have time."

"That so?" She slid her hand between their bellies and

palmed his balls. Holy shit. Blood slammed into his dick and his pulse raced faster than a runaway train.

***

Jessie couldn't believe how incredible his body felt pressed against hers, and when he'd deepened the kiss, warmth shot to her abdomen and below. She'd never felt more wanted or desired in her life, but she had to have more. Jessie opened her mouth to invite him in, and this time, he didn't hesitate. As their tongues tangled and sparred, she enjoyed the minty taste from the gum they'd found last night.

Wanting more contact, she rolled off Dax and pulled him on top of her.

"Easy there," he said. "I don't want to put too much pressure on you."

"You won't." She loved the security of his weight on her body as he balanced on his elbows. The only thing that could really harm her would be if he left, and seeing how they were trapped in this mine, that wasn't going to happen. She tugged on his shoulders, wanting—no needing—to feel him on her, and then in her.

Just as Jessie was enjoying how his fuzzy beard bristled under her palm, Dax lowered his head and dropped a kiss on her throat, his tongue sending shivers of delight up and down her body. She moaned from the exquisite tension skittering across her skin. More turned on than she'd ever been in her life, she ran her palm under his shirt to touch his chest, to feel his heat. Her fingers danced across his strong pecs, and then she explored the contours of his body. Ooh, how the man could make her feel wonderful and wickedly wanton.

"I need you," he panted.

"Then take me."

Dax half sat up and fumbled with her blouse buttons, but she was too intent on loving his sleek muscles to stop and help. The sprinkling of soft chest hair tantalized her, and the light from the lamps shimmered against the walls, creating a cozy cocoon made just for them.

"You are so sweet," he groaned. "I've wanted to touch you from the moment I saw you."

"Then how come you always pulled away when I was close?" Now probably wasn't the time for a discussion, but her curiosity had gotten the best of her.

He stabbed a hand through his hair. "It's hard to explain. Everyone I've ever cared about has died. First my father, then my fiancée, and recently my mother." He waited a second, she guessed, to see if she would ask about Laura, but now wasn't the time to let a ghost in.

She nuzzled his neck. "It might come as a surprise, but I'm not dead yet and you touching me won't change our outcome." She drew the bottom of his earlobe between her teeth then let go. "How about forgetting my question and just enjoy the moment?" She needed the release, needed his tenderness, and dare she say she needed his love?

"You got it."

He finished unbuttoning her blouse and popped open the front clasp of her bra. That was the answer she was looking for. Dax massaged and tweaked her already hard nipples, and her needy breasts burned under his touch.

She must have gasped because he immediately stopped. "Did I hurt you?" he asked.

"No! I'm excited, that's all." A red-hot burst of desire spread through her, and she clasped his powerful shoulders. Dax was so strong, rugged, and capable that her heart nearly burst for wanting him.

He leaned over and pleasured her breasts again, plucking her nipple with his teeth, then sucking hard on the sensitive nub, electrifying every nerve ending. He kneaded her other breast, ringing her nipple with his finger until she wanted to scream.

Pluck, caress, pluck, caress. The combination drove her wild with want.

Jessie raked her nails down his back then ran her palms up and down his hard corded muscles. She drew him near and arched her back to press her breasts upward for more contact. When his hard, throbbing cock rubbed against her, he created a yearning so deep, she thought she'd drown in her own lust.

"I think it's getting hot in here," he said, his eyes half closed.

Dax rolled off her and when he slipped out of his pants and boxers, Jessie couldn't help but stare at his huge cock. Heat swelled between her legs, and her inner walls cramped with lust.

"Lick me," she begged.

She'd never asked a man to do that before, but with Dax, she wanted to experience everything.

"My pleasure." Once naked, he took off her pants and panties and tossed them on the ground. "You are magnificent."

Before she could respond, he slipped between her legs and opened her folds with his thumbs. Anticipation swirled inside her. She clutched his head, ready to hang on for a wild ride. The first lick sent her spiraling out of control. "Yes, yes."

He rubbed her tiny nub, and waves of ecstasy swept through her, pushing her closer to her climax. As he licked and plucked her little pearl, he reached up and ran a palm over her breast, sending fire through her veins.

She wasn't going to last much longer. This man seemed able to make her forget everything, and for that she'd die loving him. Heat pooled and swirled inside her until she couldn't stand it any longer.

"I'm about to come." She didn't want to give into her lust without returning the pleasure first. She gently pushed on his shoulders, but like a rock boulder, she couldn't move him. "Roll over, please."

"You sure you want me to stop? I thought you were enjoying what I was doing."

"That was the problem. I was liking it too much."

He grinned and lay on his back. As if a sexy goddess guided her, she sat on her haunches, grabbed his cock, and licked his rock hard length. The army-type blanket scratched her knees, but his moaning helped her ignore her discomfort. She stroked him faster and faster while she drew him deeper into her mouth. If only this would last forever, she'd die happy.

***

Jessie's hot touch undid him the moment she opened her mouth and let him explore her sweetness. As soon as Dax had taken off her blouse and touched her breasts, he was a goner. Jessie was the perfect woman, and everything Dax ever desired.

He wanted to recite some romantic turn of phrase to describe how the tip of her breast was in perfect proportion to the rest of her body, but his mind was in a fog. He had too much pent up emotion to think clearly, especially with the way Jessie was stroking him.

He grabbed her wrist. "Sweetheart, if you want me to do justice to you, you've got to give me a break." He panted to catch his breath.

He wasn't about to admit how long it had been since he'd had sex—or rather meaningful sex. A man did have to survive. Dax could never get enough of her in a lifetime, but at the moment his lifetime looked to be rather finite. Just as he was about to question why life had turned so cruel, she dragged his head up to her mouth and kissed him with more intensity and desire that any man deserved.

Dax slipped his finger between her wet, needy folds, nearly making him come. It wouldn't be fair to her if he came first. They had all day and all night, and he had no intention of stopping.

Her kiss turned more urgent, and then she murmured, "I want all of you. Now."

With one finger flicking the bud of her core, he dug his other hand into her hair and kissed her closed lids, her nose, and chin, thrilling at every touch.

She pleaded again, sending him into a state of desperation.

"You win." *Or rather I win.*

Dax crawled on top of her, excitement racing through his veins. Just as he was about to mount her, a deep voice reverberated from far down the mine, and Dax stilled. He clasped a hand over her mouth and extinguished the light.

CHAPTER TWENTY-SIX

Jessie grabbed Dax's shoulders, her heart beating a rapid tattoo. "That sounds like Bruno."

"Bruno? How did he get here?"

"I have no idea."

Dax jumped up and helped her to her feet. She dressed faster than Houdini could get out of chains when trapped underwater —all except for her shoes. They never made it to her feet before the flashing lights arrived.

The lights along the mine wall flickered on, implying the electricity had somehow been restored.

At least ten of the townspeople stood in front of them gawking—some with joy, others with surprise. Only a few had knowing faces. From her disheveled hair and the possible glow on her face, they might be able to guess what she and Dax had been doing. It didn't seem to matter that it was fairly dark in there.

Her prayer for a rescue had been answered, but she wished they had waited another hour, just long enough for them to finish making love.

"Make way," said a very familiar voice.

Her heart lurched. "Nana?" What was she doing here? Hell,

what was anyone doing there? It wasn't possible. She had to be dreaming.

When her grandmother broke through the crowd, she shone her light around the walls, spotlighting their supplies. "Jessie? Did you plan to stay down here forever?"

She laughed and then rushed to her grandmother, giving her the biggest hug. "No, of course not, but we were trapped. The elevator exploded. The lights went out. Never mind. I just want to get out of this grave."

Nana ran her light up and down Dax. "You all right, stud?"

"Peachy keen." Jessie heard the laughter in his voice, and her spirits lifted.

Nana looked confused. "Why is all this equipment here?"

Nana's curiosity was never ending. "I'll tell you everything when we get out of here."

"Hmm. I bet the girls will love to hear all about this." She gasped. "Did you check to see if everything was made in this world?"

"Versus the alien world? Why yes, I did. I checked the cans, bottles, and stoves. Everything was made in either the good ole U.S. of A. or the Republic of China." She'd done no such thing.

"Well, you never can be too careful." Nana stepped back and grabbed Jessie's arm. "You didn't find Roberta down here, did you?"

"No, Nana. If Roberta's here, she didn't stop by, but how did you get down here?"

"Come along, and I'll show you," Nana said.

"Let me put on my shoes." Nana threw her an interesting look, one that Jessie didn't want to dissect.

Dax doused the hurricane lamps then followed everyone down the tunnel. She'd made it no more than a few hundred feet when her grandmother stopped and pushed open a door that blended into the wall. Only now could she see how the handle was shaped like a curved rock, Flintstone style.

That was really clever. "When was that door put there?"

"Your grandfather had it installed years ago. We never told you about his hidden tunnel since we didn't want you to snoop around and get lost."

Jessie smiled at Papa's ingenuity. When their group entered the tunnel, wonderful, bright fluorescent tubing lit the narrow hallway, and suddenly her aches and pains disappeared.

Dax doused his light and his shoulders relaxed as he looked around. "I'm not believing this."

Nana tapped Jessie on the arm. "Your granddaddy had a fear of mine explosions. If the main entrance ever got blocked, he wanted another way out."

Jessie looked to the ceiling and mouthed a thank you. Hopefully, Papa was good at reading lips.

Nana had to stop several times to catch her breath, but she was determined to lead the way. She should have stayed up top and let the others handle the rescue, but that was Nana—stubborn to a fault.

Bruno stepped next to her and leaned close. "You all right, Jess? I mean really all right?" He nodded toward Dax as if the man had harmed her.

"I'm fine. Shaken up maybe, but if hadn't been for Dax, I would have been buried alive. He saved me."

A scowl crossed Bruno's face. "I'm glad. Just watch yourself." With that, he pushed ahead. It was as if once he'd delivered the warning, he could move on.

"A jealous lover?" Dax asked, returning to her side.

From the look on his face, she'd say Dax was the jealous one. "Maybe, but you don't have to worry about him."

The tunnel had to be a few hundred feet long, or at least it seemed that way. Finally, they came to another elevator shaft, one that looked newer, less used. The three of them went first since the elevator couldn't hold any more.

Emerging up top, they found themselves in a small room crammed full of empty, smelly coal cars, picks, and other mining equipment. The generator implied the town's electricity might not have been restored, but all Jessie could think about was fresh air and answers.

As they stepped into the clear air at the back of the mine, Jessie shielded her eyes from the blinding sun and took in a big breath. The freshness smelled sweeter than honeysuckle and wild roses on a summer day. She spun around, only now remembering seeing that door. Grandpa had said it led to a small room where he kept dangerous chemicals. She'd bought his story and never tried to sneak in.

Lena raced up to greet them. Black and blue rings marred her eyes, nose and mouth, and her smile looked a bit lopsided. "Jessie, ohmigod, I never thought I'd see you again. Was Roberta down there?" She glanced over Jessie's shoulder, as if she expected Seth to walk out any minute.

"No. There was no kidnapping." Jessie didn't need to discuss what happened.

"There wasn't?" She enveloped Jessie in a big hug. This time, Jessie didn't pull away, but stayed an extra moment to enjoy life. "I feel like such a fool for believing Seth's story."

"It's not your fault. We were all fooled."

Dax stepped up to Nana. "Margaret, may I borrow your car again for a very important mission while you drive Jessie's cruiser back to your house?"

She brightened. "I get to be sheriff for the day?" She practically jumped up and down. "Wait until I tell the girls. They'll be so jealous."

Jessie rushed up to them. "I'm not so sure about Nana driving. It's against regulations."

"Maybe, but it's damned hard to tail someone in a police car."

"Point taken." She dug in her pocket and dropped the keys in Nana's hand. "You have to promise me you won't go over the speed limit. I know how you like to race."

"Me? You must have me mixed up with Eleanor. Why, that woman is a terror behind the wheel."

Jessie rolled her eyes then turned to Dax. "I know time is

important, but given we're covered in dirt, could I at least get a change of clothing? We'll be spotted immediately if we go to the Navy Yard looking like this."

"You're right." He turned to Margaret. "Change in plans." He told her they'd both drive back to her place but that he'd need the Cadillac afterward." He glanced at his watch. "I hope we're not too late."

"We won't know until we reach a phone and call."

He smiled. "I love how practical you are. Let's go."

***

From Jessie's house, Dax was able to contact his former partner, Jake McCray, and explain what he knew about the impending nuclear disaster. Last year, Jake had transferred from Baltimore to the Annapolis area and would be in a good position to help.

"Only one nuclear sub is scheduled to be docked," Jake said. "It's the USS Edgemont. I'll contact the Admiral and see if he can put us on the list to get in."

"I'm no longer on the Force."

"True, but you have a high security clearance and defused bombs for the military. If explosives are involved, I want you to have my six."

"Can't hurt to ask him." Jessie came down stairs, cleaned up and ready to go. "We're heading out now. See you in ninety."

"Can he help?" she asked after Dax hung up.

"He's certainly going to try. Jake has a lot of connections. His wife's father is an Admiral at Annapolis."

"That's handy." She grabbed a service revolver from a drawer, nodded, and marched outside. Dax followed, pride heavy in his chest. Jessie Nash was one helluva woman.

For most of the drive, she remained quiet, and he was worried about her. He bet she'd been trying to make sense of her near death experience, the betrayal by her friend, and the possible radiation leak.

With little traffic to speak of, they arrived at the base a few minutes early. Jake had made good on his promise as their names were on the list.

"Will your friend be here?" she asked.

"If he's not, it means he's working furiously to pull as many strings as possible to make sure nothing happens to the sub." Dax did a quick sweep of the parking area that Jake told him would give him the best access to the sub. "Let me give him a call." He punched in Jake's number, thrilled at being once more connected with technology.

The phone rang and Dax drummed his fingers on the wheel. The sun might be shining, keeping Dax's demons asleep in their coffin, but things appeared almost too calm.

"Hey, ole buddy, where are you?" Jake sounded cheerful.

Dax tilted his head to hold the cell between his ear and shoulder while he maneuvered into the lot. He spotted the ship and hoped they weren't too late. "Where are you?" As if his ex-partner were a magician, Jake stepped from behind a vehicle right into Dax's path, forcing him to slam on his brakes. His relief washed away his anger. "You are such a jerk," Dax said without any malice and hung up.

Dax parked. "Wait here," he said to Jessie. He slid out and gave his old partner a bear hug. "You look good, you sly dog."

"You too. You learn anything more?"

"Nope."

Jake had been an officer in the Navy before joining the Baltimore PD. "I spoke to the Admiral who in turn called the commander in charge of the sub. He said there's been no breach."

Relief washed through him. "That's good. Either we arrived in time or it's an inside job going on now. Given the effort they took to stop us from snitching, I doubt it was a hoax."

"The Admiral is sending men, but you know how those things take time."

Jessie slid up next to him, and he introduced them. Even

though he'd asked her to stay put, it was probably best that the two meet.

"How do you know Amanda hasn't been here and gone?" she asked, her eyes glistening in the sun.

Dax scoured the park. "If she'd harmed the sub, the person in the control room would have the entire base here. We might actually be too early."

Jake straightened. "Since this is a terrorist operation, I also called a friend of mine at the FBI, but they're even slower to react."

"I guess some things don't change. You ready?" Dax asked Jake.

"You bet."

Here goes. The shit was about to hit the fan the moment he told Jessie he wasn't taking her onto the sub. He was about to explain her role when she held out her hand and pointed to a white Ford Taurus. "That's Amanda's car."

"You sure? There must be a hundred white Ford Taurus's in the lot."

"See the little turtle on the back of her bumper?"

"Ferocious little bugger. What about it?"

"Our tenth high school reunion is in two weeks and the turtle was our mascot. Brian gave both of us stickers. When we get back, take a look at my cruiser. I put it on my bumper."

"Well, God Bless Brian. Remind me to thank him." If Amanda was nearby, they could be sitting ducks standing there. Not that he expected them to show their faces, but one couldn't be too careful. "Jess, please don't argue, but I want you to stay by the car in case Amanda manages to escape." He handed her the keys.

Her lips pursed. Crap. She wasn't going to buy it. "Fine, but only because my leg isn't strong enough to run."

Halleluiah. Dax leaned over and kissed her hard. "Wish us luck."

"Luck." She smiled, threatening to undo his resolve to leave her.

Jake grabbed his arm. "Let's go, good buddy."

***

Jessie smiled sweetly as Dax and his friend hiked to the sub platform. She couldn't believe he told her to wait by the car. After all that had happened, he didn't seem to understand her after all.

Jessie moved Nana's vehicle and parked ten cars away from Amanda's. Jessie slipped out and kept her gaze on the submarine. A guard stopped both men, checked their names on his list, and then let them enter. Jake's connections must have been very powerful. Jessie wondered who Amanda had diddled to get by the guard, assuming she personally showed up. Then again, perhaps being a former Navy person entitled her to go where she wished.

As soon as Dax and Jake disappeared into the sub, Jessie waited a few minutes then followed. Her leg ached from sitting in the car for so long, but she couldn't let a little pain get in her way.

As she made her way across the parking lot toward the guard, she saw him tap the mic on his shoulder. Hopefully, Jake didn't mention what might be happening below or he'd never let her down there. With her head held high, Jessie climbed the metal steps. When she reached the guard, she flashed her badge, hoping he wouldn't look too closely. A sheriff in West Virginia had no jurisdiction in Annapolis.

"I'm sorry, ma'am. It's not safe for you to go below."

She was afraid he'd say that. "You just let a police officer and a private investigator in there. I have it on good authority that—"

Before she could finish her sentence, gunfire rang out from inside the sub and every muscle in her body shot to alert. Indecision twisted her mind. As much as she wanted to make sure Dax wasn't hurt, she needed to be ready to stop Amanda if she managed to escape.

Jessie flipped around and nearly tripped going back down the steps. The guard was shouting to someone over his mic, and she anticipated a deluge of officers to appear any moment. Gun ready, she found cover and waited.

Shouts sounded, feet stomped, and a mass of soldiers descended. Those who entered didn't come out, and with each second that passed without seeing Dax, a piece of her heart died.

CHAPTER TWENTY-SEVEN

Sirens sounded in the background, and when Jessie spotted the ambulances, her stomach tumbled. Either someone had been injured, or the paramedics were here as a precaution.

No one had exited the sub in the last fifteen minutes, which meant Amanda was either dead, injured, had been captured, or had never been on the sub in the first place. Jessie refused to believe anything bad had happened to Dax—not with all he'd been through.

As much as Jessie wanted to see if he was okay, she'd never be admitted entry now. Several paramedics raced by her, pushing two gurneys toward the boat. She debated following them, but she didn't want to get in the way. A sub wasn't a place with lots of room.

Now that the danger seemed to be over, Jessie stood and eased closer. Six minutes later, Dax came out next to a man on a stretcher. It was Jake. Damn. Ignoring the pain in her leg, she raced toward them, and this time the guard didn't try to stop her. Lines creased Dax's face, but otherwise he looked unhurt.

She wanted to hug and kiss him, but his distant gaze made her stay back. "Dax?"

He turned toward her and a small smile lit his lips. "It's over."

He then squeezed his hand's friend. "You'll be running in no time," Dax said. Jake held up his middle finger and Dax's smile widened.

As soon as the paramedics loaded Jake into the ambulance, she faced him. "What about Amanda and the nuclear leak?"

"We stopped it in time, but I'm afraid she's dead. I'm sorry."

"I'm not sure I am. Tell me what happened."

His lips pressed together as he maneuvered them away from the entryway. "We informed the Captain of our suspicions, but he maintained there hadn't been a breach. At that point, there was nothing more we could do. As we were about to leave, the power went out."

She grabbed his arm. "Oh, no."

"Believe it or not, the panic never came. Several officers had lights, so we headed to the power station. The Captain was the one who decided our concern had merit. One man we ran into said three other people, all of whom had proper paperwork, had entered the area of the nuclear reactor earlier. Knowing time was crucial, we decided not to wait for back up, and a group of us went in. I forgot to remind the two naval officers to douse their lights, and before we could react, one of the insurgents opened fire." He swallowed.

"Was that when Jake was hit?"

Dax stabbed a hand through his hair. "Yes."

Jessie placed her head on his chest and wrapped her arms around him. "He'll be okay, right?"

Dax tightened his hold. "Yes, with rehab."

She leaned back. "You said Amanda was with two other people. What happened to them?"

"As soon as the insurgents opened fire on us, we returned shots. That's when Amanda went down, but until they remove the bullet from the body, we won't know who had the kill shot. Seth, Lena's beau, was injured, and the third man is in custody." He nodded to the gangway. "Here's Seth now."

Two paramedics carried Seth out on a gurney, an oxygen

mask covering his face and tubes coming out of him like he was some kind of human octopus. It didn't look good for him. A moment later, a man was taken off the ship in handcuffs.

Something about him tickled her mind, but she couldn't pinpoint why he looked familiar. "If Seth was involved, it was no wonder he wanted Lena to tell me about the faked kidnapping. It was a ploy to get me into the mine, and I fell for it."

He stroked her hair. "Don't be so hard on yourself."

Before Dax could say anything more, a uniformed man who might have been handsome had it not been for the black eye and bloodied lips, charged up the ramp. He was immediately detained by two MPs. "I need to speak with the Captain, goddamn it," the man yelled. "Let go of me and that's an order." The MP said something, but she couldn't make out the words. "There's been a nuclear breach."

Dax squeezed her arm and headed back up the plank. She followed.

"Sir? The leak has been contained," Dax said.

The man's legs crumpled, and both Dax and the MP helped him up. "Thank God." He twisted around. "I need to find my daughter then. That woman kidnapped her."

The word kidnapped had Jessie's pulse race. The woman he referred to was most likely Amanda. "Sir," she said, "we might be able to help."

The tall officer brushed off his uniform. He looked down at her. "And who are you?" His voice cracked.

She flashed her badge. "Sheriff Jessie Nash from Kerry, West Virginia. You said someone took your daughter?"

"Yes, a woman and a man took Kendall. I'm embarrassed to say they threatened me, saying that if I didn't give them some information that would help them sabotage the sub, they would kill her." His whole body shook.

She didn't want to say they probably planned to kill her whether he helped Amanda or not.

Dax stepped up behind her. "Do you know if she's still alive?"

"She was a little while ago. That woman let me talk to her on a satellite phone."

Dax's face brightened. "Satellite phone?"

"Yes, why?"

"If Amanda used one of those, ten bucks your daughter's back in Kerry."

"Please," the father pleaded. "Kendall is eight months pregnant. I need to find her."

Dax wrapped an arm around Jessie as he spoke to the man. "It's a ninety minute ride back. There's no guarantee that's where she is, but it's my best guess. You're welcome to come with us."

"Thank you. I'll call one of my men to meet me there so we can bring Kendall back home."

The three of them climbed into Nana's Cadillac. She rode shotgun while the officer slipped in the back. Jake's car sat empty, forlorn, abandoned. Dax might feel responsible for what happened, but it wasn't his fault. He hadn't pulled the trigger.

"I'm Dr. Mark Jalbert, by the way."

She nodded to the bruises on his face. "May I ask what happened to you?"

Dr. Jalbert explained how they'd used a lot of physical force to make him cooperate. "I could handle the pain, but I didn't want them to harm Kendall. The woman let me speak with her for only a few seconds. She then took off, leaving one man to watch me. They'd rightfully assumed I would have gone to the authorities for help. The man who tied me up didn't do a good job, and I managed to free myself. When he wasn't paying attention, I charged him."

Jessie could fill in the rest. "I'm glad you managed to escape. Did this woman have short blonde hair and a killer body?"

"Yes."

Then it had been Amanda. She turned back around. Dax was driving too fast, as though someone was on his tail, but she said nothing, letting him work through what happened.

Dax glanced in the rear view mirror at their passenger.

"When you spoke with your daughter, did she give any clue where she was being held captive?"

He shook his head. "I didn't speak with her long enough."

"The ring leader lived in Kerry, and I'm betting your daughter is somewhere in town." He glanced over at her. "Jessie, do you know where Amanda was living?"

"No, but I bet her mom knows."

***

By the time Dax pulled into town, he'd gone over the incident on the sub a hundred times. As soon as they entered the ship, Jake had pushed ahead of him and the other Navy men, claiming he was the law officer. Even if Jake had worn a flak jacket, it wouldn't have stopped the bullet to his leg. Dax sure hoped the injury wasn't too serious.

"Take a left at the next street," Jessie said jerking him out of his painful mental movie.

The road only had a few homes, all of which looked below poverty level. A strong ache twisted his gut. He used to live in a place just like one of these after his dad died.

"It's the next house on the right," she said, and Dax pulled over. "I think it would be better if I go alone. Amanda's mom can be a little, ah...mean."

Like mother like daughter, he supposed. "I'll wait outside by the front just in case something happens."

"The woman is sickly. She's not going to attack me."

"Suit yourself."

He still didn't want to be far from Jessie, so as soon as she disappeared, he piled out of the front seat. Avoiding the living room window, he rushed close to the porch. He didn't think Amanda would stash a pregnant lady at her mom's house, but one never could be sure.

When Jessie didn't come out in a reasonable time, he snuck around the back and looked in the kitchen window. Past a doorway and down a hallway, Jessie and an older lady wrapped in a blanket were chatting in the living room. He guessed Jessie needed to make some small talk before extracting the information from Amanda's mom. At some point, Jessie would have to tell Mrs. Simmons that her daughter was dead.

By the time he made it back to the front, Jessie was outside waving at the mom.

"Got it," she said with more enthusiasm than he'd heard from her in a while.

"Did she say where Kendall is?" Mr. Jalbert asked as soon as they were inside the car.

"No, but she told me where Amanda had been staying."

Jessie directed Dax to a paint chipped farmhouse in a part of town he hadn't visited before. They passed acres and acres of fallow land, unloved by the human hands, and sadness colored every leaf and blade of grass. To say the place needed some repair was an understatement. An old blue car sat in the drive.

"What's the plan?" she asked.

He appreciated Jessie was willing to let him help. Knowing how much she couldn't stand to sit still, he decided to let her take the lead. "While you knock on the front door, I'll go around back. And Mark? Care to be my backup?"

"Absolutely." The man sounded willing and able.

Jessie eased out of the front seat. She unbuttoned her jacket most likely to give her easier access to her weapon. As she knocked on the front door, he and Mark jogged to the back, where Dax quietly tested the handle and found it locked.

"Psst." Mark waved him over to the side of the house. He was smiling. "Kendall's in there," he mouthed.

Needing to assess the safety of the scene, Dax motioned Mark to move out of sight. He then chanced a look. The only occupant was a pregnant woman, tied up in a corner, seemingly unharmed, and he let out a long held breath.

She looked up and her eyes widened. He held a finger to his lips and she nodded.

Now that he knew Kendall's location in the house, Dax used hand signals to indicate they needed to go in through the back, figuring the old farmhouse probably wouldn't have state of the art locks. A quick swipe of his credit card between the jamb and the wall confirmed he was right. The back door eased opened without a sound. Had it not been for Jake's injury, he'd say it was his lucky day.

The place smelled of hotdogs and sauerkraut, which made his nose wrinkle. He never could stand the stench of cooked cabbage. Jessie was already inside, her voice chatty but a little nervous. She must know the person keeping guard over Kendall.

Keep him talking, Jessie.

Dax pulled out his Glock from his holster then handed Mark the twenty-two he kept at his ankle, hoping Kendall's dad wouldn't need to use it.

Dax held up his hand for Mark to stay put, and thankfully the man nodded his assent. With the guard's back to him, Dax slipped into the living room as quietly as he could. Jessie kept the kidnapper talking, never indicating anyone else was in the house. The man was small and would be easy to take down. From the back, he looked like a kid. Not wanting to use more force than necessary, Dax stepped behind him and wrapped his left arm around the kidnapper's neck.

"Hey!" The man struggled, grabbing Dax's arm with both hands, trying to pry his arm away. He failed. For effect more than anything, Dax shoved the gun to the kid's temple.

"Jess, go get Kendall. She's in the bedroom." He yelled to Mark to help him secure Amanda's assistant.

Footsteps pounded. "What do you want me to do?" Mark asked.

"Find some rope so we can tie him up."

Jessie must have heard him, for she yelled from the bedroom. "There's enough rope and duct tape in here to build a fort."

Once Dax secured the kid, he asked him his name.

"What's it to you?" Dax pressed the gun barrel against the

captive's neck this time. The kid groaned and Dax let up on some of the pressure.

Before he could ask him again, Jessie and Mark brought a shaking but smiling Kendall to the living room. Dax sure loved happy endings. When he used to work homicide, he rarely saw this kind of joy.

"He's Hunter Ransom, Amanda's cousin," Jessie said.

"Where's Amanda?" Hunter demanded, acting as though he wasn't about to be taken into custody.

Sympathy was written all over Jessie's face. "I'm afraid she's dead."

"You're lying."

"We aren't." Dax dragged him over to the sofa and made him sit down. "How old are you, kid?"

Hunter struck a pose of defiance. "Nineteen."

"Too bad for you." That meant prison instead of Juvie.

"What happened to the two people with her?" Hunter asked, suddenly sounding scared.

Jessie sat down on the sofa next to him. "Seth was shot, and I'm not sure if he'll make it. The other man is in custody. It's over Hunter."

Amanda's cousin closed his eyes and leaned back against the couch. "So who blew it? Seth or George?"

Jessie stilled.

"What is it, Jess?" Dax asked.

"George who?"

Hunter opened his eyes and shrugged. Dax stepped forward waving the gun. Not that he'd ever shoot a helpless person, but Hunter didn't know that.

"George Richards."

Jess's mouth dropped open. "Brian's brother?"

"Yup."

"Well, shit."

CHAPTER TWENTY-EIGHT

Jessie awoke to the rich aroma of coffee, her head still pounding from all the stress. She couldn't believe the nightmare was over —that Amanda, who'd admitted killing Clinton and Sadie, was dead. Her former friend also took credit for a lot of other crimes, but Jessie would just have to take her word she'd committed them.

Her visit to Judge Simmons seemed surreal even now. He looked almost proud when she told him the news of his daughter's death, acting as if Amanda had done something heroic for the first time in her life. It disgusted Jessie to think that kind of man was an elected officer in her town. If she'd had proof that he'd assaulted his daughter, she would have hauled his ass into jail.

She sat up in bed and remembered there was a mass and then a closed casket service for both Sadie and Clinton at six tonight. When they'd bury Amanda was anyone's guess.

Jessie shoved off the covers, shivered from the cold, and rushed to get dressed. Dax had said he'd be leaving this morning, and she wanted to say goodbye. Actually, what she really wanted was to throw herself in his arms and beg him to stay, but deep in her heart, she knew he had to leave. Kerry offered nothing for him, and she'd never abandon Nana to work in Baltimore. His hometown might be nice, but big city life wasn't for her.

Her cousin, Sky Nash, worked in New Mexico at the sheriff's department and frequently suggested she check out her neck of the woods, but Jessie had always said no. She liked the Kerry people too much because for the most part, they were hard working, honest citizens. This town represented who she was—a small town girl.

Jessie pulled on the denim skirt and sweater Amanda bought for her. *Amanda, Amanda.* Jessie decided to remember the fun loving side of her, and not the woman who'd turned bad. Some memories should be kept, while others needed to be discarded.

Jessie went downstairs, holding onto the handrail. From all the activity yesterday, her leg was bothering her, but she wouldn't let on. Dax would worry.

He and Nana were at the table talking softly. When he looked up then glanced away, her heart cracked. She couldn't tell from that quick look if he was feeling guilty for leaving or excited to get back to his fast paced life.

"Sit down, dear. Let me get you some breakfast."

"Thanks, Nana."

Jessie rubbed her forehead, trying to make the throbbing go away. Stress, depression, and frustration were doing a real number on her head. She inhaled and painted on a semi-cheery smile "So when are you taking off?"

"After I finish eating."

Say something. Tell him you've fallen in love with him. When she opened her mouth to speak her mind, the words wouldn't form, and begging wasn't her style.

Now that both murder cases had been cleared, the town would settle down and life would turn dull. It wouldn't be fair to ask him to stay.

Nana pushed open the kitchen door with her butt and carried in a feast. "I can't eat all that food," Jessie said.

"Do your best."

Maybe if she ate slowly, Dax would stay a bit longer. Aw, hell, it would serve no purpose to delay the inevitable. Whether he left in ten minutes or an hour from now the pain would be equally as intense.

The smell of scrambled eggs and bacon made her mouth water, but when she took her first bite, her appetite disappeared. Not wanting Nana to notice her listlessness, Jessie chewed each tasteless bite, one after another. Finally, she set her fork on the plate. Dax Mitchell was about to walk out of her life and she wasn't going to stop him. *What a wimp.*

"Dax, I have to get to the station, so why don't I walk you out?" she said, her gaze focused on her coffee cup. Jessie couldn't look at him, or rather wouldn't look at him, because if she did, she might cry.

"Why, Jessie Nash," Nana said. "Are you trying to get rid of your young man?"

"No, Nana, but the sooner he leaves—"

"The sooner you can get to work," Dax and Nana said in unison.

Jessie shook her head and a small smile lifted her lips. "You two are a pair."

Dax looked uncomfortable as he pushed back his chair. "Margaret, it was a pleasure meeting you. I wish it had been under better circumstances." He hugged her and Jessie swore Nana's eyes watered.

"Now, don't talk like it's so final. Maryland is but a hop, skip, and a jump away. Don't be a stranger. You know you'll always be welcome."

"Thank you. I'll try to stop by."

Dax picked up his suitcase and Jessie followed him out, her heart breaking. He stuffed his gear in the front seat of his truck, turned back toward her, and ran a callused thumb down her cheek. Her pulse fluttered. *Tell me how incredible I am and that you can't live without me.*

The breeze pushed her hair over her face, and Dax hooked a

strand behind her ear. His touch sent shivers of delight through her.

Don't cry, don't cry. Be strong.

"Hope you get the sheriff's position," Dax said lowering his hand. He opened his mouth then shut it.

Was he about to tell her he loved her but couldn't stay? He squeezed her arm and hopped in the driver's side. Jessie remained in her drive, seeing her breath frost in the air, but feeling no cold.

When his truck was out of sight, she dragged herself inside, but the second she stepped in the door, she knew there was going to be trouble. Nana stood there with her hands on her hips. "Why didn't you tell him you loved him?"

"Nana, sometimes there are things better left unsaid. Can we discuss this later? I have to get to the station and tell Brian about his brother being back in town."

"All right, but we are going to have that discussion whether you like it or not. Remember, the funeral's at six."

"I'll be there."

Nana ducked back into the kitchen.

Great. Now, even her grandmother was pissed off at her. Jessie grabbed her bag and Pea coat and headed to the cruiser. She should have been ecstatic that she'd solved all the crimes in the given time frame, only she wasn't. She wanted to crawl in a hole and mourn the loss of her friend, mourn the loss of the one man she'd grown to love in such a short period, and mourn the loss of the town's innocence.

She parked in her usual spot in front of the office, and as she trod up the steps, she frowned at the wilted flowers, once so pretty but now dried up. They were like her—the dried up part, not the once pretty part.

When she entered the office, the former deputy, Frank, had his feet propped up on the desk and Lena was pouring him coffee. The domestic scene almost made her smile.

As quickly as was possible for Frank, he dropped his feet to the floor. "Oh, hi, Jessie. Didn't expect you in today after all that happened."

"I have work to do."

Hunter sat in one cell, Brian in the other, and both looked miserable.

She turned to Brian. "Did Hunter tell you about George coming back to town?" Jessie asked.

Brian looked sheepish. "Yeah, but Hunter didn't let the cat out of the bag. I knew George was here. Hell, he'd already moved into the house before I arrived in town."

"He had? Why didn't you tell me?"

"I didn't want to get him into any more trouble. He was the one who created the meth lab. Not me. I wanted to tell you, Jess, I swear, but I couldn't. He's my brother."

She stepped up to his cell. "Did you know he planned to sabotage the nuclear sub?" She couldn't believe Brian would keep such a secret, especially when National Security was involved.

"No! I swear. George never breathed a word about why he was here. You've got to believe me."

The desperation in his voice broke her heart.

"Jessie," Lena said. "You've got to let Brian go. He's innocent."

"Innocent of making meth, perhaps, but not of harboring a criminal or knowing about the lab."

"She's right, Lena," Brian said. "I'll take whatever punishment is due."

Jessie turned back to Brian. "Why didn't you tell me you'd been arrested for stealing guns?"

"Brian?" Lena said. The softness in her tone implied she'd gone sweet on him.

"I was framed. I know you won't believe me, but as God is my witness, it's the truth."

"We will have to wait for the new judge to decide." First, she had to call the mayor and report what Amanda said about her father. With her death, it might be a case of he said, she said, but it would be a real shame if the man got off. While Judge Simmons was being investigated—by hopefully an unbiased sheriff from a different town—Kerry would need to bring in someone else to settle the disputes.

"Thanks."

A knock sounded on the door, and Jessie turned, half expecting the loving duo of Kreplick and Lucas to prance into her office and tell her they didn't care that she'd solved the crimes. They wanted a man to be sheriff.

But it wasn't them. It was... "Roberta?" Joy raced through her. She couldn't believe Nana's friend was alive.

The sleeve of her dress was torn, her hair looked like rats had taken up residence, and her face was smudged with dirt. But damn if the woman wasn't smiling and seemed to have more pep in her step than ever.

Lena and she rushed over to greet her. "Roberta? Are you okay?"

"Hi, Jess, Lena," Roberta said in a rather dreamy way. She looked up at Frank. "Hi, Frank." Roberta tugged on her blouse as if she were flirting with the old guy.

Jessie dragged over a chair. "Please, sit down. We've all been so worried about you."

Roberta sat. "I don't know why. I've had the most wonderful adventure."

Jessie couldn't fathom how something that left a person a mess could be so wonderful. "Tell me what happened."

"I fell in love."

"You did? So where is Mr. Wonderful?"

Roberta glanced upward. "He had to go back to his home planet."

Home planet? She had to be kidding. All the joy drained out of Jessie. Someone had stolen the woman's mind and replaced it with oatmeal. "Roberta, tell me what really happened," she pleaded.

Roberta stood, and as if she were in a trance, walked over to

Clinton's desk. The bomb detector with its colorfully lit buttons sat on top, and Roberta picked it up. "Where did you get this?" Her eyes shone with excitement.

"We found it in Cyril Harper's barn." Amanda must have dropped it. "Why?"

"My alien used it on me. I can't tell you how wonderful I felt afterwards."

Refusing to dwell on the implications, Jessie didn't know whether to laugh or cry.

**

With every mile Dax drove away from Kerry, his heart grew heavier. Yes, Jessie was the woman for him, but if he'd stayed, he'd only be in her way. She liked her space and liked to take control. He couldn't ask her to change—for him.

Ask her, fool. Find out for sure what she wants.

Mile after mile, Dax ignored his conscience. He was doing what was best for both of them. As he neared home, he pulled into a gas station to fill up. When he was about to slide up to a vacant pump, a shiny, black Mercedes slipped in front of him and took his spot. Nerves frayed, anger blasted him. He bet that level of rudeness would never happen in Kerry.

Dax jerked the gear into reverse, backed up, and waited for another pump to free up. Once he finished, he opened his wallet to put back his credit card, and the photo of his fiancée smiled up at him. This time the familiar rush of seeing her face didn't materialize. While Laura had been a pretty woman, she'd never been as warm as Jessie. Sure, Laura and he enjoyed each other, but Jessie and he were soul mates on a molecular level. She understood him like no one else ever had.

He fingered the photo, regretting he'd never taken even one picture of Jessie.

Jessie.

A small smile lifted his lips. Never once had she made fun of his limp or for him not having a *real* job as his brother David would say. Hell, Jessie didn't even mock him when she'd learned of his panic attacks. Dax shook his head. When he had been with Laura, his hormones had ruled him, not love. After meeting Jessie, he finally understood what a true relationship could be like.

I love her. Plain and simple.

Yet, here he was, about to return to Baltimore to be surrounded by people he never spoke to. Hell, he barely knew the man who lived next door to him. That wasn't any way to live. Odd as it sounded, he knew more people in Kerry than he did in his own town where he'd lived in for so many years.

Go back to her. If she shoots you down at least you tried.

Decision made. Dax charged out of the station and headed back the way he came, hoping he wasn't going to make a fool of himself. Happy he was letting his heart be his guide, he studied his surroundings. As he neared Kerry, the leaves appeared greener, the houses neater, and the sky brighter. The ride back grew prettier and prettier the closer he came to Kerry—pretty, just like Jessie.

With no clouds to block the sun, Dax rolled down his windows and turned on the truck's heater. He wanted to feel the air on his face, smell the freshness of the air, and enjoy the fact he was alive.

As he approached the town, he pulled over before he crossed the bridge to Kerry and stepped out. He looked down at the town like he had before. For some reason, the one road in and one road out didn't bother him anymore. This time, the glistening water spoke of welcome and not of some dark evil. He knew what he had to do, and if Jessie said no, he'd stay until she changed her mind.

Dax Mitchell wasn't going to let the best thing in his life get away from him.

***

Jessie was tired and hungry. She leaned back in the office chair, pleased Brian wasn't the bad man she thought after all. She would have felt guilty if she'd had a hand in putting him away for a few years if he had been innocent.

Even better news, Lena hadn't gone to pieces when she'd learned about Seth's injury. In fact, she too seemed pleased that he got what he deserved. But perhaps the most astonishing news was that Roberta had come back safe and sound. Nana was going to be the happiest woman alive when she learned of her friend's adventure.

Frank must have noticed Roberta for the first time because he offered to escort her home, and knowing him, he'd probably ask her out to dinner. Frank might not be an alien, but she bet he'd give Roberta some much-needed attention. Somehow, Roberta would have to figure out a way to let Doc down and not hurt his feelings.

Jessie closed her eyes and sighed. The circle had closed on so many issues. The only hole left open was for Mayor Kreplick to stop by and drop the bomb that she could kiss her job goodbye.

Hell, maybe it would be a good thing if they kicked her out of town. If Nana were willing, perhaps they'd sell the house and move to New Mexico. She hadn't seen her cousin in years, but Sky always said they were looking for more officers.

On the other hand, Jessie could go to Baltimore and look up Dax, or had finding Sadie been just another job to him? Sure, when he was trapped in the mine and thought they would die, he treated her like no other man ever had, but if he'd really cared, he wouldn't have left.

She hated self-pity, but right now she wasn't in the mood for anything else. She'd wallow in sorrow for a while, then pick herself up, dust herself off, and go on as if none of this nastiness had ever happened. It was how the Nash women handled life.

The door creaked open, and she sagged against her seat. *Here comes the brush off from the mayor.* Jessie swiveled around to face the next tragedy in Kerry.

"Hello," said the sexiest man alive.

"D-Dax! What are you doing here?" Jessie shot up out of her chair and pressed her hands down her skirt then tried to detangle her hair, but adrenaline, lust, and excitement, ripped the air from her lungs.

He walked toward her with a gleam in his eye. "I want you to come with me." He held out his hand.

"Where?"

He let out a loud breath. "Jessie, trust me. Okay?"

"I want to but I can't leave."

The door opened again and Frank strolled in. "Heard you needed some coverage."

Dax glanced back and nodded. Wasn't he the sly old dog? "Okay then," she said with a smile.

"Better bring your coat," Dax said. "There's a chill in the air."

She nabbed her purse too, just in case. In case of what, she didn't know, but she wanted to be prepared. Holding hands, they crossed the street and headed south, which meant they weren't going to the diner. His truck was parked in front, so they probably weren't going far. Jessie couldn't fathom what he was up to, but as long as that something involved Dax, she was willing.

Peter Lucas stepped out of the bank, waved, and walked down the street. She expected him to rush over and rant about how the town had suffered so much because of her incompetence, but instead he smiled and strolled on. After all, Kerry had lost electricity for several hours because she'd pissed off Amanda, and no telling if Mr. Catchman would sue once he found out his precious mine had been ruined.

Cars dashed down the street, people honked, and the fresh smell of fall filled the air. Dax kept looking down at her and smiling, and she wanted to ask him what was going on, but then decided to let him take the lead.

When he turned into the Kerry Hotel, she halted. "Are you crazy? I can't just waltz into the hotel with you?"

"Why not?"

"How would that look to the good citizens of Kerry if I spent an afternoon in a room with a man?"

He had the gall to laugh. "I think they'd clap. I'm sure most of the town is waiting to see that in-control veneer of yours crack. Come on, Jessie. Lighten up. It's the twenty-first century, not the eighteen hundreds."

She looked around. The clerk at the front desk was on the phone not paying her any mind, and two city councilmen were having a drink in the front parlor seemingly unaware they'd even come in. Aw hell. Life was too short, as Sadie always said. "Lead the way."

"Yes." Dax practically raced toward the elevator.

When he pushed the button several times, she had to laugh. "It doesn't come any faster if you press it more than once."

"I know, but I don't want you to change your mind."

"Me change my mind? Why would I do that? You haven't told me what you have planned." Well, okay, she could guess—Dax, bed, sex, wow.

The elevator doors opened and she and Dax stepped in. She almost expected him to kiss her in the confined space until she remembered he probably wasn't comfortable in the three-foot by four-foot box.

As soon as they reached his floor, he rushed out and led her down the corridor where the soft carpet cushioned her tired feet. Dax stopped at room 304, swiped the keycard, and twisted the handle.

When Jessie stepped in, her heart almost stopped.

CHAPTER TWENTY-NINE

"You like it?" Dax held his breath.

"Like it? Are you kidding? It's incredible. What woman wouldn't love a room lined with candles and a bed sprinkled with rose petals? It's dark, yet light at the same time. Cozy, comforting, wonderful. When did you have time to do this?"

"I called the hotel. The concierge has many talents."

"I never knew."

He smiled. "One of the reasons I wanted to hurry was that I didn't want to burn down the hotel. They'd fire you for sure."

She huffed out a laugh. "I don't know what to say."

He turned Jessie around to face him, loving her vulnerability, her strength, and her honesty. She was everything he wanted in a woman. She might act tough, but inside she was marshmallow soft. He dragged a thumb across her lips, and her dreamy eyes almost melted him to the spot. "You don't have to say anything."

"Dax, I'm not sure about this." She swept a hand at the bed and candles.

A rush of anxiety nearly crushed him. "What about *this* aren't you sure?"

"I mean. Once we make love, what will happen to *us*?"

Jumping out of a plane couldn't match the rush he got from that one word—us.

He drew her face to him and lightly kissed her supple, sexy lips. "What will happen? I'm no fortune-teller, but I can take a guess. First, we'll buy a house of our own then we'll populate it with about a dozen kids. Who knows what will happen after that." He edged her against the bed.

Her expression slowly changed from concern to joy. "You want to stay here, with me?"

He laughed. "I want to more than stay with you. I want to marry you, make love to you every day of our lives, and share all the wonders of the world with you."

"Marry me?"

"Yes, but you'll need to wait for a ring."

"But what will you do for a living?" She didn't care about the ring—at least not yet.

He dragged a finger down her forehead then tapped her on the nose. "Do you have to be so practical all the time?"

She bit her lower lip and his dick shot to attention. He pressed on her shoulder, forcing her to sit and then slid next to her. He gathered her in his arms and loved how her body molded against his.

Jessie glanced down and fumbled with his jacket. "I guess not, but how are we ever going to buy a house without money?" she asked, worry lines creasing her forehead.

He released his hold for a moment, slipped off her jacket then tugged off his own. "I guess I could get a job or I can always commute to Baltimore if I have to," he said.

"But then I'd miss you too much."

"Is that so?" Joy shot through every part of him. He took off her pretty sweater, trying not to rush, and then leaned her back onto the petals, her perky breasts begging to be suckled and caressed. "I've never touched the life insurance money from when my father died. It's been building interest for close to thirty years. It's more than enough to buy a mansion for our dozen kids."

"I wouldn't want you to do that."

"Then maybe you'd let me work with you, huh? Be your deputy?"

She grabbed his arms. "Really? You'd work for me? Do as I say?"

He laughed. "I'd be willing to work for you. Let's not get carried away with the doing-what-you-say part."

"Hmm. I guess I could ask the town council what they think."

Dax unhooked her bra and lowered the straps over her shoulders. "You have the most beautiful tits." He dipped his head and licked her brown nipples, first the right one and then the left, and her moans made his balls draw up tight. "You know, you never answered me about whether you'd be willing to marry me," he murmured trying not to pressure her.

"I never answered?" She rolled out of his grasp, stretched onto her side, and faced him. She ran a hand from his Adam's apple across his abs and straight to the bulge in his pants.

"No, you haven't, but I'm willing to wait for as long as you need."

"I thought it would be more fun to show you my answer instead."

He did a mental fist pump. "I like that idea."

"Don't move."

Dax wasn't sure he could handle her hands all over his body and not taste her, touch her, and love her. Jessie sat up, unbuttoned his pants, and pulled them down over his knees. He swore she purposely let her knuckles rub against his cock just to torment him even more. Her warm hands then slid down his thigh almost causing him to prematurely go off—something he wanted to avoid at all cost. She then struggled to take off his boots.

"Let me help." Dax jerked off his footwear then discarded his jeans and briefs. All that was left was his shirt. "You want to do the honors?" He must be a masochist because delaying their lovemaking was killing him.

Jessie dragged her palms under his shirt, setting his skin on fire, and slowly lifted the material over his head. As soon as she tossed it aside, she smiled. "I love your chest and your abs." Her gaze lowered.

"And?"

She grabbed his dick. "This looks like something I might like to test drive."

"I'll be driving it into you in a moment. Now it's my turn to divest you of your clothes."

He tugged off her shoes and socks then pulled down her skirt. His pulse soared as he imagined plunging into her. The only thing preventing that from happening was her pretty lace panties. He ran a finger along the edge and inhaled deeply, enjoying her feminine scent.

"I love you, Jessie Nash." Dax held his breath waiting for her to answer, but all she did was smile. He slid on top of her, taking most of his weight on his elbows.

"I can't wait any longer," she panted.

That wasn't the answer he was looking for, but he was a patient man.

"I want to take my time and enjoy every inch of your body." He kissed her neck and worked his way up to her lips.

She grabbed his head and drew him closer. "I've wanted to make love with you since that moment in the mine. I'm more than ready now." She shook her head. "Who am I kidding? I've wanted you for a lot longer than that."

He hoped that meant she loved him. "Let's get you out of those panties then."

Jessie wiggled out of them before he had a chance to take them off. She reached between them and grabbed his raging hard-on. Dear God how his woman could drive him wild.

"Get on your back," she commanded.

The last time he let her suck on his cock, he was barely able to hold on. "I thought you were ready."

"I'm more than ready." Jessie pressed on his chest, a determined look on her face.

Heaven help him. On her knees, Jessie drew him deep into her mouth, and he nearly came off the bed. He fisted her hair with one hand, reached around to the side with the other, and cupped her breast. He rubbed his thumb across her distended nipple, loving how the tips hardened under his caress.

Her pumping motion increased to the point where he was about to explode. He grabbed her wrist and flipped her over. "My turn."

***

"Hurry," she said.

"Not on your life." Damn man had the audacity to smile.

Jessie grabbed the sheets as Dax slid between her legs, reached up, and twirled a nipple, sending sparks of need straight to her core. She'd fantasized about doing this all last night, but her imagination didn't come close to the reality.

With his other hand, he threaded his fingers through her curls and opened her folds wide. The first touch had her reeling. Electric pulses skittered over her belly, igniting her deep inside. She planted her feet on the bed and scooted closer, wanting more of his mouth, more of him. "I love you, Dax Mitchell," she whispered.

While she couldn't see him smile, his response was to flick his tongue over her sensitive bud until heat swamped her. Releasing the sheet, she clawed his shoulders, and then lifted her hips. Each swipe sent her closer to that climactic edge as chaos swirled inside her.

When he slipped his fingers into her, she fought not to come. This first time, she wanted it to be special in finding their total bliss together. She wiggled her butt, loving the soft, velvet rose petals caressing her skin. "I need you."

Dax lifted up and grinned. "Do you want me to use a condom?"

"I'm on the pill." Though she could see stopping that in the future. "I need you now."

Instead of impaling her, he dragged his tongue up her belly, leaving goose bumps in its wake. She reached between them and tugged, trying to line up their bodies, but he ignored her.

"Let me love you the only way I know how."

His sensuous words caused a torrent of ecstasy to shoot through her. "Oh, yes."

Dax settled over her and kissed her deeply, his tongue making love to her mouth. When he opened her thighs with his knees, she couldn't get enough oxygen into her lungs. Overwhelmed with desire, passion, and love, she wrapped her arms around his waist and lifted up to meet him. She clutched his corded muscles and pressed her chest to his.

The moment his cock entered her, the world seemed to stop rotating. He forged into her, stretching her inner walls to the max, each inch taking her closer to that perfect moment. Their lips met again, but this time, his kisses were butterfly soft. She nipped at his and their breaths mingled.

"I need you, Jess, forever."

With that, he drove into her again, and her heart and body shattered. Each piece connected with him on the most elemental level. It was if they were one. They held on tight and loved each other hard. Each time he thrust into her, she soared higher and higher. He palmed her face and kissed her with such passion, her love bloomed even more. When he drove in to the hilt, Jessie could no longer hold on. Waves of ecstasy washed over her as her climax took hold.

Dax lifted his head and grunted as his seed spilled into her. He then rolled them over. Too tired to move, she lay on top of him, never happier in her life.

Once she regained some energy, she lifted her head. "The answer to your question is yes. I will marry you. I love you more than you can know."

.

"Come on, Jess. It's time to get ready for the funeral." Dax lowered his feet from on top of Clinton's desk. He looked ready to take over the job already. Frank was by the cells, chatting with the prisoners.

She couldn't help but smile at Dax's take charge attitude. Actually, she hadn't stopped smiling since they'd left the hotel. The hot shower they'd taken together had been decadent, exciting, and oh so sensual. And to think he wanted a repeat performance every day for the rest of their lives. If she let Dax have his way, crime in Kerry would soar, as they wouldn't be out keeping the wild ones under control.

"I'm coming."

No sooner had she stood than a knock sounded on the door. Come next week, she was going to buy a sign that read, *Enter. No knocking allowed.* "Come in."

The Mayor strode in. Oh, shit. Not only had she forgotten to call about the accusations against the judge, she didn't want to hear what the Mayor had to say.

"Good day, Jessie." He turned to Dax. "Mr. Mitchell."

She was surprised he didn't sound angry. Jessie straightened her shoulders. "How can I help you?"

"I came by to say the City Council and I were discussing a few things and we want to offer you the job as sheriff—permanently. If you'll take it."

She waited a beat, expecting to hear the conditions attached to the job, but none came. "I accept under one condition."

"What would that be?"

"I'll need help," she said.

"Who do you have in mind? If I recall, the last person you hired was a bit of a rogue."

That was quite the understatement. "True. Amanda wasn't who I thought she was, but Dax here has decided to stay on in Kerry. He's well qualified, I assure you. Why, I couldn't have solved those—"

Mayor Kreplick held up his hand. "Say no more." He turned to Dax. "Mr. Mitchell? What do you say?"

"I would be honored to work with our new sheriff," he replied. His smile dimpled his cheeks, but she bet he didn't realize what an incredibly sexy man he was.

Bob Kreplick extended a hand and shook hers, and then Dax's. "Welcome aboard."

The moment the Mayor left, they hugged and kissed, making sure they were out of sight of both Brian and Hunter. Frank could watch all he liked.

"Oh, I forgot to mention that Roberta came back," Jessie said, as she gathered her purse and coat.

"Really? Where was she?" Dax cocked a brow.

"Well, if you believe Roberta, she was on an alien spaceship getting experimented on. She even claimed that the triangular piece we found in the barn—the one with the stones on it—was a sexual tool. Can you believe it?"

"Sweetheart, nothing surprises me anymore about the citizens of Kerry, especially the elderly ones." He looked around. "So where is the instrument of delight. Maybe I can use it on you."

"Like you need help."

"Oh, you never know."

Jessie opened her desk drawer. "I'll be damned. It's gone. I bet that scoundrel Roberta stole it." She looked over at Frank. "Do you know anything about this?"

"Absolutely not."

Dax placed a hand on her back. "Well, she'll probably put it to good use, though only if a bomb is nearby."

Jessie ran her hands down his face. "Did I mention that I love you?"

"Not in the last, oh, ten minutes."

Jessie couldn't believe love could be this sweet. "Well, I guess I'll just have to prove it to you again tonight."

***

EXCERPT-BLACK OPS &LINGERIE

Don't forget to sign up for my newsletter to receive a free book, as well as up-to-date information on my stories. If you prefer to only receive notices regarding my releases, follow me on BookBub.

***

I hope you enjoyed Jessie and Dax's story. Next up is Sky and Kane's story in BLACK OPS AND LINGERIE(Nash Mystery Series, book 2).

Here is Chapter One.

Officer Sky Nash might enjoy supervising the Navajo Open Market, a place where the local tribes sold their silver jewelry, woven blankets, and pottery to the public on the third Wednesday of the month, but it wouldn't earn her any points toward becoming a detective. Neither would checking Earl Chee's story about a UFO sighting last night, but at least it would give her a chance to check up on the old man.

Sky turned off Arizona's route 98, a few miles past Savory's town limits, onto the rutted dirt drive of his farm. Rocks pinged off the undercarriage and dust coated the newly washed cruiser.

Sky skidded to a stop in front of Earl's house, sending a huge dust cloud into the air. Cutting the engine, she scanned the area to see if the reported UFO was in plain sight, though she didn't expect to see anything.

As she waited for the air to clear, the front door opened, and Earl rolled his wheelchair down the wooden incline to the driveway and sent her a toothless grin. Sky eased out, trying not to sink too far into the powdery dirt.

While Earl had an open and imaginative mind, she wouldn't call him a crackpot like her boss did. She believed in the possibility that life could exist elsewhere, but she wasn't ready to say there were aliens walking around on the face of the earth.

Earl stopped in front of her. "Thanks for coming out so quickly."

"No problem. I've been meaning to stop by this week anyway. Do you need anything? Want me to pick up some feed for the animals?" Being handicapped made his life extra hard, especially since his wife's death six months ago.

"Nah. I'm doin' okay, considering."

She pulled out her pad to show him she would take his report seriously. "So tell me what happened." The sun beat down on her face, warming the fifty-degree chill in the air.

He rubbed his thigh above the amputation. "Last night, I was getting ready for bed when the sky lit up on the north side of the property."

"Uh-huh." She glanced in the direction of his finger, but the wooden house blocked her view. There had been a lightening storm a little before midnight, so perhaps that was what he'd seen. "Go on."

"When I seen this craft, I got real excited thinking maybe my friends had come for me."

His *friends* he'd told her, lived forty-seven light years away, so she doubted they'd come for a visit. "But it wasn't them?" she asked.

Earl had claimed he'd been to a far away planet in some kind of exchange program with the aliens back in 1975. The extra dose of radiation on the trip back from the Zeta Reticuli solar system had caused him to get cancer and lose his leg—or so he believed.

"Afraid not. Anyway, I was about to check out the craft, when this big eighteen-wheeler pulls up next to the ship. I waited a bit to see what they were going to do when these two guys jump out of the truck."

"Were they human?" She could never tell when she spoke with Earl.

"Hell, yeah, they were human, and they had themselves some big rifles, so I decided it best to stay inside with the lights off."

Sky jotted this down. "Smart. You saw the craft land?"

"No, dammit, I didn't." He hung his head. "I was looking for my special binoculars."

"Could you tell what they were doing?" *They* could mean either the men or the supposed aliens.

"Sure could. The two men were takin' apart the craft using a blowtorch and some big ass hydraulic wrench, and then putting the parts in their truck. Then someone else showed up. I didn't see no other car, so maybe this new guy had been hidin'."

She was surprised Earl didn't conclude the third person was a passenger on the spacecraft or had beamed down. Sky didn't dare mention that a news article back in the late forties claimed alien space crafts were made of a material that couldn't be torn, burned, or punctured, and that they had no bolts or screws to undo.

"So were your binoculars night vision goggles or something?" Binoculars alone wouldn't cut it.

"Or something." He winked.

It was just like Earl to keep a secret. She glanced at the house and noted the spotlights mounted in the corners of the roof. "Then what?"

"Once the men were done, the three of them got into a whoppin' shoutin' match."

"Could you hear what they said?" She almost forgot to take notes.

"They were too far away."

"How far is too far?" A gust of wind whipped her hair into a frenzy, and she swatted the strands away from her face.

"'Bout fifty yards."

Not close enough to hear but apparently near enough to see. "And then?"

"One of them knocked the newcomer down and leaned over him. The first guy grabs a shovel and starts digging a hole, but at the time I didn't know why. Not wanting them there, I grabbed my shotgun just in case they decided to come in and take me. I got to the back bedroom, opened the window, and fired a few shots at them. I mentioned that when I called it in."

"The Chief didn't tell me." No surprise there. She decided to refrain from saying it might not have been the smartest thing for Earl to have drawn attention to himself. She wasn't convinced Earl's eyes weren't playing tricks on him. *Two men fight with a third and start digging a hole,* she noted. *Earl fires shots.* "Did they return fire?" If they did, she'd need to find the casings.

"Nope. They got back in the truck and took off. They didn't seem to give a hog's butt I was trying to take 'em down." He shrugged. "Maybe they were wearing them vests like on those crime shows."

"Probably. Can I see where the craft landed?"

"Sure, lemme pull up the cart."

As she turned to follow Earl, a burst of gunfire shattered the cruiser's windows and put holes in the side panel. Holy shit. The crack of glass and metal was louder than Fourth of July fireworks. She shoved his wheelchair behind the cruiser, away from the spray of fire. "Duck down," she shouted.

She did a tuck and roll to get out of the way, sucked in a breath, and dropped to all fours.

"Sky?"

She looked up. Flashes of light came from the rocky hills

about five hundred yards away, and the sand in front of Earl's house rippled. Damn. She drew her gun and took cover at the back of the cruiser, her breath caught in her throat. Her Glock 23 didn't have the range to reach the attacker, but she needed to protect Earl somehow. Just as she leaned out into the open to take aim, a bullet grazed her tricep. "Dammit." The sharp burn made her jolt upright.

"Sky!"

The stinging ebbed as blood dripped down the inside of her sleeve. She holstered her weapon and crouched next to him. "I'm good." An extra dose of adrenaline flooded her body and blocked some of the pain. "You okay?" she asked.

"Sure am. We need to get you inside." He nodded to her arm.

"Let's wait a minute." She had to make sure he was safe. No telling who they were after—her or Earl. When no more gunfire sounded, her breathing slowed. She covered her wound with her right hand to stem the flow. *Think.* "Whoever is out there might be waiting to see our next move." Her heart wouldn't stop racing, and her fingers shook. "I need to call for backup. You have any idea who's shooting at us?" Using her good arm, she fumbled for the cell phone in her top jacket pocket, and her bloody fingerprints smeared the screen. Crap.

"Could be the aliens," Earl mumbled, his head nearly between his legs.

"I don't think the aliens would have lasers on their guns. Only a sniper weapon could shoot that far with such accuracy."

He twisted his face toward her. "You're right. When I stayed on planet Serpo, I never saw a more peaceful civilization. They had no reason for guns."

She refrained from rolling her eyes. "It's clear our attacker or attackers are human. Keep low, I don't want you to be next." She called the office and got through—a rare event in this remote area of Arizona. "Hey, Harriet. It's me." She gritted her teeth against a quick blast of pain.

"Ask for medical help," Earl whispered. "My skills are a might rusty."

Sky covered the phone. She wouldn't ask what kind of medical skills Earl had. He'd most likely tell her he'd gotten a medical degree somewhere in Zeta Reticuli. "It's a scratch. I've had worse." She told Harriet about the shots fired, but not that the cruiser was damaged or that she'd been injured. If the Chief found out about his precious vehicle, he'd be here faster than a missile warhead, and that would delay, or rather end, her dream of becoming a detective.

The dispatcher assured her she'd send the best, but since the only other officer on the day shift was Harvey, she wouldn't get any real help.

Sky disconnected but kept watch on the far hill where the shots had come from. "You piss off anyone lately?" she asked. The natives around here would never shoot at the law.

Earl shrugged. "Could be the two men from last night who killed their partner. Maybe they don't want a witness."

"What? Someone's dead?" She stared at him.

"I told the Chief."

She slapped the bumper and cursed. She and the Chief needed to have a talk about him keeping her in the loop. She couldn't do her job properly if her boss didn't give her all the information and show her the same respect he showed his male officers.

"On second thought, the men could have found out the aliens were trying to contact *me*," Earl said.

"That must be it." She lifted her hand from the wound. The bleeding was down to a trickle.

Earl wheeled backward. "We need to get you fixed up right quick." He held up a finger. "And no arguing, young lady. I've seen enough infections in my time to kill a whole slew of pigs." He smiled. "The barn animals, not—"

"I got it." The distant rumble of an engine rolled over the mountains away from them. "Sounds like our snipers might be leaving." The telltale sign of billowing dust added to her conclusion. Earl kept a long-handled grabber in the side pocket of his wheelchair. "Hand me that metal claw." Sky slipped off her jacket, and using Earl's extension rod, she waved the material in the open to see if she could draw fire, but no more shots rang out. She nodded at the cruiser. "You realize the Chief is going to kill me for this."

"It don't look too bad. I bet Morton's Garage can fix this up in no time. Come on inside. We'll worry about the cruiser later."

"Easy for you to say." She stepped behind his chair and pushed him to the door, keeping an eye on the hills in case she'd been wrong about their attackers' departure.

Inside, she checked the damage to her wound and to the jacket while Earl located a small first aid kit. The hole in the wool ruined the coat, so she'd have to wear her slick leather coat to work for a few days until she ordered a new one.

He handed her a tin metal box. "Looks like you just got grazed."

Needle pricks pulsated along her arm, and she sucked in a breath. The morning had started out so well, and now she'd been shot. "Yeah."

Sky took out the iodine and cleaned the wound the best she could, but it stung like a bitch. Earl then helped her wrap the injury in gauze.

Gravel sounded on the drive, and colored flashing lights speared the front window. "That was quick. Harvey must have been nearby." She stood up so fast her vision blurred. Holding onto the top of the chair, she waited until her balance returned to normal then slipped on her coat. "Let's hope we can get to the bottom of this."

They both headed outside. At six-three and three hundred plus pounds, one hundred of which spilled over his waistband, Harvey Bonner huffed as he ambled up to them.

"You okay?" he asked, raking a gaze along the cruiser's side.

At least his tone had been tinged with concern. "Better than my vehicle." She pulled out her notepad and listed the events that led up to the shooting, including the fact Earl had found a body.

Harvey's eyes widened. "Where is he?"

Earl moved toward them. "Out back. Let's take the golf cart. It's the only way I can get around out there with the stones and scrub brush. My wheelchair's not built for the rough terrain."

"I'll walk," Sky offered. The two-seater golf cart wouldn't fit all three of them.

Harvey didn't argue. She hurried behind them to make sure her coworker didn't do anything stupid when he arrived out back. She'd heard he'd once been a great officer, but his zest for the job evaporated after his son overdosed.

They all reached the site three minutes later. With her mouth open, she stared at the corpse only half buried. "Dear God."

It sure wasn't what she'd expected.

The end

ABOUT THE AUTHOR

Love it HOT and STEAMY? Sign up for my newsletter and receive MONTANA DESIRE for FREE. Click here

OR Are you a fan of quirky PARANORMAL COZY MYSTERIES? Sign up for this newsletter. Click Here

Not only do I love to read, write, and dream, I'm an extrovert. I enjoy being around people and am always trying to understand what makes them tick. Not only must my romance books have a happily ever after, I need characters I can relate to. My men are wonderful, dynamic, smart, strong, and the best lovers in the world (of course).

My Paranormal Cozy Mysteries are where I let my imagination run wild with witches and a talking pink iguana who believes he's a real sleuth.

I believe I am the luckiest woman. I do what I love and I have a wonderful, supportive husband, who happens to be hot!

Fun facts about me

(1) I'm a math nerd who loves spreadsheets. Give me numbers and I'll find a pattern.

(2) I live on a Costa Rica beach!

(3) I also like to exercise. Yes, I know I'm odd.

I love hearing from readers either on FB or via email (hint, hint).

Social Media Sites

Website: www.velladay.com
FB: www.facebook.com/vella.day.90
Twitter: velladay4
Gmail: velladayauthor@gmail.com
Tiktok: Velladayauthor1
Bookbub: https://www.bookbub.com/authors/vella-day

ALSO BY VELLA DAY

SILVER LAKE SERIES (3 OF THEM)

(1). **HIDDEN REALMS OF SILVER LAKE** (Paranormal Romance)

Awakened By Flames (book 1)

Seduced By Flames (book 2)

Kissed By Flames (book 3)

Destiny In Flames (book 4)

Box Set (books 1-4)

Passionate Flames (book 5)

Ignited By Flames (book 6)

Touched By Flames (book 7)

Box Set (books 5-7)

Bound By Flames (book 8)

Fueled By Flames (book 9)

Scorched By Flames (book 10)

(2). **GODDESSES OF DESTINY** Paranormal Romance)

Slade (book 1)

Rafe (book 2)

Will (book 3)

Josh (book 4)

Jace (book 5)

Tanner (book 6)

(3). **WERES AND WITCHES OF SILVER LAKE** (Paranormal Romance)

A Magical Shift (book 1)

Catching Her Bear (book 2)

OTHER PARANORMAL SERIES

PACK WARS (Paranormal Romance)

PACK WARS-THE GRANGERS

Meant for forever (book 3)

Meant for her (book 4)

HIDDEN HILLS SHIFTERS (Paranormal Romance)

An Unexpected Diversion (book 1)

Bare Instincts (book 2)

Shifting Destinies (book 3)

Embracing Fate (book 4)

Promises Unbroken (book 5)

Bare 'N Dirty (book 6)

Hidden Hills Shifters Complete Box Set (books 1-6)

CONTEMPORARY SERIES

MONTANA PROMISES (Full length contemporary Romance)

Promises of Mercy (book 1)

Foundations For Three (book 2)

Montana Fire (book 3)

Montana Promises Box Set (books 1-3)

Hart To Hart (Book 4)

Burning Seduction (Book 5)

Montana Promises Complete Box Set (books 1-5)

Novellas:

Montana Desire (book 1)

Awakening Passions (book 2)

PLEDGED TO PROTECT (contemporary romantic suspense)

From Panic To Passion (book 1)

From Danger To Desire (book 2)

From Terror To Temptation (book 3)

BURIED SERIES (contemporary romantic suspense)

Buried Alive (book 1)

Buried Secrets (book 2)

Buried Deep (book 3)

The Buried Series Complete Box Set (books 1-3)

A NASH MYSTERY (Contemporary Romance)

Sidearms and Silk(book 1)

Black Ops and Lingerie(book 2)

A Nash Mystery Box Set (books 1-2)

STARTER SETS (Romance)

Contemporary

Paranormal

www.ingramcontent.com/pod-product-compliance
Lightning Source LLC
Chambersburg PA
CBHW020258200626
46816CB00001BA/357